Prelude

"Stop! Please stop! Why are you doing this? I'm begging you, please stop!"

"Shut up! This is entirely your fault! I was so happy; but you've destroyed everything; you brought this on yourself!"

She had no clue why this was happening to her; and frantically looked for an escape as she edged closer and closer to the top of the cliff. She quickly glanced over the bluff as the waves crashed below knowing that the water was not an option. As she tried to construct another escape route, the voice let out a barely audible grunt and she before she could scream, Rachel found herself crashing into the waves below, and her final resting ground. The voice looked over the edge, smiled and disappeared into the night.

Chapter 1

"Jared, I've found it! We've got to go see it!"

"Slow down Nicki, take a deep breath, and tell me what you've found."

"Our new house!," she said enthusiastically. "Listen to this description: Sacrifice sale; just listed and won't last long. Custom built 1940's estate overlooking Oneida Lake. This lovely home offers the ambitious buyer 4 bedrooms, 3 baths, eat-in kitchen, ample sized formal dining room; library and living room, wonderful lake view, and is nestled on four wooded acres

Nicki pranced about their tiny kitchen as she described the listing. "Honey, I've got to have it," she squealed with sheer delight.

"Okay, okay Nicole, we'll go look at it sometime; but before you start mentally decorating it, you failed to mention one little detail," Jared mused. "What's the price?"

Taking a deep breath, "Well, it's listed for Two ninety nine; but according to Gwen, the price is probably negotiable. She said that an elderly woman has lived there for the past thirty years. I guess she recently passed away and the estate was willed to her niece, who, according to Gwen, hasn't even been inside it since the funeral and has let it be known that she wants it sold ASAP. I know you'll love it so I told Gwen we'd meet her there at 7pm tonight. Love you; bye!"

Before Jared could say another word, Nicole hung up in his ear; then set about making his favorite meal.

"I can see it now; I'm about to buy someone else's headache," Jared thought to himself as he set out for home.

Nicole was also thinking about the house that afternoon. She wondered how she was going to persuade Jared to view the property with an open mind. She knew how practical he was regarding decisions in life. She also knew that she and Jared were just what the house at 1990 Sycamore Lane needed as they could emotionally and monetarily make the commitment it would take to fix up a still charming, but definitely run down home.

Nicole, a Registered Nurse at Lee Memorial Hospital for the past seven years; was not only angelic in looks and personality; but in bedside manner as well. Loving her job, she treated all patients the same, with genuine care and compassion. Jared, a project manager with a large aerospace company located just outside of Syracuse, also loved his job. But being introverted in nature, he was more content working in his cubicle than surrounded by people.

Nicole, a natural extrovert, and her real estate confidant Gwen, had been friends for years. From beach volleyball and roller-blading, to hang gliding at the shore; Gwen and Nicki had done it all. During their senior year in college, Nicole met a shy, almost nerdy engineering student. If one acknowledges proverbial phrases such as "opposites attract", then anyone who met Jared and Nicole knew that they were meant for one another. Where Jared lacked in originality and spunk, Nicole made up for it with spontaneity, energy and zest for living. The relationship that blossomed between the two was quickly unchallenged; and from Gwen's viewpoint, nothing short of a miracle.

Nicole and Jared were married shortly after graduating from St. Lawrence University. The young couple both agreed that Syracuse would be an ideal city in which to start their careers. Nicole had originally wanted to work at Albany Med and live in a downtown flat, but Jared thought that a smaller city would be a good place to call home. After a month of hemming and hawing, compromising and downright fighting, they both agreed upon Syracuse. Shortly after starting their respective careers, they bought a townhouse and for the past seven years had had a relatively maintenance free way of life; and that had suited Jared just fine. Now Nicki wanted a house, and a house meant painting, yard work in the summer, snow blowing in the winter, and the list went on and on in Jared's mind. But Nicole Rose certainly knew what she wanted, and almost always got it.

Nicole was raised in a hardworking middle class Irish Catholic family. She was adopted into the family when her biological mother decided that she couldn't afford to keep her without a husband around for financial and emotional support. The young single mother had found herself shunned by her family and community and unable to give her infant daughter a stable home. Although a heartbreaking decision by her mother; it paved the way for Nicole entering the Flanahan family as their sixth child, making her the baby of the family, and the only girl. When not being picked on by her older brothers, Nicole could be found climbing trees or playing ball with the neighborhood boys. Her mother tried to raise a lady but Nicki was destined from birth, and family circumstance, to be a free spirited, independent tomboy.

Jared on the other hand, was the mirror image of his father. Hardworking and well-respected, Jared's parents raised their only child to prioritize and be mature beyond his years. Jarod's youthful days weren't filled with baseball games and fishing by the lake; but with science camps, schoolwork and an occasional chess tournament.

When college decisions had to be finalized during their senior year of high school, both Jared and Nicole chose St. Lawrence University in upstate New York, Nicole chose it not only for its' nursing program but also for its' reputation for partying. With numerous fraternities, sororities and their social events, Nicole knew that not only would she receive an excellent nursing education, she would also "broaden her horizons" as she ever so often told her mother.

Jared chose St. Lawrence for its' outstanding reputation for producing top engineers and because he had received a full scholarship to attend the university. Coincidence and circumstance had brought Nicole and Jared together, but destiny ensured their union.

Jared pulled into the drive at precisely 5:35pm to find Nicole popping burritos into the microwave. "Hi honey," Nicole gleamed. Everything about Nicole Rose was vibrant and full of life. Her voice was quick and pert, but her body was tall and slender, with just the right amount of curves. In Jared's eyes, everything about Nicole was in impeccable good taste. He especially like the way she pouted to get what she wanted and he always anticipated her way of saying "thank you" afterwards.

'Hi Nicki, How was your day in paradise?" Jared enjoyed teasing her frequently about her work because he knew that she took her job so seriously.

"It was fine. Now go change so I can tell you about the house."

"And here we go..." Jared muttered to himself as he hurried upstairs to remove his steel toed shoes and slightly worn-out suit. Though reserved and plain by all outward appearances, under the work clothes lay a well sculpted physique. Exercise and toning had never been, in Jared's mind, as important as eating right and working hard; but during the course of their marriage, Nicole 'nd transformed Jared in mind, body and spirit. Jared's body was as fit and trim as Nicole's was well proportioned.

Throwing on a pair of khaki's and a polo shirt, he could hear Nicole's voice radiating from the kitchen that dinner was ready.

"Great," he thought to himself, "a tofu salad, carrot juice, frozen burritos and a hard sell on a money pit she wants to call home. This should be some evening."

As Jared entered the kitchen though, his palate became alive with the distinctive smell of chives and cayenne. Instead of the usual healthy meals Jared had grown accustomed to, Nicole had outdone herself. In front of him lie nacho appetizers, a huge taco salad, steaming hot burritos and a tall Corona. Nicole watched his expression as he evaluated the spread, and smiled to herself knowing she had scored points with her well thought out menu.

"Well, what do you think?" Nicole asked; knowing full well what the response would be.

"I think I'm in trouble," he responded with a grin that bordered on a smirk. "And when you cook all of my favorites in one setting, I know you're up to something."

With that, they ate their dinner and set off for 1990 Sycamore Lane.

The drive to the south side of Syracuse took longer than both had anticipated. Their GPS announcing the last turn, Nicole could hardly contain her excitement. As they rounded the final corner, the home materialized in front of them. They pulled in next to Gwen who was waiting in her fire engine red Saab.

"What took you so long?" Gwen scolded as she got out of her car. "I thought you'd forgotten about me!"

Shorter and stockier in comparison to Nicole, Gwen had always been able to make them laugh. Gwen's jokes covered her insecurity about her weight and Nicki had learned back in college that there were some subjects that even the best of friends didn't brooch.

"Come on, let's go see your new house," Gwen chirped as she slid the remainder of her Snicker's Bar into her coat pocket.

Gwen and Nicki bolted off towards the front door, but weren't quick enough to avoid hearing Jared inquiring as to why the property were listed below value. From the outside, the house didn't look to be in need of any major repairs.

"There has to be a reason," he thought to himself as he set off to catch up with the girls.

Once inside, Gwen answered his question.

"The only reason this house hasn't sold yet is because some people are just stupid enough to believe in superstitions," and turned away to avoid Jared's puzzled look.

"What superstitions Gwen?"

"Well," Gwen paused, "About thirty years ago, the old lady who just passed away didn't live here; her sister and her family did. Rumor has it that her ghost is still seen around here sometimes. Isn't that the silliest thing you've ever heard?"

"Unbelievable," Jared exclaimed as he started to pace around the entranceway in frustration. "You brought me halfway across the county after I put in a stressful and crazy day to show me a haunted house? Forget it, I'm out of here!"

Jared turned away from Nicole and Gwen to make his escape off the landing and back to his truck. Before he could exit, Nicole had Jared by the shirtsleeve pleading her case.

"Honey, you know there are no such things as ghosts. People just like to talk that's all."

Gwen glanced over to observe Jared's posture and expression and then intervened.

"Jared, you know me, I would never waste your time and drag you out here if I didn't think that this is the investment of a lifetime. You can't possibly believe that this place is haunted?"

Jared looked at both women and their pitiful expressions, then shrugged his broad shoulders and laughed.

"Okay, you're both right as usual. Of course, I don't believe in ghosts. Come on, let's see the house."

As Jared started walking inside ahead of Nicole and Gwen, the ladies silently gave each other high fives before catching up to him, and entering the house together.

Once all three had absorbed everything about the interior of the home, they made their way outside again and headed towards the boathouse and lake. With dusk rapidly approaching, the stars began to light up the evening sky over the water. The aroma of freshly cut grass and lilac filled the air as they approached the dock.

"I love it here Jared. This place makes me forget about the city and all the worries of the day. Don't you think this would be an ideal place to raise a family?"

Before Jared could answer, he felt a cold chill shoot through his body. At the same time, he impulsively glanced over his shoulder, looking back at the house. "Jared, did you hear me?" Nicole asked impatiently.

"Yeah I heard you. I just had a funny feeling that's all." Dismissing the feeling, the three of them headed for their respective vehicles.

"In answer to your question Nicole, yes; I do believe that this would be a wonderful place to raise children but I'm not ready to commit to this home quite yet. We can talk about it more when we get home."

With that said, Nicole and Gwen said good night. Gwen promised to call in the morning with answers to Jared's laundry list of questions. The night sky glistened as the two cars pulled out of the stone drive and onto the road leading back to the city. Nicole turned to take one last look at the home and did it just in time to see the upstairs bedroom curtain fall back into place. Unsure what she had seen, Nicole remained silent as the home faded from view.

Chapter 2

Nicole rose the following morning, exercised, showered and ate before Jared's alarm went off. She woke him with the smell of freshly brewed coffee, a ham & cheese omelet and toast. Before Jared was completely awake, Nicole dropped her robe at the base of their bed and slithered in next to him. The feel of her hot flesh and warm mouth on his neck and chest made his hormones explode with excitement. He didn't say a word and let Nicole take full control of the moment. Nicole, confident in her sexuality and secure with her body, could do things to Jared that most men only fantasize about. It wasn't that she was knockout gorgeous, but at 5'6" and 118 pounds, Nicole personified sexy when she let her auburn hair down. Her eyes were what had first attracted Jared. He had always told her that her green cat eyes could stop a train; and he still found them and her, irresistible.

When they finally relaxed in each other's arms and caught their breath, both laughed at the cold breakfast still sitting on the tray beside the bed. "Thanks for breakfast Nicki."

"Oh Jared, I did make you a wonderful breakfast. I just got a little sidetracked in giving it to you."

"You can get sidetracked anytime you want," Jared replied as he smiled and rose to shower.

Jared could be heard humming to the radio as Nicole straightened up their king-sized bed, remembering the first time they had made love in it so many years before. Many things had changed in their lives since the day they were married; yet their love for one another had only grown deeper. Once the room was in presentable shape, Nicole tiptoed into the bathroom to surprise Jared once more. Jared's humming soon turned to laughing, panting, and gasping simultaneously when Nicole started to work her seductive magic again. The entire bathroom was filled with steam from the hot shower and from the even hotter scenario being played out under the shower massage. Nicole and Jared were so enthralled in their own world that neither of them heard the phone ring, or the answering machine pick up.

"Nicole, it's Gwen; pick up if you're there…. Nicki, I guess you must be busy or gone; anyway, I have all the information that you wanted on the house. I'm leaving for appointments shortly, call me when you get in. Oh, and don't let me forget to tell you about what I found out about the murder."

Gwen had no sooner hung up when she started regretting leaving the message. She knew that Nicole would be fascinated with the details, but Jared would use the information as an excuse as to why they shouldn't put in an offer.

"Well, what's done is done," Gwen thought to herself as she set off for her first appointment of the morning. As she stopped for a red light at the intersection, she glanced over at the teenage in the adjacent car, smiled, then reached for a CD to throw in. The light turned green as she pushed the disc into the player and started to accelerate. Eric Church started playing as the teenager and his Camaro blew by her. His music was blaring, and she only deciphered the words "learn the truth" as he sped out of sight. "Teenagers and their music" she thought to herself as she shifted gears and merged with traffic onto the interstate.

Jared and Nicole both dressed quickly as the sun rose higher in the cloudless sky. Due to their morning diversions, Jared skipped breakfast, kissed Nicole good-bye and left for work contentedly humming the same song that had previously lured Nicole into the shower. Nicole was off for three days, so she decided to dress leisurely and relax. She no sooner sat down to read the morning paper, and the phone rang. "Great, I can't even relax on my day off!" she thought to herself as she rose to answer the phone. Before she could even get the word hello out, Nicole heard Gwen's sign of relief.

"Nicki, thank God it's you. I was afraid that you might have gone out for a jog or some other healthy thing you skinny people do."

"Yes, Gwen, it's me. What's up?"

Nicole tried not to let Gwen's constant sarcastic comments about her healthy habits get to her, yet sometimes she simply wished Gwen would join her instead of knocking her for taking care of herself. "I take it you didn't listen to my message yet?" Gwen mused.

"No. Jared and I were kind of tied up this morning and got a late start. He rushed out of here since he was cutting it close for work and I just sat down."

"So now you're into ropes huh Nicki?" Gwen teased. "Just kidding Nicole Rose" Gwen quickly responded to downplay her previously snide comment. "I left you a message this morning and after I hung up, I realized that Jared could possibly listen to it and that would be disastrous!"

"What was so destructive in the message Gwen?"

"Look, why don't you just meet me at the office later and we'll do lunch, say 12:30?"

"Just tell me what you found out Gwen."

"Well, according to my sources, the previous owners, the Hartemans, had only lived in the home for a few years before Mrs. Harteman died. Apparently they had originally moved there to be closer to her family." Nicole listened intently as Gwen rambled on. "The Harteman's had two children, and Mrs. Harteman longed for a third child. Her doctor advised against it since their son had been born with some kind of physical impairment."

"Gwen, what's that got to do with the house? I don't really care that a previous owner didn't or couldn't have any more children," Nicole dryly commented half reading the morning paper.

"I'm getting to that part Nicole." Gwen seemed excited in telling Nicole the vintage gossip and readily blurted out "As the story goes, Mr. Harteman supposedly got himself snipped" she said enthusiastically and somewhat sarcastically. "That way he ensured that they wouldn't have any more children after their son was diagnosed; yet when the autopsy was performed on Mrs. Harteman, she was four months pregnant. Guess he found out and killed her!"

"What? You mean he murdered her Gwen? Killed the mother of his children?" Nicole exclaimed in disbelief.

"It certainly would appear that way. And it must have appeared that way to the jury who convicted him too, since he was sentenced to life in prison" Gwen reiterated.

Nicole sat back in her chair trying to absorb everything that she had just heard. Being illegitimate herself, she knew what an unexpected and unwanted pregnancy could do to a family. Her birth had caused her parent's to end their relationship and go their separate ways. She had reconnected with her birthmother while in college, but even after all the years since her adoption, she adamantly refused to divulge Nicole's father's name; stating that he'd betrayed her like her entire community had.

"How did he kill her Gwen?" Nicole inquired, not really sure if she want to know. "And what about the children; whatever happened to them?" Nicole asked before Gwen even had a chance to answer the first question. Nicole suddenly felt saddened by the entire scenario. Two young children had lost their mother, and ultimately their father. Nicole listened to the remaining details that Gwen had obtained and felt sympathetic for the woman who had died so long ago.

"The way the story was explained to me," Gwen started, "Is that the couple used to take evening strolls along the bluff overlooking the lake, and loved to watch the sunset. As we saw, the lake is gorgeous when the sky is full of stars. Supposedly, they went for one of their moonlight walks, and began to argue about the baby. Their argument grew louder and he must have pushed, or thrown her off the bluff. The sad part about it," Gwen added, "Is that she didn't even die from the fall, she drowned."

"What do you mean she drowned?"

"I mean, she couldn't swim. She was alive when she hit the water, could be heard crying for help, and then she vanished into the lake."

There was a long silence on both ends. Gwen sat wondering if she had divulged too much information, scaring Nicole off. On the other end, Nicole remained silent, filled with great sadness, trying to imagine the pain the family had experienced with this tragedy. Even with such a traumatic history, Nicole still felt drawn to the house at 1990 Sycamore Lane. Now, more than ever, she wanted to live there; and make happier memories for the home and its' neighbors.

Chapter 3

Betty Langhorne was outside absorbing the fresh spring air when her husband of forty three years came to join her. He chuckled at the sight of her, covered with dirt from planting several dozen gladiola bulbs. Betty and Bart had a formidable relationship. She tinkered around outside, planting bulbs, flowers and garden vegetables, and he let her. Betty's philosophy was simple; she had spent twenty plus years being trapped inside, raising their three boys, and now it was her turn to get outside and enjoy nature during the time that she had left. Betty had been diagnosed with breast cancer three years prior, and had successfully completed radiation and chemo after undergoing a partial mastectomy. On the day of her diagnosis, Betty had vowed to beat Cancer and against the odds, she had. Presently Cancer free and healthy again, both she and her husband took advantage of her second lease on life. They enjoyed each other more, yet also realized the importance of each other's hobbies and independence. For years, Betty had dreamt of lavishly decorating their home with exotic ferns, flowers and ornamental trees; but her children and their needs had always hampered her plans. Now with children grown and married, every spring, Betty and Bart sowed and planted the flowers of Betty's dreams. Today was no exception. Betty was up to her knees in dirt with hoe in one hand and bulb in the other. Bart looked at her with the same boyish smile that she had fallen in love with so many years before. He lived for her and never realized it until their brush with death had almost taken her from him.

"What are you looking at, you old fool?" Betty teased. "Haven't you ever seen dirt before?"

"I was just looking at you. You're as beautiful as the day I married you."

"I guess I must have looked pretty bad back then. Or your eyesight has faded over the years," Betty joked, smiling at her first love, and then tossed him a pair of gloves.

"Come on, help me plant these before the wind kicks up anymore" Betty said as she dug into the loose soil.

"The lake sure is rough today," Bart observed as he looked across the bluff at the water. "Those boaters are crazy to be out there on a day like this. Someone is sure to drown." Even after all these years, as the words left Bart's lips, he realized that he should have phrased his statement differently. Betty's expression transcended what words could not. Quickly Bart changed the topic and the two planted the remaining bulbs in silence.

Nicole finished picking up the townhouse after hanging up with Gwen. Try as she might, she couldn't stop thinking about what Gwen had divulged had happened so long ago at the house. Being a nurse, Nicole had always wondered how one person could take the life of another, when people like herself and her coworkers were devoted to saving others. As the unanswered questions continued to mount within her brain, Nicole realized that she could only do one thing, and with that she got her purse, grabbed her jacket and headed for the library. She knew she could have researched it on her PC but for some reason felt that whatever she learned about the murder should be kept separate from her home life, a separation of sorts.

The reference section bustled with the silent scurrying of the librarian's feet as Nicole entered the library. Within moments, she was tucked away in a corner, with a look of determination on her face. Though not exactly sure why she was compelled to learn more, Nicole yearned to read about that tragic night and what became of the family that once occupied her future home on Sycamore Lane. It only took a few minutes to find the article that she was looking for. Nicole read the article, absorbing the details regarding the murder. First slated as an accident; the reporter seemed to take great delight in presenting the gruesome facts about the death of the young mother. Nicole rubbed her strained eyes and reread the article one last time.

Upon completing the article, Nicole picked up her notepad, and purse. She thought about going home, meeting Gwen for lunch, running errands or finishing up a few projects at home; but decided that her time would be better spent revisiting the house. After a quick call to Gwen, she was on 81 heading south.

The forty minute drive passed quickly as she exited the interstate and headed towards the lake. The radio was playing classics of the 80's all day; yet Nicole seemed oblivious to the tunes radiating from the speakers. She drove in silence towards the home she so desperately wanted. As she neared the drive, she noticed a woman who reminded her of her grandmother watching as she approached. She smiled and waved out of politeness as the woman gave a half wave back. "Well, at least I know the neighbors are friendly," she thought to herself as she pulled into the drive.

"Who do you think that is?" Betty inquired as she stood shaking the dirt from her hands. Rubbing the sweat from his brow, Bart earnestly responded, "I've seen her here before with another couple. She's probably just another potential buyer who liked the asking price but won't want to undertake the work that place needs to make it habitable again."

"True. Or she's just another curiosity seeker from the city" Betty added dryly as she returned to her work.

Nicole had planned on waiting in her car until Gwen arrived, but as usual, her best friend was running late. Anxious to look around again, Nicole decided to look around the yard to pass the time until she arrived. The sun was hiding behind the clouds, which were quickly moving in. The wind was intense compared to their previous visit. Nicole wandered into the back yard, taking in the gorgeous; though overcast views of the lake. From the bluff, the waves could be heard crashing against the rocks below as she approached the edge. The water appeared so rough, menacing and angry; as Nicole glanced out, she noted only a few boats challenging the approaching storm. "Definitely not a good boating day, or day for swimming," Nicole thought to herself as she turned and started heading for the driveway. She had taken a few steps as a few monster waves hit the shore and pierced the rocks, creating a whistling sound as water was forced thru the large boulders. Creating a high pitched sound, it startled Nicole causing her to spin around thinking someone was calling her. Cautiously, she took a few steps back towards the cliff's edge and viewed the spectacle for herself. She chuckled, when she realized how foolish she'd been to think that someone had called out from the water below.

"Miss, you had better be careful out there." This time Nicole did hear a voice and quickly whipped around to come face to face with a cute, but very dirty elderly gentleman. He wiped the dirt from his hand onto his trousers and extended it to greet her.

"I hope I didn't frighten you; but this bluff can be very dangerous when the wind is blowing as it is right now," Bart added when he saw how pale Nicole had become. "I'm Bart and my wife Betty and I live next door," he said as he nodded toward the partially obscured home behind them.

Nicole regained her composure and reached out to take his extended hand. Just from her firm handshake and graceful poise, Bart sensed right away that Betty had been wrong about her; she was definitely not just a curiosity seeker. This woman had substance and a kindness in her eyes.

"Hello," Nicole smiled confidently back. "I'm Nicole Brentwood. It's very nice to meet you."

"Hey Nicki, what are you doing out there? Can't you see it's about to rain?" Gwen shouted as she approached the pair. Out of breath from her fast paced walk, Gwen eyed Bart up and down before introducing herself, and suggested that she and Nicole should get inside before the storm hit. Nicole excused herself so that she and Gwen could head back towards the house. Bart paused before returning home so that he would watch Nicole depart out of view. Something about her was strangely familiar but he couldn't pinpoint what it was.

"What was that all about?" Gwen inquired once inside.

"What do you mean?" Nicole retorted as she looked around the parlor.

"Don't tell me you didn't see the way that creepy old man looked at you Nicki?"

"Don't be sick Gwen; he's old enough to be my father," Nicole snapped in disgust.

"I don't mean it that way. He looked at you as if he knew you; like you were his long lost friend," Gwen said apologetically.

"He probably looked at me that way because he's seen me here before. Or maybe at the hospital; who knows. Or maybe I just have one of those familiar looking faces."

Nicole dismissed the conversation and started looking at each room again. She studied every line and piece of woodwork as if trying to absorb the feeling of the house. The main house was a fine example of the architecture of its' day. From its' ornate built in china cabinet, to the sweeping front and back staircases; this home reveled with class. The twelve foot ceilings would be expensive to heat in the winter but between that and the Rochester hardwoods covering the floors; the home exemplified the homes grandeur. As Nicole made her way upstairs, Gwen snooped around the kitchen. Nicole went to the smaller bedrooms first to look around. Though sparsely furnished, the rooms gave off a feeling of warmth and love with their neutral colors and ornate crown molding.

"This must have been their daughter's room," Nicole pondered as she noticed the miniature crib and doll resting within it. She bent over to pick up the doll just as the rain starting pelting down on the tin roof outside. Before she would examine the fine porcelain face of the doll, she could hear Gwen's voice from below.

"Nicole, I'm still in the kitchen; what do you want?" Gwen asked as she approached the stairwell.

"I didn't say anything."

"Well, then who did?" Gwen questioned impatiently.

"The wind is really blowing outside, you probably just heard it blowing through the trees or something," Nicole reassuringly said as she gently placed the antique doll back into its' resting place. Nicole scanned the room one last time before meeting up with Gwen in the hallway.

"Are you through looking around? I want to get out of here before the storm gets any worse. Besides, this place is beginning to give me the creeps with the wind howling like that."

"Don't tell me super realtor gets spooked by a little rain?" Nicole teased as she started her descent towards the front foyer.

"Funny!" Gwen snapped back, in a half serious tone as she locked up behind them. The rain pelted down as the hastily made their way to their cars and started down the drive.

Next door, Bart and Betty scurried onto their covered porch just as the blackened sky opened up with the full force of its' rainy wrath. Bart stood silently, drying his bifocals as Betty cursed incessantly about not being able to finish her planting. Still wringing wet and sputtering away, Bart quietly wrapped a towel around her and kissed her gently but passionately.

"What was that for?" Betty pondered with a hint of disgust still in her voice.

"Kissing you has been the only way I've ever known to shut you up," he replied and winked.

With that, both laughed and settled down into the porch swing beside them.

Jared packed up his briefcase and tried to reach Nicole one last time before leaving the office. His day had been uneventful compared to most of them recently, with only two conference calls and one drawn out meeting. He just yearned to get home...

The drive took longer than usual, leaving him nothing to do but mull over the prospect of becoming a homeowner. Sure, they already owned a townhouse, but this would be different; and a much bigger investment. Jared couldn't help but admit to himself that the house did have merit and would be a good investment, yet he still wasn't sold on the idea. Pulling into the drive, he took a deep breathe, exhaled, and prepared himself for Nicole's sales pitch.

Upon entering their townhouse, he was saddened to find it empty. Quickly he changed and on the spur of the moment, decided to turn the tables and surprise her. Before she arrived, he made several phone calls, and then set out to prepare the room's setting. When he heard the garage door open, he doused the lights, adding to his intended effect.

Nicole entered the kitchen to the aroma of burning candles and vanilla. Taken back by the soft music and candlelight, she first was startled, then pleasantly surprised when Jared greeted her with a glass of wine and a rose. So untypical of him, she smiled coyly when she finally noted his lack of attire. Without saying a word, he took her into his arms and kissed her first passionately, then hungrily, as first her purse, then her wet jacket fell to the floor, followed by the remainder of her clothing. Telling her to stay still, and saying nothing more, he slowly and methodically caressed and suckled every inch of her still damp body while she writhed with pleasure. So used to being the aggressor, Nicole surrendered herself to him freely, enjoying her husband's sexual transformation. Jared even surprised himself as he took pleasure in his conquest. They made love first on the kitchen table, a first for both of them, then on the couch, and finally in their bed. With exhaustion in her voice, Nicole whispered a soft "Thank You" to her lover and held him close.

"No, thank you Nicole" Jared whispered back as he held her gently, stroking her auburn hair.

"What are you thanking me for? You're the one who made this evening so special. And I'm not sure what got into you, but I like it!" Nicki teased.

"You're the one who made me realize that we need to take more chances, and life isn't always structured and predictable. I've been thinking and you're right, we should go for it; let's turn that rickety house into a home" Jared said as he turned to face Nicole.

"Do you really mean it?" she asked as she bolted upright in bed.

"Yes, I really mean it; I want a bigger place so we can start on that family we've been talking about."

With that, Nicole leaped with joy as she grabbed Jared and hugged him tightly. Jared laughed as they lost their balance and fell onto the floor.

Chapter 4

"Good evening Henry," the guard uttered as he made his rounds through the library.

"Good evening to you Officer Barnes. It sure is a wet one out there," Henry remarked as the guard continued on his way.

"Yeah, for once, I'm glad I'm in here with you guys," the guard replied wryly.

"Yeah, me too!" Henry chuckled as the guard left his sight.

Henry went back to his reading after taking one last glance at the rain outside. He attempted to concentrate on the article but the guard's harmless interruption had made him lose his concentration. "Maybe after tomorrow, I'll be able to not only see the rain, but feel and taste it too," Henry thought to himself as he once again tried to resume his reading. Up for parole again, he refused to believe that freedom could actually be less than twenty-four hours away.

"Hey Henry, is tomorrow the big day?" Jim whispered as he peeked out of his cubicle.

"Yes, as a matter of fact it is," Henry responded with a hint of his Irish brogue coming out, as he tried to choke back any emotion from his voice.

"Well I certainly wish you the best of luck buddy."

ı." With that, both men returned to their books.

With the rain finally subsiding, the sky remained overcast with few stars overhead when Henry retired for the night. Lights out had been called hours before, but Henry, though emotionally exhausted, lay awake in his bunk. His mind raced at the possibility of parole, of being a father again, having some resemblance of family again, and what freedom would mean. He tried to prioritize what he would do first and who he'd visit; yet he was petrified at the thought of returning to society after all these years. Three decades had passed; so many things had changed since his incarceration; society itself had changed. And he couldn't help but remember that it was society and his fellow peers that had convicted him of a crime that he hadn't committed in the first place.

The trial had lasted only a few days, and then his life was over with one swing of the gavel. He had lost his wife, children, and his freedom. In the beginning he frequently had visitors. Though mostly family, it was still appreciated. Slowly, over the years, one by one, they stopped coming. Henry's parents had always believed in his innocence. When they passed on in a car accident, part of him died too. Even he started believing that it was possible that he might have done it; he just couldn't remember the events of that dreadful night.

"Maybe it will be over tomorrow," he thought to himself as he turned over one last time. "Maybe tomorrow is the start of a new chapter of my life."

Chapter 5

It was mid-afternoon when Nicole finally had a chance to call Gwen during her break at work. After a brief exchange, they agreed to write up the purchase offer later that evening at Nicole and Jared's. That would give Gwen enough time to print out comps and still get back to the office to fax the offer over to the listing agent. Subconsciously, Gwen felt a hint of urgency to get this deal done before anything went wrong, or it got sold out from under them or Jared got cold feet. She felt confident that the seller wouldn't counter if the offer was decent and encouraged her clients to write it as a one time, highest and best type offer. Once off the phone with Gwen, Nicole called Jared to let him know that they'd be meeting Gwen at their own home.

"Hi there; I thought you'd forgotten about me honey," Jared answered with a smile. "How could I ever forget about you?" she teased back.

"Look, I don't have a lot of time, but I wanted to let you know that Gwen will meet us promptly at seven so that we can sign to purchase offer. So PLEASE don't be late; she wants to finish this up tonight if possible."

Why is she rushing so much Nicki?" Jared questioned impetuously.

"No rush honey; it's just that I would like to start on that family you were talking about as soon as possible and I want to do it in our new house," Nicole responded, diverting his question.

"If the sex is anything like it's been lately, I want to do it anywhere!"

"You're a pig Jared Brentwood!" Nicole exclaimed half giggling.

"Yeah, but I'm your pig Nicki. I'll see you tonight," and the receiver promptly went dead in Nicole's ear.

"That you are Jared "Nicole mouthed to the receiver as she placed it down.

The remainder of the day flew by for Gwen, Nicole and Jared. Before they realized it, it was quickly approaching 7:00PM. Nicole finished up her shift and pulled into the drive just as Jared rounded the corner. Both looked exhausted as they made their way into the townhouse. The day had been draining for both of them as their wearied expressions revealed.

"You look awful Jared."

"You aren't looking so great yourself Nicole" Jared retorted back as he helped her off with her jacket. "Maybe you shouldn't work as much overtime as you do," his voice revealing genuine concern.

"I'm okay; just mentally fatigued, and I guess, a little physically fatigued as well," she reassuringly replied back. "Come on; help me thrown something together before Gwen arrives.

The words had no sooner left her lips when the doorbell chimed.

"That must be Gwen. We'll just have to eat later," Nicole muttered as she made her way towards the door.

"Greetings Brentwoods," Gwen chimed as she barged into the room. "I've come bearing gifts" she continued as she made her way to the living room. "God you look terrible Nicole; and you look even worse honey," she noted as she made eye contact with Jared. With that, she leaned over and withdrew a bottle of Pinot Noir from her bag. She set the pizza that she had been carrying on the coffee table and handed the bottle to Jared. "Be a good boy would you, open this and grab some glasses for us. From the looks of your wife, maybe you ought to just get Nicki a straw" she quipped as Nicole scowled.

"Just kidding honey" Gwen chuckled; not giving Nicole enough time to get angry. "Look inside my bag, there's something else in there for you Nicole."

Nicole eyes lit up as she withdrew a magnificent looking antipasto salad.

"See, I'm always thinking of my best friend," Gwen smoothly added, trying to make amends for her previous comments. "Come on, let's eat!" Gwen exclaimed jubilantly as she began to salivate at the smell of the pepperoni pizza in front of them.

After the pizza was devoured and the bottle was empty, the well fed trio got down to the business at hand. Upon reviewing the standard sales contract, both Jared and Nicole smiled triumphantly as they signed the papers. The only thing needed now was an acceptance of their offer.

Chapter 6

Claire's presence could be felt as he entered the foyer. He had both anticipated and dreaded today, for he knew that he would have to deal with her fury if the day's events didn't end favorably for her. Even after all these years of marriage, he still didn't understand fully how she could hold so much hatred towards one person. Being an attorney, she had tried numerous cases far more heinous; yet she cringed with the very mention of his name or case. Granted, this case was personal, but all the more reason that she should come to terms with her feelings; after all, he was still her father. Richard loved his wife but truly loathed the woman she became whenever the subject was broached. Today he knew would be no exception. He quietly climbed the stairs in hopes of avoiding her for a few more minutes. Methodically, he hung up his suit jacket and changed into something more casual and less restricting.

As he walked to the window, he saw her. Like a statue, she sat solemnly poised on the terrace. With her back to him, he was unable to determine her present state of mind, but the empty Martini glass at her side gave him a good indication. He looked at her with heavy heart for he knew that even though she appeared to be one tough and indestructible lady on the outside; somewhere deep in the crevices of her heart, she still loved her father.

The subject of her mother's murder was never broached in their home. He had met her while working as an Assistant DA. Back then, she was referred to as the "Black Widow" of the courthouse. She was an aspiring, young, and very talented lawyer who won practically every case she tried. Most of her peers labeled her as conceded because of her aloofness towards them; but Richard had sensed early on that this was a woman with not only a chip on her shoulder, but someone who had been terribly hurt in the past. Despite her obvious coldness towards him, he still felt drawn towards her. After numerous rejections, one night after a long day in court, she finally conceded to go with him for pizza. Remarkably, she found that they had several interests other than law in common. That first date opened the door to many others and eventually they became a couple.

When the time came to plan their wedding, Claire was forced to discuss the subject that she had so intelligently avoided over the course of their relationship. She simply explained that she was an only child who was raised by her aunt following her parents' deaths in a boating accident. She told him about her life attending various boarding schools, her spinster aunt but never gave any other details regarding her childhood. She invited her aunt, at Richard's insistence to the wedding, but at the last minute the aunt inexplicably canceled. Richard didn't give it a second thought until he saw the mostly empty pews on the bride's side of the church.

Now almost twenty years, and two children later, Richard stared down at his wife with the same pain he had felt for her on their wedding day.

Unable to avoid her any longer, he slowly made his way down the stairs and outside. Her eyes met his but she remained silent. Her long thin fingers fumbled for her glass, only to throw it once she realized it was empty. Richard winced as it smashed into minute pieces on the bricks.

"So tell me how your day was honey," she sarcastically inquired as she attempted to stand. "Mine was splendid, can't you tell" she continued.

"Come on Claire, I'll help you inside before the neighbors see you" he empathically said as he approached her.

"To hell with the neighbors" she snapped back! "The only help I want from you is the information you're keeping from me. Did they let that bastard out or not?"

"No, no they didn't Claire," he responded without hesitation. "And just so you know, this is the last time I'm pulling strings for you. Your father has paid his debt to society; he's been there over 30 years and deserves to live what's left of his life as a free man. I'm done being part of your vendetta."

"Eloquent speech your honor; save it for the courtroom," she snipped back with hatred in her voice. "Hopefully he doesn't live long enough to be up for parole again" she stated coldly as she made her way into their home.

Once alone, Richard stood silently, wondering if he had gone too far for her this time.

Chapter 7

Nicole tossed and turned throughout the night. Full of anticipation, she rose at dawn to start her morning workout. Jared pushed himself out of bed as she finished up on the treadmill. Though un-showered and sweaty, she still looked radiant as she moved in her leggings and tank top. Knowing that they didn't have time for diversions this morning, Jared headed towards the shower to eliminate the urge to take her in his arms.

"Hey honey, when do you think we'll hear from Gwen?" Nicole shouted over the sound of the water. "I'm going to call her after work if I haven't heard from her by then," she continued.

"Nicole, you've got to be patient. We gave the seller forty-eight hours to respond to the offer and they might not even take what we offered. You can't expedite their response so stop stressing about it. It is what it is."

"Jared, I absolutely hate it when you're so practical," Nicole said as her lips met his as she stepped into the shower. I'm just excited, that's all."

"I'm excited too; but getting all nervous over something you can't change isn't healthy you know," he responded as he gave her another kiss and then quickly exited the shower in order to avoid getting sidetracked.

Gwen was also anxious this morning. She had emailed the offer to the Drake's Realtor the evening prior and had hoped to get a response right away. She wanted to finalize the deal and close on the property as quickly as possible. Gwen still couldn't dismiss the overwhelming feeling she had about the estate but couldn't pinpoint what it was about the place that bothered her, and since

Nicole absolutely had her heart set on buying it, she kept her unfounded feelings about it, to herself. If the seller accepted Nicole and Jared's offer, they would be getting a fabulous deal; and making an investment that would do nothing but appreciate in value. Even if their offer was countered, she knew in her heart that they would agree to whatever the counter was.

"I'm sure once it's cleaned out and fixed up, I'll feel better about the place," she thought to herself as she made her way to the office.

Claire greeted Mrs. Hanks her Realtor dryly as she opened the door. Her head was still pounding from the evening before. They made their way to the study where, with bloodshot eyes, she reviewed the contract. Having scanned it quickly, she opened her desk drawer and pulled out a pen.

"What are you doing Mrs. Drake?" Mrs. Hanks asked quickly as she saw the pen nearing the contract.

"I'm accepting the offer Jean; that is why you're here at such an ungodly hour isn't it?" she snapped back as she started to sign the document.

"Don't you at least want to counter or discuss it with Mr. Drake first?" Mrs. Hanks inquired meekly.

"Look," Claire snapped, catching the middle aged realtor off guard "Let me make one thing perfectly clear. I own the house on Sycamore Lane. Not Mr. Drake. I have read a legal document or two in my 20 plus years practicing law, so I think I can understand all the mumbo jumbo in this sales contract. I do NOT need my husband's advice, or blessing, nor do I need to discuss the offer with him. So if you would like your commission, keep your mouth shut and let me sign the damn thing before I change my mind."

Embarrassed and appalled by the reprimand, Jean Hanks sat silently as Claire signed and initialed where appropriate. When she was finished, she handed the contract back to the still shaken, but silent agent. Once she had the agreement in hand, she quickly made her way to the front door.

"I will get this to your attorney and we should be able to close within sixty days max."

"Get it expedited; my attorney already has the deed and abstract. I want this over with!"

"Bitch," Jean thought to herself as she expediently made her way to her car.

Chapter 8

Henry spent the night following his parole hearing, again, behind bars. This denial hadn't affected him as much as the previous ones, even though his lawyer had felt he'd surely be paroled this time around. Henry didn't have much faith in the judicial system anymore. So, when his parole was inexplicably denied again, he was saddened, but not surprised.

The years had been hard on him. Incarceration changes a man, and the change is never for the better. As Henry aged and remained a "model prisoner", over time, he was allowed more freedom during his work program. His greatest joy came when he was allowed to spend extra time in the library. He had always loved to read, and spent most of his waking hours tucked inside a cubicle perusing the pages of technical books. A salesman by trade, he had always felt that knowledge was power; and the only power that he

-32-

would ever obtain was through the knowledge he gained while reading. When he was a free man, he had sold his wares door-to-door. Unlike most salesmen, his laid back, non-pushy manner and ability to hold a conversation on any topic quickly earned him a reputation throughout his neighborhood. Though they weren't rich by any means, Henry and Rachel Harteman lived very comfortably on his income. They lived in a row home on the south east side of Syracuse during the first years of their marriage. The birth of their daughter brought the realization that they would eventually need a larger home, but that dream didn't become a reality until Rachel was carrying their second child.

After their daughter's birth, Henry took a second, part time job running errands and making deliveries for a local union leader. Rachel didn't like Henry's new employer and vocalized her concerns on various occasions. She had heard that he had ties with organized crime and she didn't want her family associated with anyone remotely dishonest. Henry had continuously reassured her that everything he was doing was completely legal and that the rumors she had heard were simply that, rumors. Still, Rachel was leery of Mr. Carelli and his associates. She always felt that he could see through her outfits when she would catch him staring at her. Even some of his conversational remarks reflected sexual overtones that made her feel very uncomfortable. Often she discussed the way she felt with her husband, but Henry dismissed it by simply saying that it was just Mr. Carelli's way and that he was always warm and affectionate toward women in general. Still, Rachel knew a come-on when she heard one. She remained skeptical, even with the numerous gifts he presented to their little girl on holidays and birthdays. Rachel's opinion of Henry's boss finally changed the day he gave Henry a large bonus and they were able to put a down payment on their dream home. Mr. Carelli had always graciously denied it, but Rachel knew Henry couldn't possibly have saved that substantial amount of money. None-the-less, Rachel; was grateful to be able to move out of Syracuse and into the country. They moved into their new home on Sycamore Lane less than one month before the birth of their son Robert.

The delivery had been grueling on Rachel. After twenty hours of labor, Robert finally entered the world. Cyanotic and frail looking, the nurse quickly removed him from the room before Rachel could hold her son. Dazed from the medications, Rachel woke to find Henry sitting beside her, crying quietly. A feeling of deep despair come over her as she waited for Henry and the Doctor to explain what was wrong. The physician flatly stated that their son appeared to be born with a congenital syndrome that caused mental retardation, without any cure. Rachel sat in disbelief as she listened to this unsympathetic doctor explain that maybe they should consider letting their son become a ward of the state, to avoid the financial implications of trying to raise him at home. The final blow was when the physician stated that she should avoid having any further children as the syndrome was believed to be hereditary. Devastated and furious at this nonchalant attitude, Rachel insisted on seeing her son. Reluctantly, the nurse in attendance brought him into her. Rachel cuddled her newborn son as he slept. Tears streamed down her face as she felt all of her hopes and dreams of her son slowly fade away. Henry cautiously made his way to the head of the bed. Tentatively he pulled back the blanket to get his first view of his only son. Robert awoke and appeared to make eye contact with the object above him. Henry felt instant unconditional love for his child as he cooed in his mother's arms. He knew that this child would never be placed in an institution; he would be cared for, and loved in his own home. Given only a few minutes with their newborn son, a stern looking, gray haired nurse abruptly entered the room and took Robert away. It was only then that the young couple embraced and cried together.

Against everyone's advice. Henry and Rachel did take Robert home. Life was very difficult at first. Robert required constant attention and care, but they quickly adjusted their lives to meet his needs. In the beginning they were unable to afford anyone to assist in his care. After a few months of barely getting by, Mr. Carelli offered to hire a nanny to assist Rachel at home. He first approached Henry with regards to hiring someone but when Henry said that Rachel would never accept charity, he decided to visit her himself. Henry never understood what Mr. Carelli had said to convince her, but before he knew it, they had a full time nanny. Suddenly, part of the burden was lifted off of Rachel's shoulders and once again she had time for not only Robert but their daughter.

The years went by and Robert did remarkable well. The child that they were told would most likely die as an infant or young child, learned to walk and talk; much to everyone's surprise. Slowly, one by one, Rachel dared to allow her dreams for her son to be realized. Rachel became so caught up in Robert's accomplishments that she didn't notice the subtle changes occurring in Clarissa Anne.

The biggest hurdle Robert overcame even astonished his parents. Clarissa, at a young age had become an accomplished swimmer, and every time Robert saw his big sister enter the water for her swimming lessons, he fought to get into the water as well. After numerous refusals from various instructors, the Hartemans finally found a young instructor who was willing to give Robert a chance to learn. Though cognitively slow, swimming came naturally for Robert. From the moment he jumped into the pool, all traces of any handicaps were gone. Quickly he learned the proper strokes and was swimming laps within weeks. Rachel and Henry couldn't believe their eyes the first time they saw their son go off the diving board. When Robert was in the water, he was free from any stigmas. The pool held no bounds for him; and in it, he was just like the other boys and girls his age.

The family spent many summer nights under the stars swimming in the lake beside their home. Henry would join his children frolicking in the cold water while Rachel admired them from the dock. Deathly afraid of the water, she was so thankful that both Clarissa and Robert would never have to fear the water the way she did. The children spent endless days doing something she so desperately wished she had mastered as a youth.

Soon it was fall and Rachel enrolled Robert in school. As his self-confidence grew, so did his ability to learn. Gradually, and with remedial assistance, even his teachers saw his potential. His grammar expanded and his cognitive skills continued to expand. Rachel was so proud of her only son the day he came home from school and eagerly read a paragraph from a book. Each child was thriving; and while Robert was learning fundamentals; Clarissa was winning essay contests in her advanced classes. The achievements were of vastly different magnitude, but Henry and Rachel were equally proud of both of their children. Their lives were finally in order until that fateful night.

Chapter 9

"Henry, I just wanted you to know that all the guys here put in a good word for you yesterday, and we're sorry it didn't work out. Hey, look, I'm sure you'll beat it and get out the next time. Again, sorry," Officer Danbarry's voice was full of genuine empathy and sincerity as he spoke with Henry. "Officer Danbarry, can I ask you something; and you give me your honest answer?" Henry asked somberly.

"Yeah sure" the officer responded inquisitively.

Hesitantly, Henry asked the guard he had come to consider a pseudo friend "I've been in here for a long time, and you've been here for my entire incarceration, so you've seen me every day that you've worked right? Well what I'm trying to say is" Henry said timidly, "Do you think I'm capable of killing anyone?" Almost afraid of his response, Henry studied the guard's face as he waited momentarily for his response.

"Henry, to be honest with you" Officer Danbarry said slowly, carefully choosing his words, "When you first came here, all of the evidence pointed to you. But to answer your question; no, no I don't think you are capable of taking another's life, let alone your wife's."

Surprised at what he had just heard, Henry looked dumbfound as the officer continued. "When you first came here, I had read about you in the papers. Murders interest anyone in law enforcement, but your case particularly interested me because of your little boy.

"Robert?" Henry asked surprisingly. "What has he got to do with anything?"

"You see," the officer continued. "I wanted to know what was going to happen to your children, mainly because the misses and I had a son just like him. Miles didn't accomplish as much as the paper said that your son did, but we were proud of him just the same," Officer Danbarry quickly wiped a tear from his cheek as he passionately spoke of his son.

"You speak of your son in the past tense," Henry inquired quietly. "He died just before his tenth birthday," the officer responded as the wiped his nose.

"He had a simple cold, and the next thing we knew, he was dead. The doctors said that he was immunocompromised and what had appeared to be a simple cold turned into pneumonia and that killed him."

Henry sat silently absorbing what the officer had just shared with him, and also thinking of his own son. He felt ill when he thought about what had become of his son and daughter.

His sister-in-law had taken both children in after the trial, but soon Robert's care became too much for her and she had him institutionalized. Clarissa was old enough to fend for herself, and she went off to a boarding school to finish her education. During the early years, his sister-in-law would write only to inform him of the children's progress, but that too soon ended. Faithfully, every week Henry wrote to his son and daughter in their new homes, but neither ever responded. As the years passed, he began to give up hopes of ever seeing them again and eventually stopped writing. It wasn't until he read about his daughter's engagement to a handsome young lawyer that he attempted to reconcile with her. When he built up the courage to send her a wedding card and letter, she had already gotten married. Fate was not in Clarissa's corner on the day the letter arrived. Richard picked up the mail and opened the letter from his supposedly dead father-in-law. The compassion expressed within the pages of Henry's letter moved him as he read about his unknown brother-in-law and Clarissa's father. Furious at this intrusion into her life, Claire ripped up the letter without reading it. Her explanation for her omission of the truth during their courtship was simple; she didn't want the scandal brought up, nor did she want to embarrass him because of her family. Often he wondered what could have happened during her childhood to create such hatred for her only brother and her father.

Henry took a deep breath after reminiscing about his children for a moment. "Officer Danbarry," Henry said sincerely, "I swear to you on my life that I did not kill my wife. I never ever even laid a hand on her, let alone, kill her." Henry's expressions and words were full of sincerity as he spoke; the officer sat down next to him and smiled. "Why don't you tell me in your own words what happened that night Henry," the guard spoke softly as Henry looked up at him. "Tell me what you remember about that night; that is if you want to talk about it."

"After the trial, I vowed to never think about what happened that night; but if you really think you can help me..." Henry rambled on as Officer Danbarry interrupted him. "Wait a minute Henry," the officer said compassionately but sternly, I'm not making any promises that I may not be able to keep, but I do want to hear your side of it. My nephew is some hot shot lawyer here in town and if he's interested enough, he might look into your case. That is if he thinks he's got enough evidence to have the case reopened," the officer interjected. "So, take a deep breathe, and tell me exactly what happened the night your wife was killed, and don't leave out any details no matter how irrelevant they seem." The guard sat back watching Henry as the color left his face as his story began.

"It was a beautiful fall evening the night of Rachel's accident" Henry said softly, almost a whisper, as if the words were coming from someone else. "We were out on our evening stroll just as the sun started to set. The moon could be seen peeking through the clouds as the night air become crisper. Rachel said that she had something she wanted to discuss with me but that she wanted to go for our walk first. She had been distant all evening and I thought that something was wrong with one of the kids, but she kept reassuring me that they were both fine. She had seemed distant and nervous ever since I got home that night. I never understood why I she looked so stressed out when I saw her at home with my boss out on the veranda. "That man," Henry said smiling, "was always stopping by, bringing something for her or the kids," Henry continued on, shifting his weight nervously, "by the time she got around to telling me what was wrong, it was practically dark outside and downright cold out."

"What did she tell you Henry," the guard prodded.

"She told me that she was pregnant; Henry blurted out disgustingly.

"Yeah, so, what's one more mouth to feed?" the guard responded innocently.

"It wasn't that she was pregnant; it's the fact that I knew it wasn't mine! I had a vasectomy right after Robert was born because the doctors said that if we had any other children, they'd probably be just like Robert," Henry continued on sadly, "So when my wife told me that she was pregnant, I knew that she was carrying someone else's child." Henry's voice broke as he spoke.

"Henry, what you're telling me isn't going to help your case, only hurt it. You, my friend, had the perfect motive to commit murder. What did you do when she told you about her affair Henry?" the guard asked.

"She denied ever having an affair of course, and swore to me that the child must be mine. She begged me to go see our doctor to have him see if maybe the operation hadn't worked but I wouldn't have my intelligence be insulted that way," Henry said almost in regret.

"Were you mad Henry?" the guard asked, drilling the convict.

"Only as mad as any man would be; yes of course, I was mad" Henry responded back. "Mad enough to kill her?" Danbarry shouted before Henry had time to regain his composure.

"Yes, yes I was mad enough to kill her; but I didn't" Henry blurted out. "I swear I did not kill my wife." By now Henry was sobbing as the guard stood up. "If you're up to it Henry, tell me how she died?" the guard spoke softly as he paced slowly about the corridor, allowing the obviously rattled man enough time to regain his wits. Henry began to speak again recalling the final moments before his wife's demise.

"I remember shouting at her, yelling at her, asking her how she could have done this to us. I wanted to know who the man was, how far along she was and if anyone else knew. She continued to adamantly deny having any affair and I knew she was scared because she was shaking. We were bickering back and forth and just as we decided to take the conversation inside, we heard a noise" Henry's eyes lit up as he began recalling the last details of the night. "We thought we'd better go inside because the topic wasn't something you'd want the neighbors to hear you know; besides our immediate neighbor was a busy body and would have loved nothing more than to trash our name around. Rachel decided that we should continue our fight outside even though we may be overheard because she didn't want the children to hear us. She was shivering so I went inside to get her a sweater and also because I just wanted to get away from her and the situation for a moment.

How I wish I had let her go inside," Henry said as he hung his head as the tears started to once again flow.

"I was only gone a moment and as I started back off the porch I heard her scream and just like that, she was gone."

"What do you mean, she was gone Henry; the autopsy said that she drown, she didn't disappear."

"She did drown. But we had been standing on the top of the bluff when I left her. The next thing I know, I heard her scream and heard the splash in the lake below. I ran as fast as I could to reach the dock but by the time I got down there, she had gone under. I dove in after her but it was so dark that I couldn't get to her in time. I tried and tried but I just couldn't find her," Henry's voice trailed off as he dropped his face into his hands. "She couldn't swim you know," Henry said softly. "She insisted that the children learn to swim; but she couldn't swim a stroke" Henry added.

"Henry, the autopsy showed bruising consistent with a struggle" Officer Danbarry said matter of factly.

"I know," Henry said dryly, "I can't explain the bruising, except to say that maybe she got it from the fall. I just know that I had nothing to do with it."

"Do you think she lost her footing or jumped?"

"She would never have killed herself; either she lost her footing or was scared off the bluff" Henry said confidently. She knew the path along the bluff. She would never lose her way, even in the dark," he added.

"What would scare a woman off a cliff and into water that she couldn't survive in?"

"I wish I knew," Henry responded back as he shook his weary head.

Chapter 10

Nicole and Jared dressed for their respective jobs in silence. They both knew that they could possibly hear news about their offer and both were filled with anticipation, joy and dread. They had spent half the night lying in bed pondering whether or not the offer would be accepted and if it was, when they could close and start renovations. Jared went over in his head the financing involved, what needed to be fixed up immediately and other technical details, while Nicole dreamt of decorating the rooms and giving it her touch to make it truly their home. Both were so full of excitement that they couldn't broach the subject any more that morning. Nicole headed off to work while Jared worked on the computer. Throughout her drive into work, Nicole tried to focus on anything but the house but couldn't. She already felt such a strong bond with that dilapidated home and knew it was meant to become their forever home...

Nicole was racing around between her assigned rooms when she was paged to the nurse's station to take the call. Praying it was Gwen with good news, she snatched up the phone. "Hi Nicki, I'll cut right to the chase," Gwen said enthusiastically. "They took your offer without countering. You my friends, are about to become the new owner of 1990 Sycamore Lane!"

"Nicole, hey Nicki, did you hear me?" Gwen asked when the line remained silent.

After what she had just heard sunk in, Nicole let out a loud "YES" right at the nurse's station. Patients passing in the hallway stopped dead in their tracks trying to figure out what the outburst was all about. Trying to contain her emotions, Nicole started firing questing at Gwen without even giving her a chance to respond.

"When can we close? When can we move in? Can we have early occupancy? You think we could have gotten it any cheaper? What about the furniture? We added the contingency that the furniture stayed; did they accept that as part of the offer too?" Nicole asked quickly, barely stopping to catch her breath.

"Nicole Rose; shut up would you!" Gwen finally shouted into the receiver to get Nicole's attention. Once she was quiet, Gwen proceeded to answer her questions one by one. "If you stay quiet for one minute, I will answer all of your questions one by one. First of all, you can close once you have a mortgage commitment and are cleared to close, which usually takes approximately 45 days. You can move in after you close, but the seller did grant you access to the property to make cosmetic improvements but not structural ones. I don't know if you could have gotten it any cheaper, but you stole it as it is. And yes, the furniture all stays as per our offer. The seller was asked if she wanted anything from the house for sentimental reasons, and the answer was a resounding NO. Jean Hanks, her realtor says that she's a real bitch and just wanted to be rid of the house so Congrats, it's yours!" Gwen concluded, nearly out of breath.

"Why is she such a bitch and why does she have to have such an attitude towards her late aunt?" Nicole asked, feeling defensive.

"It wasn't her aunt's house; it was hers all along. Her aunt just had life use of it. You are buying the house directly from Claire Drake, the daughter of the murdered woman," Gwen cautiously explained. Without hesitation, Nicole responded, "I would have offered her less if I had known that. Oh well, doesn't matter who owned it; it's mine now!" With that, the conversation was completed and Nicole immediately called Jared to fill him in on the good news. Nicole deliberately omitted the fact that the owner was none other than the victim's daughter. She wanted Jared to keep an open mind and love the house as much as she already did, and wanted him to move into their new home without any misgivings. He was so damn superstitious that she didn't want anything to possibly spoil the moment.

Upon the real estate agent's departure, Claire made her way towards the liquor cabinet. Lately, it seemed the only escape from Richard, her job, and the pain of her mother's death could be found within a bottle. Slowly and methodically she poured herself a glass of bourbon, then lifted the glass and gazed into the fluid within. Tears flooded her eyes when she thought of the past and her present; and with one quick thrust of her wrist, the glass and its' contents were thrown across the room.

"Good morning Claire, with a wrist like that, maybe you should try out for the local farm team. I hear they're recruiting" Richard joked as he made his way past the library. He felt great despair when he saw her in such a state that sometimes he felt that joking around was the only way he could keep from breaking down. Deep down, he still loved and needed her, but slowly he saw the woman that he'd fallen in love with, slipping away. Many nights he tried to reach out for her, to console her, but she always stoically pushed him away. Claire had become so cold in the last few years that even her own children felt the after-effects and had stopped caring.

Both Jared and Nicole thought of nothing else as they made their way through the day. When they were finally home together, both exploded with excitement, and a little concern on Jared's side.

Nicole had spent the day not only taking care of patients, but picking out color schemes for the rooms, and how she was doing to update the kitchen and bathes. Jared, on the other hand, had thought about financing, and what they would need to do next to secure it. Nicole was talking away and when Jared didn't respond, she turned to see that she was talking to an empty room.

Before she could figure out where he'd went, he returned from the garage with a dozen yellow roses in one arm and a package in the other. Nicole lunged at him, kissing him passionately.

"Thanks Nicki, but you haven't even opened your gift yet."

"The kiss wasn't for the gift, or the roses. It was for you being you. I love you so very much Jared Daniel and I know we'll be so very happy in our new home."

"I love you too Nicole and I would love you even if we continued to live here, in our car or in a cave. I just love you," he said sincerely. "Now open your present."

Nicole quickly opened her gift and removed the box lid. She gasped as she saw what lay inside. Carefully tucked within the tissue paper was an ornate wind chime covered with dragonflies and angels. The chime gracefully jingled as she picked it up.

"The lady at the boutique said that angels and dragonflies are supposed to bring good luck so I thought we should hang it at the new house" Jared said sheepishly. "I thought they were kind of pretty and I know how you like dragonflies."

"You have got to be the best husband anyone could ask for" Nicole responded as her lips once again met his. Nicole's kiss was long and hot and Jared became immediately aroused as her slender body pressed against his. Feeling his obvious excitement, she quickly began unbuttoning his dress shirt without ever disrupting the motion of her tongue and body against his. She no sooner started working on his Dockers, when the phone began to ring. Both ignored the annoyance of the noise until they heard Gwen's voice on the other end. Nicole reached for the phone without letting Jared out of her grasp and breathlessly answered it. Gwen's message was short and brief. Nicole reassured her that they were making application in the morning and hung up, returning to more pressing matters. Once Nicole hung up the phone, Jared took it off the receiver again and whisked her into his arms. "No more unnecessary interruptions," he whispered as he carried her into their bedroom.

Chapter 11

Henry spent the day in the library. With the exception of acknowledging other prisoner's condolences regarding his denial, he barely spoke to anyone. Absorbed in self-pity, frustration and anger, Henry tried to forget his conversation with George Danbarry. Until the guard got back in touch with him, hoping that someone might help him get acquitted was too painful a venture. As Henry sat alone, he was greeted by Mac, another prisoner who had been incarcerated nearly as long as he had. Suddenly, Henry's moment of solitude was shattered by a loud blast just outside the library door. Unsure of what to do, Henry impulsively dove underneath the cubicle and listened to the commotion coming from the hallway. For a brief moment the only sound he heard was the heavy pounding of his own heart. Another gunshot blast suddenly echoed in his ears, followed by a heavy thud. Perspiration rose on his brow as he tried to fathom what was commencing just beyond the door, but fear kept him from venturing out of his hiding place. Within the library, the few other inmates were scurrying about, some seeking shelter, while others inquisitively peered out from behind book shelves. Within seconds a siren could be heard, partially concealing the noises coming from within the compound. In between the siren's wails, Henry could make out the pounding of feet up and down the hall; yet he remained frozen in place trying to absorb what was taking place. In all of the years that he had been incarcerated, no one had ever been shot or attempted to break out. Henry looked quickly at his watch, trying to determine how long he'd been under the desk when he heard a familiar sound. Mac, his longtime friend had crawled over to Henry's hiding place.

"What the hell is going on out there?" Henry whispered as he stared into Mac's ashen face. "Do you have any idea who's out there shooting up the place?"

"I heard a few guys in sector B bragging the other day about getting some guns and going hunting, but I thought Stellar was just talking smack like always." Mac's hands were trembling as he continued. "Shit, do you think this is going to turn into something bad Henry?" Mac asked nervously. "I mean, I would have told someone if I really thought they were actually serious and gonna do something. Henry, if we get out of this alive, promise me you won't tell anyone what I overheard. I'm up for parole in a few months and I don't want to blow it. Please Henry, don't say anything." Mac was on the verge of pleading and whining all at the same time when Henry quickly put his hand over Mac's mouth.

"Shut up, someone's coming" Henry mouthed into Mac's wide blood shot eyes.

Henry no sooner mouthed the words when three burly looking prisoners rounded the corner heading in their direction. Mac and Henry held their breath as the men stopped a few feet away from the cubicle under which they were hiding.

"Do you think the cops are on their way yet Stellar? Maybe we'd better take some more guards hostage instead of killing them all" Dillon sarcastically said as he wiped the perspiration from his forehead. "Seems to me they are more valuable alive than full of holes."

"Shut the fuck up would you" Stellar screamed at the teenage boy standing beside him. If I wanted your fucking opinion, I would have asked for it."

Henry suddenly recognized the squeaky voice emanating from above him. He gasped silently as he listened to the boy trying to talk like a lifer. The kid had only been in the system less than a year, and yet, now it was obvious that he had attached himself to one of the biggest assholes in the facility. The third inmate interjected his opinion of the two's exchanged only after Stellar was out of earshot. "I agree with you kid but mouthing off to him might get you killed you know," he said as he cast his eyes upon the obvious leader of the group.

"I know Gus, but who's he gonna fuck tonight if he kills me" Dillon replied confidently.

"He's had plenty others before you kid and he'll find someone else if he kills you. Just remember that whenever you're feeling cocky," Gus said with a smirk as he made his way to the window where Stellar was perched like a cougar looking for his next prey. Momentarily Dillon allowed the words to register in his already jumbled brain and then he set off to join the others.

Henry and Mac remained frozen for what seemed like hours until the three men finally left the library. Slowly Henry made his way toward the same window that had transfixed Stellar for so long. Hoping to see help coming, Henry became visibly distraught over the absence of humans outside. Mac paced nervously as he spoke in a barely audible tone.

"Henry, please promise me you won't tell anyone. I swear I didn't think they were serious. I can't stay in this place any longer than I already have. I've gotta get out of here with this next parole hearing. If the board got wind that I knew and didn't say anything, I'd never be paroled." Mac's eyes were genuinely full of despair as he pleaded with Henry who knew all too well what it was like to have freedom so close, then snatched away. He couldn't help but feel envious of the sorrowful looking man beside him. "Mac, lets concentrate on getting out of here alive. Come on, we're no threat to Stellar and the others. Let's see what's going on out there and try to get a handle on how many men are involved in this mess."

Cautiously Mac followed Henry's lead and made his way toward the doorway. The sound of sheer commotion emanated from the corridor but Henry was determined to regain some form of control over what was happening within his environment. The only way to do that was to obtain information. Mac, on the other hand, would have been just as content to remain hidden under the cubicle for the remainder of the night. Henry slowly and quietly cracked the door leading into the hallway. Men were running around everyone; some carrying crudely made knives and other weapons. Henry quickly surmised that any guards that had been in their immediate area were either long gone or dead. The floor and walls were splattered with blood and reeked of death. Henry motioned for Mac to follow him into the hallway as he quickly blended in with the others. No one seemed to notice the two older men as they made their way down the hallway.

Laughter and obscenities filled the air with an occasional distant gunshot blast piercing the commotion. Henry felt his composure slipping away as he searched the area trying to find the source of the riot. Before he was psychologically ready, he rounded the corner and came face to face with Stellar.

"What's going on Stellar?" Henry muttered, trying to sound matter of fact.

"What the fuck does it look like old man? We're settling a few scores with a few guards and getting the fuck out of here. What's it to you anyway?" Stellar barked as he evaluated the two men's faces.

"It's nothing to me Stellar; I just want to get out of here too. Shit, I've been in here longer than most of you and I know every nook and cranny of this place, so count me in if you want my help," Henry stated in a monotone voice, trying not to irritate the already irrational man. Mac glared in disbelief as he listened to Henry offering his assistance to this arrogant and obviously crazy man. Mac stood frozen as he watched his own execution unfold in his mind. He didn't return to reality until Stellar hit him with the butt of his shotgun screaming out a question that Mac hadn't heard the first time.

"What about you Mail boy, are you gonna help us too or should we lock you up with the other pricks or slit your throat right now?" Stellar laughingly asked as his piercing blue eyes glared at Macs. Mac remained frozen, momentarily evaluating his options. In front of him stood a six foot four inch lunatic with a gun; and beside him were his sidekicks who were also armed, dangerous and stupid. There was no way out. Acceptance of his fate had just been made remarkably easy. Knowing he had no choice, he just put on his best poker face. "Of course I want in Stellar. I want out of this fucking joint just as much as anyone else," Mac responded, trying to sound confident.

"Right answer Mail boy. You can start by using your little mailroom key ring to unlock some doors around here. And if you don't have keys to get in each room, you know how to pick a lock right; cause that's what you're in for remember? If you're too old to handle it, give me the keys and we'll kill you right now," he added with a smile. "We'll start with the kitchen stockroom cause I'm starving" Stellar said as he made his way down the corridor.

Mac gave Henry a hateful glare before setting off to catch up with his new pseudo friend. Henry shrugged his shoulders and exhaled as he waited for the other two hoodlums to exit before he fell in line. On their way to the dining hall, the men passed a few groups of inmates banding together, tearing up the place. They had already trashed the warden's office, along with desecrating the adjoining meeting rooms. To Henry, the outward violence seemed ridiculous, but to the men participating in the destruction, it appeared invigorating. Henry tried to make a mental note of each area they passed but the entire day was fading into one terrible blur.

Once the men reached the kitchen, Stellar waited for Mac to make his way toward the locked doorway. Quickly Stellar pushed him closer to the door and motioned for him to get to work opening it. Mac fumbled with the key ring before finally finding the correct one. With shaking hands, he jostled the handle and within seconds, the storeroom door opened up to reveal a cornucopia of canned and boxed foods. Stellar's eyes lit up as he pushed his way inside. He ran from shelf to shelf like a kid in a candy store, laughing in delight. Henry couldn't help but think how pathetic he looked. With the men distracted momentarily, Henry got Mac's attention. "I have no intention of helping these idiots Mac, and I didn't mean to involve you in this mess but what choice did we have. If we didn't play along, we'd already be dead. At least now we should have free rein of the prison and might be able to help end this fiasco. Oh, and Mac, of course I'm not going to tell anyone about you overhearing anything," Henry reassuringly said to his longtime friend. Mac admired Henry's sincerity but wished that he was still under the sanctity of his cubicle. "It's okay Henry, I know you wouldn't intentionally throw me to the wolves; or in this case, to an asshole," Mac finally replied, revealing a partial smile. "Come on, let's see what stuff the cook has hidden back here," Mac said as he made his way into the storeroom. Henry followed, though not at all interested in the room's contents. He wanted to speak with Stellar again. As they examined the boxes, Stellar and Dillon could be heard gorging themselves. Casually Henry called to Stellar "Hey, want us to check to see if these keys open up the infirmary so we can see what goodies Nurse Ratchet has in there? Stellar pondered the idea for a few seconds, then walked to where Henry and Mac were standing. "Yeah, you do that."

"What about the guards," Henry asked. "What do we do with them; I don't want to get shot you know; nor do I want to get locked up if they see me."

"Don't worry about them asshole guards," Dillon spoke up before Stellar could swallow his mouthful. "We shot a bunch of them and threw them in a cell and locked their asses up. So you don't have to worry about any dumbass guards, they're incapacitated so to speak."

"Would you shut up kid," Stellar screamed. "He's stupid most of the time," Stellar scowled, "But he's right this time. They're all locked up in this cell block and we haven't heard shit from the other sections. "But remember this old man, and mail boy; if you try to outsmart me and keep any of the pills for yourself, I will kill you; understand?"

"We understand completely Stellar" Henry replied as he made his way toward the hallway. Mac was once again quivering as he hustled to catch up with Henry and get away from the madmen as soon as possible. Once out of earshot, Henry divulged his true intention.

"You've got your key ring right?" Henry quickly inquired.

"Yeah, it's right here, why?" Mac responded as he patted his pant leg gently.

"Come with me then, we've got a job to do."

Chapter 12

The Drake's home was unusually lit up when Richard pulled into the drive. The lights were illuminated both inside and out. Unaware of any special circumstances or impending company, Richard quickly pulled into the garage and made his way into the house to find out what was going on. Rosa, their housekeeper was busy dusting the already meticulous china when he entered the kitchen. A short, pudgy woman in her late sixties, she had been employed by the Drake's from the time their children were infants. Upon seeing him arrive, she never missed a beat humming her Latin tune, but smiled and motioned towards the billiard's room. Trying to remember if it was his or one of the children's birthdays, he racked his brain trying to determine what was going on.

Upon entering the room, he saw her. Claire was crouched on the sofa, fixated on the TV screen. She acknowledged his presence without saying a word and continued to take in every word the reporter was saying. Richard scanned the area to see if she had been drinking before he focused on the news story that had Claire mesmerized. As she stared at the TV, he noted that her face wasn't flushed and she wasn't acting the usual jittery way that had become so commonplace whenever she indulged. When he finally focused his attention on the TV, he could not believe what he was hearing. The news reporter seemed out of breath as she was describing the deadly riot that was unfolding in the prison that Claire's father was incarcerated. Finally Richard realized what had caught Claire's attention.

When the anchorman finished reporting, Richard sat down by Claire trying to determine if her face expressed fear for her father or satisfaction at the possibility that he could be among the dead. "I can't believe that there's a riot," Richard said quietly. "Did they say how many casualties?"

Finally Claire spoke in a barely audible voice, "They've got negotiators down there now; but all they know is that there are several guards somewhere inside and the one that escaped from the area where it's taking place said that he knew of at least two guards, and half dozen prisoners who were dead. The warden issued a statement just before you got here saying that not all of the prisoners are roaming freely. Supposedly, the leader of this mess is some crazy lifer who put the prison on lockdown himself. The only other thing that he said was that the core group is heavily armed and that shots are continuously being heard from inside."

Not quite sure what to do or say, Richard spoke softly "I'm sure he's ok honey. He's a strong man or he wouldn't have survived in there as long as he has already."

"Sure you're right dear. Bet if he'd been the one pushed off the cliff, he would have survived with barely a bruise, unlike my mother," she replied trying to sound uninterested and uncaring. "Who cares what happens to him anyways?"

"You do Claire, "Henry thought to himself as he watched her leave. "You do."

Chapter 13

Jared lay exhausted in their bed as Nicki returned from the kitchen. He admired the self-confidence she had as she strolled around their townhouse in her birthday suit, totally comfortable in her nakedness. Sometimes after a grueling workout, he'd find her on the back patio cooling down with nothing but a towel on. It wasn't that Nicole was an exhibitionist; she just felt comfortable with her body. Settling down on the bed beside him, Nicole grabbed the remote control and turned on the TV. Jared sat up to eat and couldn't help but notice Nicole's long legs as the light of the television screen reflected off them. Suddenly his attention was diverted as Nicki changed the channel and word of the riot was announced. Both listened as the news anchor provided the information that was streaming in. After a few minutes, Nicole changed the station to a sitcom which was less depressing than the news. Jared picked up their now empty dishes and headed for the kitchen. He no sooner left the room when Nicki screamed to him. Running back, thinking something was wrong, he found Nicki springing off the bed.

"Oh my God Jared, I knew that I had read something about that prison recently, and I just remembered! I just read an article that stated that that's where the guy convicted of killing his wife went. You know the one who's house we're buying!"

"When did you read about that Nick," Jared asked in amazement. "I'd rather forget the fact that a murder took place in our new house."

"How could anyone forget it? It's part of the house's history. And Mr. Harteman and his kids have had to live with that fact for all these years. Nobody should forget the story; he has maintained his innocence all these years you know."

Jared decided to drop the subject as she padded the bed and welcomed him back in beside her. They drifted off to sleep in each other's embrace; neither dwelling on the news story.

Chapter 14

As soon as Mac and Henry were out of the kitchen, Henry turned to face Mac and with an outreached hand asked for the key ring. Puzzled and still trembling from Stellar's threat, he quickly reached inside his trousers to retrieve the keys. Once in Henry's possession, he jerked the kitchen door shut and with a quick flip of his hand locked it behind him. Mac's jaw dropped when he realized what Henry had done but before he could say a word, Henry grabbed his arm and yanked him into the corridor.

"Come on Mac, we need to find a way to end this before it gets any worse," Henry said as he headed down the hallway.

"You're worrying about it getting worse?" Do you realize what you just did? You just signed our death warrants with Stellar! We have got to go back and unlock that door. We'll tell him it was a joke or something," Mac pleaded as he caught up to his friend.

"No Mac. What's done is done. This is the only way to get us out of here alive. Stellar may be insane, but he's also very smart. Everyone is afraid of him so they go along with whatever he tells them to do.

Now that he's not available to call the shots, hopefully everyone will remain idle just long enough for us to get some help in here. We've got to get help to the injured guards and hopefully end this madness."

"I just want to know who's going to help us if he gets out of that kitchen stockroom" Mac asked, his voice full of concern. "Pretty soon his buddies are going to notice he's missing and go looking for him; then what'll we do?"

"Nobody's going to think to look in the kitchen's stockroom," Henry replied calmly, trying to persuade both Mac and himself. "They're too busy destroying the place and each other. Come on, let's go find the guards and see if we can get some help in here."

"Henry, just one last question, couldn't Stellar just shoot his way out of the stockroom?" Mac asked inquisitively.

"It'll be tough. Dillon and Jake left their shotguns in the kitchen when they went into the stockroom, and Stellar seems to be missing this" Henry said, holding up the clip and smiling.

Even Mac laughed as the two men entered the corridor and started careening their way through the hordes of men loitering in the hallways. Some were beating up on others, while a few stood bewildered at what was happening around them. Both men filed past the other prisoners swiftly and silently. Neither dared stop for fear of being questioned by the other prisoners. Once around the corner, they made their way toward solitary, where they thought Stellar had mentioned they'd thrown the guards. Henry let out a sigh of relief as he noted the empty halls. As he attempted to push open the door leading to the next corridor, Henry suddenly realized why no one else was there. Stellar or someone else had locked the steel door leading to where the guards were being held. A feeling of deep despair overtook him as he felt as if he's knees were giving out. Before Henry became more upset, Mac giggled the keys out in front of Henry.

"Today might be your lucky day old man," Henry chuckled as he positioned himself in front of the locked door.

"You mean you really have a key to get in here too?" Henry asked in amazement.

"Yup; I'm the mail boy remember? I have keys to get into just about everywhere, including the warden's john!" Mac relied with a laugh. Methodically Mac flipped the key ring around in his hand until his eyes spotted what he was looking for. With key in hand, Mac opened the heavy door leading to solitary. When the two men took a second to catch their breath, they looked at each other momentarily and smiled in agreement. Neither knew what the immediate future held, but both men knew what they had to do. With only one door to go, the men rushed to the area they believed housed the captured guards. Standing on his tiptoes, Henry was the first to peak into the small window set high in the door. He scanned the room, which was in deed housing the captured guards. Before he had finished scanning the walls, his eyes zeroed in on something he never expected. In front of him lay one of his only true friends. Gary Danbarry sat propped up against the wall with another officer at his side. His color was ashen white and from what Henry saw, he appeared to be in great pain. As soon as Henry realized that his friend had been severely injured, he desperately wanted to go to his aid. Suddenly the magnitude of the riot took on a whole new meaning. Henry quickly tapped on the window, catching everyone's attention. The men looked ready to pounce on whoever entered the door but Henry watched them back off when Officer Danbarry focused on Henry's eyes and then mouth something to the other guards. Henry stepped back and allowed Mac to fumble with the keys. Within seconds, Mac had the door open and Henry ignored the others and made his way to his injured friend. A few of the guards cautiously glanced outside the cell while majority blocked Henry's passage to his friend. Danbarry motioned to his comrades and they reluctantly backed off. Once the commotion died down, Mac and Henry tried to explain what had been going on within the prison. They explained who was behind the riot and where they had left him and his sidekicks. Even Officer Danbarry laughed, despite the pain, at the thought of someone double-crossing Stellar. They went on to explain how many cellblocks were involved and that they hadn't seen any sign of help coming from the outside. Mac did most of the talking while Henry crouched at Officer Danbarry's side. Officer Danbarry had been stabbed in the chest, though from what Henry could surmise, it was not a deep wound and apparently missed any vital organs. Henry felt that his friend had definitely lost a great deal of blood for his uniform was bloodstained through the makeshift compress against the wound. A few other guards had injuries, but of those within the cell, none appeared life threatening except for his friend's. Henry told the guards that Stellar had bragged about killing some of the other guards. As he spoke, he felt the tension rise from within the tiny cell, and suddenly wished that he had remained silent.

Sergeant Wilkes was the first to speak. He analyzed both Mac and Henry while he questioned them; skill skeptical as to why two inmates would have gone out of their way to help them.

"Do you have any idea how many men are locked up and how many of these assholes are still roaming free? Also, how many guns do they have and how much ammunition? Do they have enough to hold off a SWAT team's entry?" Before he allowed the men a chance to answer, his tone changed and the questions became an interrogation.

"By the way," the husky guard asked, nearly in Mac's face, "why are you here helping us anyway? Why are you risking your necks for us? And how do we know that this isn't a set up to kill the rest of us?"

The Sergeants voice was incriminating as he hovered over Mac. The middle-aged man looked like a little boy compared to the giant above him. Sure he was about to get slugged, strangled or roughed up; Mac momentarily thought that maybe he should have stayed with Stellar where at least he had some degree of protection. This guard who was practically on top of him made it evident that he didn't trust the two men even thou they had just freed them from the confines of the cell. Instead of being grateful, he was accusing them of being part of a conspiracy. Henry pushed himself in between the two men before the scene escalated any further, and quickly put the guard in his place.

"Look Wilkes," Henry said sternly, "You are absolutely right. We didn't have to come down here and save your sorry ass. We did it because we wanted to; and because we wanted your input on how to stop this mess. Mac here is up for parole soon and whether you believe it or not, I'm not an advocate of violence. I just want this thing to get resolved as soon as possible so my wonderful life can get back to normal. Now, if you're ready to listen, we'll tell you everything we know about the riot and the men involved."

Sargent Wilkes and the other guards backed off and motioned for Henry to give them what details they had acquired. The men listened intently as both Mac and Henry told them about the events that had transpired thus far. When the two had finished, everyone agreed on two things; first, the riot needed to end quickly; and secondly, Henry and Mac would die if somehow Stellar got out and found them. The guards sat in silence reviewing what they had been told. Finally Gary spoke to his longtime friend. His voice was full of emotion and conviction when he spoke; yet the sound was barely audible.

"Henry, me and the other guys are really grateful to you and Mac. I think I speak for everyone when I say that if and when we come out of this alive, we will have your backs. As I've told you in the past, I never really thought you belonged in here. You, Mac, on the other hand" Danbarry said jokingly, "I know you deserved to be in here and I don't think they really ever determined how many robberies you actually committed, but you too, deserve to be a free man."

Henry appreciated what the officer had said but felt that before the moment was lost, he needed to say one thing to all of them. "Gary, Sargent Wilkes, Officer Jones, and the rest of you; I just want to tell you one thing and I mean it from the bottom of my heart. I know that this mess could get worse, and if something happens that I don't make it out; I want you to know that as God as my witness, I did not kill my wife. I loved that woman with all of my heart and she was my soul mate. If I die during this fiasco, please promise me that someone will reiterate that to my son and daughter." Henry's eyes filled with emotion at the mention of his children.

He reminisced silently about his children and the happy times they had shared. "Maybe, he thought to himself, "if I do make it out of here alive, I will be given another chance at freedom." Sargent Wilkes broke the silence, "I know that you two have done a lot already, but there is one other thing I need you to do." The guard had the men's attention as he proceeded with his request. "We need you to get into the infirmary and retrieve a cell phone. The nurse has one stored there. We turn in our personal cells when we start our shifts, so if you can make it to the gate, they're there; but I don't think you could get that far. Your best bet to get us in touch with the outside is thru the infirmary."

"Forget it" Mac screamed in a high pitched voice. "No way am I risking my neck another time for you without a guarantee of freedom. If I go back out there and Stellar has been set free, I don't want to tell you what he said he'd do to us if we double-crossed him. Do you know that he actually likes fucking men? Think of what he'd do to Henry and me if he got out. And that's only one risk. Right now, there are a whole lot of idiots running wild within this compound. Who's to say that one of them won't turn on us huh? No guarantees; no way!"

"Wilkes," Henry said passively. "You are the highest ranked in here, and you're in good with the warden; if Mac and I go out there to get the phone, can you guarantee us that you'll do everything in your power to get us paroled?" Before Henry had a chance to answer, Gary Danbarry called Henry over to his side. With ashen face, he gazed deeply into Henry's eyes and with great effort, he spoke to his old friend.

"Henry, you don't have to risk your neck again. You're not one of them. You don't know how to think like the predators out there. You and Mac are targets, simply because of your age and passive nature. It's too dangerous for you and Mac" the officer whispered before a coughing spell started. When Henry saw the amount of blood that his friend was coughing up, his mind was made up. He reached over and grasped his friend's hand. The officer's hand was cold and clammy, and Henry dropped it impulsively, fearing that his friend was dying right before his eyes. Even Mac understood the urgency of the situation. Without hesitation, the two men made their way towards the doorway.

"I'm gonna lock you boys back up for your own safety," Mac said as he started to close the steel door. Henry paused, looking back at his dying friend. "Don't let him die before I come back."

"Be smart and be careful" Officer Jones cautioned as Mac closed the heavy door.

"No, don't go" Officer Danbarry whispered as he regained momentary consciousness, and just as quickly, slipped under again.

Chapter 15

Nicole's dreams were full of demons as she tossed within her bed. More than once Jared had to wake her from her troubled sleep. Jared watched her face contort and grimace, then relax. He wondered what she could possibly be dreaming about that caused her such emotional swings. After laying still for a brief interval, her body again began to tense within their bed. Before Jared could wake her for a third time, Nicole screamed out and sat upright in bed. The noise was so piercing; she woke herself and tried to get oriented.

"What's wrong Nicole? What's with the nightmares lately? And what did you mean "Don't go?" Nicole, still half asleep, looked at her husband's concerned face.

"Honey, I just had a silly dream about that riot we saw on the news. Not a big deal," she slyly smiled. "Now that we're both awake, I can think of something we should be doing instead of talking," she purred as she snuggled up to her husband.

"Nicki," Jared said as he delicately pushed her away, "I can't. It's the middle of the night and I've got a meeting I'm running first thing in the morning. It's not that I don't want to, but I'm exhausted and need some sleep."

"Party pooper," Nicole mused as she rolled over to her side of the bed. Once undisturbed, Jared lay awake for a few moments himself thinking about what must be occurring at that prison during the riot.

Well after 1:00AM, Richard made his way to his bedroom. He hadn't spoken with Claire since their brief exchange in the library during the news bulletin. Quietly he made his way into their room and slipped into his closet to change. Within minutes he approached their bed where Claire slept and stared down at her. He noted that although she wasn't moving, her breathing was rapid and slightly labored. He lay next to her, studying her face and wondering what she was feeling. Deep down, he knew she still cared about her father, her own flesh and blood, and the only parent she had left. Suddenly he felt great sadness for his spouse of so many years. He yearned to reach out and hold her, but fearful of her rejection, he chose to just slide in next to her and let her rest. Once situated in bed, he began to feel the strain of the day settling in. Concern for his wife and his father-in-law began to escalate within him and he felt such empathy and sympathy for them both. As he started to drift off, he suddenly felt the warmth of a hand on his back side. Richard disregarded the feeling but was completely awake when the hand traveled around to his crotch. Unsure of what to do, Richard played possum until his wife started to caress his thigh. His long dormant libido was now awake and alert, begging her to make the next move. Richard practically held his breath so as to not spoil the moment as Claire silently started exploring an area that she had evaded for so long. Richard felt his temperature rise immensely as she methodically stimulated every nerve in this most sensitive area. Slowly her lips made their way up to his mouth as her breast brushed against his chest. Unable to restrain himself any further, Richard wrapped his arms around her still firm derriere as his lips met hers. There embrace was not only long but also intense. All the built up emotion within Claire seemed to be released through her actions. She continued to kiss and caress his body for what seemed like eternity until he was about to explode. Just when he thought he was about to climax, Claire did something that surprised them both. Unable to contain herself any longer, she looker her husband momentarily in the eyes and with a magnitude of emotion flowing through her, she sincerely and passionately whispered "I still love you" and sat on top of him, taking him in in one swift motion. The feeling was more than he could handle and within seconds, both Richard and Claire reach ecstasy together. When both finally caught their breath, Richard, still not sure of what had transpired just moments before, decided to take advantage of the moment. As they lay intertwined in their bed, Richard turned to face Claire, and touched her gently.

"I love you so much Claire; with all of my heart and soul. Welcome back."

Tears welled up in both of their eyes as they remained in each other's embrace. Claire finally allowed the emotions that she had kept locked up for so long to flow freely. Richard held his wife tenderly as she let her emotions free.

"Richard, I'm so scared for him and for me. Besides you and the kids, he's all I've got. Lord knows the kids feel alienated from me. I don't blame them. I've been very good at pushing everyone away from me. Why did you stay all these years?" she asked, wiping tears from her eyes. "I let alcohol cover my pain; and I allowed it to turn me into someone who was incapable of loving. Yet you never wavered; you never left…"

"Oh Claire," Richard said empathetically, "Don't you know why I stayed? I stayed because you are the love of my life. Your mother's death, and your father's conviction aren't your fault; yet you seemed to act like they were. You can't control what happened to them back then; but you can influence what happens to him in the future."

"What if he dies? I'll have his blood on my hands. I'm the reason he's still in there. Maybe if I had told him what my mother was doing when he was away, maybe none of this would have ever happened and they wouldn't have fought that night and she wouldn't have died and he wouldn't be rotting in jail. I heard them fighting that night you know. Heard them; and did nothing. "

"Claire, you never told me that your heard them that night."

"You never asked. It happened so long ago and I had suppressed it so deep that up until a few days ago, I had forgotten about it."

"Maybe," Richard said excitedly, "You saw or heard something that could help you father."

Claire held her face in despair when she realized the severity of her actions against her own father. Her hatred of what happened to her mother had become focused and projected upon her father. When he was first convicted, even she didn't think her father was capable of murder, but somehow over the years, her need to have her mother back had become blurred with her need to blame someone for her senseless death. "But what if he doesn't make it out of there alive?" Claire asked softly through her sobs. "If he dies, we both know it's my fault."

The years and the alcohol had somehow made her forget the profound love that she had once had for her father. And now she realized that it might be too late.

"Richard," Claire asked pleadingly, "Is there any way you can find out more about what's going on there?" Claire looked at her husband with pleading eyes as she continued. "I swear to you that I never meant for this to happen to him. I just wanted him to feel the loss that I have had to live with all these years. First my brother took up all of her time, then her stupid boyfriend." Claire looked up at Richard, shocked. "Did I just say my mother had a boyfriend? My God, I had completely forgotten about him."

"Do you know who he was Claire? Do you think your father knew about the affair?"

"No, until now, I had completely forgotten about him. Shit, that's right. He was a horrible man, but my father thought the world of him. He absolutely gave me the creeps; and I think he knew it, because he was always giving me beautiful gifts. What did we call him?" Claire said, scratching her head.

"Uncle Antonio. Yes, that's it," Claire responded, smiling.

"Your mother really had a boyfriend and you knew about it?" Richard asked, somewhat dismayed.

"She always laughed my accusations off; but I clearly remember how weird she would get when he'd unexpectedly drop by. She'd get all uptight and he'd no sooner get there, and our nanny would whisk Robert and me off for a few hours. Many times, when we'd get back home, I'd find her crying. I always assumed it was because she missed him already and wanted to be with him."

"Claire, this is important. Do you think your father knew?"

"No. I am sure he didn't; and she made us promise to never mention it if Uncle Antonio had been around."

"Oh Claire, both you and your father have suffered so much. Your father has felt the same loss that you have; only his is even greater. The day of his conviction, he not only had already lost a wife, but on that day, he lost a daughter and son as well; along with his freedom. I'm sorry to say it Claire, but he lost much more than you or I can ever imagine. Hope, he didn't lose his will to survive."

As Claire's sobbing intensified, Richard pulled her close and felt a few tears of his own well up. "Please don't have it be too late for Henry" he thought silently as he held his wife, and eventually faded off to sleep.

Chapter 16

After securing the cell that housed the guards, Henry and Mac made their way back out into the corridor. The noise emitting from the hallways as they neared the infirmary was loud and offensive. The two men concentrated on blending in as they made their way towards their destination. Henry had made the decision to make it their first stop to pick up the cell phone and scavenge for some bandages and painkillers. Mac seconded the motion, but more for his own reasons. He knew that within the confines of the infirmary, he could find something to help his nerves. This whole ordeal was more than he wanted to deal with and he knew that the nurses probably had some Valium tucked away somewhere. When he had been a free man, Mac had always bragged that his best jobs were done when he was stoned. None the less, Mac thought if there was ever a time that he needed a little help relaxing, it was now.

As the men neared the infirmary, they came along another group of young men loitering in the hallway. They didn't look to be more than eighteen or nineteen and Henry recognized only one of their young faces. Henry felt his stomach tighten as they approached the men. Just as they were about to pass the group without saying a word, one of the boys jumped into Henry's path. Henry and Mac stopped dead in their tracks, trying to control their fears. Henry and the teenager stared at one another momentarily until the boy finally spoke.

"Hey, you got a smoke old man?" He asked coyly.

"Yeah, I've got one right here" Mac spoke up and passed it to the kid. Seizing the opportunity, Mac asked nonchalantly, "Have you heard anything about what's going on outside yet? Thought this place would be crawling with cops by now."

"Nah, haven't heard a thing yet; been too busy settling a few scores," the teenager laughingly said as he flashed the blade he was carrying. Just as the men were about to make their exit, the kid shouted back "Hey, have either of you seen Stellar? He was supposed to meet us over an hour ago and no one knows where the fuck he is. Those fuckers better not have broken out of here without us!"

Mac was the first to respond. "Yeah, I just saw him a few minutes ago. He was over by the exercise room using a dumb bell on someone's head."

Once out of earshot, Henry breathed a sigh of relief as he looked at Mac's smiling face. Proud of his quick thinking, Mac beamed from ear to ear. "Sending them in the opposite direction ought to detain them for a bit, don't you think?"

"Yeah, until they get there and some other inmate tells then that Stellar hasn't been in there all day."

"Shit, I didn't think of that," Mac said as the smile quickly faded from his weathered looking face. "We'd better get that phone and get the hell out of here before they come back."

"I couldn't agree with you more my friend," Henry responded as both men headed down the hall with an even brisker pace.

Within minutes Mac and Henry had made their way to the infirmary. To their surprise, the area was empty and didn't appear to have been destroyed yet. The men entered the room and methodically shut and locked the door. The area was dark but neither man turned the lights on for fear of being discovered. They fumbled their way around searching for medical supplies. Mac found the narcotic box and had it opened in under a minute, complimenting himself on still being the best in his former profession. Henry looked at this partner but said nothing. He just wanted to find painkillers and the phone and get back to the injured. Henry searched the area frantically but couldn't find the phone. Meanwhile, Mac stayed still, scanning the area with his eyes now adjusted to the dark. Honing in on something out of place, Mac moved over to study a picture more carefully, then grabbed it with both hands and lifted it off the wall, to reveal an indent in the wall that housed a shelf. On the shelf lay two items; the phone and a map. Upon determining that it was in working order, he spontaneously hugged Mac, smiled, and turned to leave. Mac, smiled back as he grabbed the map and tucked it into his sock.

Checking for noise before they left, the two men quickly departed the area as soon as they felt safe. Once outside the infirmary, Henry asked Mac how he had known where to find the phone. Mac chuckled and reminded Henry what he had done for a living prior to being the prison's mail carrier. Both men laughed and set off for solitary.

Back in their own prison, the captive guards paced anxiously, waiting for Mac and Henry's return. Some had voiced concerns that the whole thing could very easily be a set up. Sargent Wilkes himself came to the two men's defense when he reminded the other guards that neither Mac nor Henry were forced to risk their necks in coming down to find them in the first place. He then reminded them that if the men really had locked Stellar up as they said they had, they truly had put their lives on the line to save the officers. Officer Jones seconded what Wilkes had said and the younger guards dropped the subject. While Officer Jones was speaking to the group, Gary regained consciousness enough to comprehend the conversation taking place. He motioned the officer to his side. As soon as the man was within hearing distance, Officer Danbarry spoke.

"I know that some of you look at Mac and Henry as two inmates, and no different from the majority of the scum in here and because of that; I want you to know how proud I am of you for standing your ground in their defense. As his voice became weaker, the older officer continued, "I don't think I'm going to be here much longer, and before I die, I want you and the other men to promise me one thing. The officer tried to sit up to gain everyone's attention, but the searing pain within his chest kept him from moving more than a few inches at a time. "I want every one of you to promise me that you'll do everything within your powers to prevent bodily injury to the two men who are trying to save our asses right now. And I want you to make sure the warden and parole board hears about the heroics that they have done to save us. I believe with all of my heart that Henry did not murder his wife and if I live through this, I intend to prove it. But boys, I don't think I'm gonna make it through, so it's up to you to get them pardoned." The words had barely left his mouth when the officer drifted back into unconsciousness. His breathing became more irregular and shallow as the men looked on in horror, knowing they were watching their friend die. Jones squeezed his hand and leaned over towards his ear.

"Hold on just a little longer Gary. Help will be here soon."

As the young officer spoke, his voice trailed off as he felt Officer Danbarry's hand go limb and fall to the floor.

Henry glanced out the few windows they passed in hopes of seeing help from the outside. The compound looked vacant but Henry surmised that the area was probably full of sharp shooters and troopers. Inside the prison, the few that were not in lockdown were starting to become noisy again. As Mac and Henry approached their destination, Henry silently prayed that Stellar and his partners were still locked up in the stockroom of the kitchen. He knew the risks involved when he originally locked the lunatic up, but now he had to face the reality of his demise if in fact Stellar had somehow gotten free. Just thinking about it made Henry's pace quicken and Mac had to struggle to keep up. Once they neared the corridor leading to solitary, Henry slowly his pace slightly but continued to look over his should every couple of feet. They had encountered several small groups of inmates but no one had bothered with them. Once they rounded the final corner, the men relaxed and didn't' notice they were being followed by a lone shadow. Neither noticed their fatal mistake until they were about to unlock the door leading to the guards.

"Don't move another inch or I'll blow you two away."

Both men turned in disbelief. Neither could fathom how they could have been so stupid. Mac started trembling when he realized who the sinister sounding voice belonged to. Henry, on the other hand tried to evaluate the situation. Standing merely five paces from them was one of Stellar's main enforcers. Latham, or Viper as his buddies called him, was snickering as he leaned against the wall pointing a shotgun directly at them. Too frightened to move Mac turned to face Henry who didn't appear rattled by the confrontation. Henry slowly stepped forward towards Latham and was the first to speak.

"Hey Viper, what are you doing down here? Mac and I were just snooping around trying to see what was going on." Henry's voice sounded poised and confident as he continued. "Why are you wandering down to this neck of the woods?"

"Cause I wanted to settle a score for Stellar" the aloft man maliciously responded. And if you wanted to snoop around looking for trouble, well asshole, you've found it!" Both Henry and Mac suddenly realized that this confrontation was not going to end well.

"What do you mean?" Henry asked, never taking his eyes off the gun being pointed in his direction.

"You know exactly what I mean," the man sneered as he continued. "I ran into one of the kids who said that two old men told him that Stellar was in a place he'd never been in. You two match the description. Now, before I kill you both, I want to know why you gave false info and what happened to Stellar. What the fuck did you do with him?"

"Well, if you put it that way, we locked him up in here to let him cool down for a while" Mac responded, pointing his head in the direction of the solitary cell door.

"No!" Henry shouted. "They're not in there he screamed as he approached the armed man.

"Back off old man" the gunman shouted back as he raised the gun directly at Henry's chest. "So if Stellar's not in there, then who is that you're protecting" he asked as he motioned for Henry and Mack to back away from the door.

"Move out of the way Henry. Do as he says," Mac said as he quickly winked at him. Reluctantly Henry backed away from the door and Latham started to approach it. Without warning Henry leaped toward Latham but before he could deliver a blow, Viper spun back around and fired a shot. The blast knocked Henry off his feet and against the wall. Watching in horror, Mac seized the momentary distraction and reached into his trouser pocket. Before Latham realized what was happening, Mac thrust the contents of his pocket deep into the man's chest. Puncturing this aorta with the thrust of the blade, Latham dropped to his knees and fell face first onto the cold pavement. Mac jumped over him and bent at his friend's side. Henry lay motionless in a puddle of blood. Before he could speak, Mac turned to face the cell when he finally heard the pounding coming from inside. Quickly he got to his feet and fumbled for the key. With trembling hands, it took what seemed like forever for him to open the door. Once opened, Mac quickly told the guard what had transpired. Jones was the first to step outside the cell. He gasped when he saw the two lifeless looking bodies just beyond the doorway. Viper lay in front of him with his lifeless eyes staring into space, and the blade still thrust into his chest wall. As Jones evaluated the situation, Mac pleaded his care. "I did it to him. I ain't never killed anybody before. Shit, I'm just a burglar but I had to do something to stop him from killing Henry. Oh my God, Henry!" the man cried as he rushed over to his friend's side.

Henry lay face down against the wall. When Officer Jones and Mac gently rolled him over, the extent of his injuries became very clear. Latham's bullet appeared to have ripped through Henry's upper chest and gone straight through. His arm lay at his side at a precarious angle, with both muscle and bone exposed. The bullet appeared to have shattered his collarbone before exiting, ripping off half of his arm on the way. Tears welled up in Mac's eyes as Officer Jones felt for a pulse. After a few seconds of silence, Jones's face lit up as he exclaimed that Henry still was alive, his pulse was weak and irregular but at least he was alive. Even the once skeptical guards broke out in laughter and high fives at the news.

"Where's the phone Mac. We need to get help in here now if Henry and Gary have any chance of making it," Sargent Wilkes quickly asked the still emotionally overcome inmate.

"It's in Henry's pocket" Mac mumbled as he motioned towards Henry's pant leg.

"God I hope it didn't get crushed when he fell" the older man retorted as he gently rolled Henry while reaching for the phone.

The hallway was once again silent as they flipped open the phone and listened for a dial tone. A smile came across Jones's face as he gave the men a thumb's up sign and dialed. Mac remained at Henry's side trying to wake him up. Henry lay motionless with his chest slowly rising and falling in an irregular fashion. His breathing looked familiarly similar to Officer Danbarry's. After watching him for a few moments, Mac leaned over to Henry's ear and started talking to his friend, not at all sure if he could even hear him.

"What the hell did you do that for Henry? There's no way I was gonna let Viper hurt the guards, I just needed his back to us. You didn't need to jump him you know; I would have stopped him from hurting anyone. Now look what he's done to you! Hang on buddy, help's just a phone call away."

Mac stared down at his friend, waiting for a response, but Henry remained motionless on the cold concrete floor. After a brief moment, Mac diverted his eyes toward Officer Jones who by now was involved in a noisy conversation on the phone. Trying to get the joist of the call, he looked back at Henry to monitor his breathing, but kept his ear peeled toward the phone. One of the younger guards knelt down beside Henry, offering to hold pressure on Henry's wound, giving Mac a rest. Mac looked up at the young guard, who was no more than twenty one or twenty two and by the look on the man's face, surmised that he probably had never seen anyone dying before. Mac remained silent as he tried to evaluate in his head why this had to happen. From the start of the riot, Henry's main concern was to find a solution to the situation, and do so with the minimum amount of bloodshed. Looking down at this bloodstained shirt and ghastly appearance, Mac suddenly felt guilt, remorse and rage at the same time.

Upon completing his call, Officer Jones and Sargent Wilkes joined Mac at Henry's side. Briefly he explained what was about to transpire in regards to the police taking back the prison. With their location being established, the swat team was poised to enter the compound and subdue the inmates. Wilkes instructed a few of the guards to secure the door at the end of the hallway and motioned to a few others to assist him in moving Henry next to Danbarry and out of harm's way. Mac jumped up to help, making sure his friend knew what was happening. Henry groaned in agony with any movement and through still unconscious, appeared to nod when Mac explained what was going on.

While the guards and Mac were preparing to hopefully be rescued, the entry team was getting set up on the roof. Four policemen had already penetrated the prison through a hole they had blasted within a perimeter wall. Eight more men were positioned on the roof waiting for their signal. Once everyone was in place, the plan went into action. With tear gas and weapons at the ready, the team entered the now smoldering compound.

"How long's this gonna take?" Mac whispered. He still was unaware that the rescue was already in progress. "I don't think either's got much time left."

"I know," the sergeant replied. "But don't write them off just yet. I think both are tougher than you think. We will be out of here soon and there's a trauma team waiting for them at the hospital. On a different subject; I think you should know that when we get out of here, they're probably gonna lock you back up until this mess is resolved and we can tell the Warden and parole board what you and Henry did.

"Yeah, I know" Mac laughed. "Just don't let me share a cell with Stellar," Mac joked.

Within moments, the intensity outside their solitary domain seemed to increase and suddenly, it appeared that a war was being carried on around them. The younger guards huddled together, trying to protect themselves while the more seasoned guards waited anxiously for their rescuers. The entire time, Mac remained frozen at Henry and Danbarry's side. Soon the rest of the group joined him as they made their way toward the back of the cell where the injured men were lying. The guards were instructed to huddle around the two men lying on the floor to protect them from flying debris. As soon as the men formed a make shift barricade, a small blast seared the cell door off its hinges and four members of the entry team clad in full body armor barged in. Mac stood as he noticed the 12 gauge Remington pointed in his direction. Sargent Wilkes quickly intervened. After what seemed like hours, the man lowered his weapon and Mac breathed a sigh of relief.

"Hold on Henry, they're going to get you both to the hospital real soon. Just hang on a little longer."

"Yeah," Sargent Wilkes added, "Both of you better pull through this shit. Don't either of you dare die now!" As he spoke, Sargent Wilkes was interrupted as the second round of men rushed in with stretchers in tow.

As they made their way towards the roof, they passed body after body lining the hallways. Mac covered his nose at the smell of death and the lingering remnants of the tear gas and wished that he could have covered his eyes as well. Some of the inmates had been shot, some stabbed and some had been beaten to death. Mac had never seen so much violence before and felt nauseous by the time they had reached the rooftop.

"Once we step out there, you know they're only going to see you as an inmate."

"Yeah I know. Just don't let them shoot me. I'm one of the good guys remember?"

"Don't worry, I've taken care of that but according to them, you're still a convicted felon until you're officially paroled or pardoned. But hey, play the game a little longer and you will hopefully be a free man before you know it."

"Can you promise me that I'm finally getting out of this hell hole once and for all?" Mac asked as his hopes were lifted.

"I can't say for certain, but my guess would be yes; you'll both be free men soon enough. That is, if Henry makes it."

"He's gonna live, damn it!" Mac responded in a louder than anticipated voice as they watched the two injured men being loaded into choppers and whisked away.

Within a few seconds, Mac winced at the intensity of the sun, but welcomed it just the same. He stood in the morning light, relieved to be able to take a breath of fresh air.

"Take care Henry," Mac mumbled under his breath as he watched the chopper depart out of sight.

Chapter 17

Nicole mulled around her unit, trying to get motivated for her long shift ahead. She felt drained this morning and attributed it to staying up late and not getting a sound night's sleep. Jared had even commented on how exhausted she looked. Her assignment wasn't overwhelming, yet she just couldn't muster up the energy to tackle it with her usual vitality. Even her co-workers noticed that she wasn't her usual perky self and when a few teased her about it, she found herself snapping back in retaliation.

"Hey, I'm really sorry. I didn't mean to snap, it's just that I didn't get much sleep last night and I think that this whole house buying thing is starting to stress me out. Forgive me okay," she said with a sly smile.

"Forgiven," Vivian responded back. "I was just hoping that you and that gorgeous husband of yours had split so I could have a chance at him. Oh well," she teased, "I guess I'll just have to wait a little longer" she said with a wink.

"Yeah, I guess you'll have to wait just a little bit longer Viv," Nicole answered back, now laughing.

"Hey guys; how come I'm running around like a crazy woman this morning and you two are just standing around gabbing?" Sarah asked jokingly as she approached her co-workers.

"Because Heather gave you the toughest assignment Sarah, that's why" the older nurse responded.

"Yeah right; she just knows I'm younger and more efficient than some middle aged nurse," Sarah retaliated back and she sped off with her computer on wheels towards her next patient's room.

"Wise ass," Vivian quipped as she too set off to tackle the morning ahead of her. Nicole returned to her pod and got organized for her first med pass. She, though physically and emotionally exhausted, greeted each patient with a smile and warmth in her voice. Nicole was a nurse who was loved both by the patients under her care, and by their families as well. Her efficiency was noticed in her actions. Even her peers looked up to Nicole for her knowledge and dedication to their profession.

Nicole continued passing her meds and assessing her patients when the intercom overhead paged all nurses to the front nursing station. Nicole, Sarah, Vivian, Michelle and Jorja made their way towards the desk. Heather, who was in charge, stood waiting for them with a long puss on her face. By her expression, everyone instantly knew that her news wasn't good news.

"We just got a call from the supervisor. She needs a nurse from each unit to report to Critical care."

"What, can't those bitches handle their own assignments. Whenever they break a nail or have more than one patient, they whine for backup. Christ, their patients are on vents so it's not like you have to do much for them. I'm tired of getting pulled there to do their work all the time" Vivian snapped in a sarcastic voice.

"I couldn't agree with you more Viv, but this time it's legitimate. They're pulling from all units so it's not just here. They've got several critically injured patients arriving and are treating this as a Code D but didn't want to announce it overhead due to the type of people coming in. I don't know any details yet but I do know that the injured are all coming from the prison and the injured are both guards and inmates."

"Oh come on Heather," Michelle groaned. "You could have told her no. We've all got full assignments already and now you want us to absorb one of our assignments so one of us can go help save an inmate? WTF?"

"I know Michelle, it's getting old but those inmates, and especially the guards; they all have families and all deserve care. So do I have a volunteer or am I choosing who floats?

"I'll go" Nicole spoke up. But who's going to pick up my assignment?" Nicole asked.

"I'll take half your assignment and cover charge" Heather spoke up. "You guys," she said, looking at the remaining nurses, "Figure out who is taking who."

"No." Vivian spoke up, "I'm curious and haven't been down there in a while. I need to catch up on the latest gossip anyways. Say, is Tom still messing around with that blonde RT?"

"I think so," Sarah quietly added.

"Wouldn't you if you were him?" Michelle interjected. His ex is a first class bitch.

"You guys are awful. It's not her fault that she got so bitchy after gaining so much weight during her pregnancy. Are you going to say the same about me when I'm pregnant too?" Nicki asked.

"What?" Vivian squealed in delight, "Are you knocked up Nicki?"

"No," she answered, blushing. "Not yet anyway."

"Are you trying?" Sarah coyly asked.

"Well, not exactly. We're going thru the motions but not actively trying to have a baby. We thought we'd try as soon as we're settled into the new house."

"I think that's great," Vivian said as she handed off her assignment so she could report off and get to CCU. "I think you should get pregnant, gain about seventy pounds and make the rest of us feel better about ourselves. Then maybe that gorgeous husband of yours will look my way."

"Not in your lifetime Viv; not in your lifetime."

"Yeah, yeah; story of my life," Vivian sighed as she headed off the unit towards Critical Care.

After Vivian departed, Nicole and the rest of the staff returned to work, each in their own pods. The hours passed quickly as they were busy. Nicole didn't mind her assignment, nor would she have minded being pulled. Most of the patients in their CCU were either victims of car accidents or the aggressive actions of others. Syracuse as a whole had recently seen only a slight increase in crime but their hospital had the level 3 trauma unit so most of the victims came to their facility. If they made it out of CCU, many of the patients ended up on Nicole's unit; if they made it at all. But for now, Nicole and the others weren't worrying about admissions; they were just trying to stay caught up with their work.

As the hours passed and Vivian didn't return, Nicole's thoughts wandered from thinking about the house, to thinking about having a baby, to thinking about the strange dreams she had had during the night. Unable to explain why, she had the underlying feeling that she should have taken the float. Maybe if she had, she would have been busier and not had time to stand around worrying about thinking about things she couldn't change and ridiculous dreams. Regardless, she didn't take the pull and decided to venture over to Sarah's area to give her a hand. Even then, she still was bored and volunteered to go to first lunch after she finished helping Sarah. Before she left, she snuck away to call Gwen to check on their loan application. After speaking with Gwen, she phoned Jared.

"Hi honey, did I call at a bad time?"

"No time is a bad time to speak with you Nicole."

"You're so sweet. By the way, Vivian wants me to get fat so she can have a chance with you."

"Nicki, Vivian wants anything that's breathing and has a zipper."

"Jared, now that's not fair. Maybe true, but not fair," Nicole said as she laughed. "Anyway, I just got off the phone with Gwen and she said the mortgage should be approved quickly. She said that she has the key so we can start cleaning and painting like the early occupancy agreement states. We can directly there from work tonight if you want."

"Do you think that's such a good idea Nicole? I mean, you must be exhausted by now. You hardly slept last night and when you were asleep, you did nothing but toss and turn. I don't know about you, but I am really beat today."

"Yeah, I'm a little tired too but don't you want to start fixing up the house as soon as possible. I can't wait to get in there and start rearranging furniture."

"What little furniture we own Nicki, can easily fit into one of the rooms. Besides, the dirt will still be there tomorrow."

"Well, you don't have to come" Nicole huffed, "But I'm going to meet Gwen there right after work."

The phone went dead in Jared's ear. "Guess I know what I'm doing tonight too," he thought as he hung up the phone and returned to his computer terminal.

Frustrated that Jared didn't' appear to share her enthusiasm for their new home, Nicole reported off to Heather and left for lunch. Once she sat down for lunch, she tried to unwind. She thought about her conversation with Jared and decided that maybe she'd been a little too harsh, but the house was so important to her and she just wanted him to be as excited as she was. Part way through her lunch, she spotted Vivian and motioned her over. Originally desiring solitude, Nicole now longed for company to provide a distraction from her ever-consuming thoughts about the house. Within moments, Vivian made her way through the cafeteria and joined Nicole. Her face looked tired as she sat down beside her co-worker.

"What's the matter Viv; you look awful."

"I feel awful. You should have taken the pull. I'm getting too old to work my ass off."

"What kind of assignment do you have? Did they dump the admissions on you or what?"

"No, mine are relatively stable ones that had been there but the one weighs half a ton and killed my back turning her. Nancy took one of the ones that came in, our buddy Tom took another and Meg took two. Two of the ones they took to surgery never made it off the table; I guess a guard and an inmate."

Vivian glanced over at Nicole who sat silently after Vivian's finished talking. Vivian studied her face momentarily while waiting for her to respond. "Hey, are you in a trance or what? Did you hear anything I just said to you?" she asked gruffly.

"Nicole snapped out of it and answered her friend. "Yes, I heard everything you said. You said that an inmate and a guard were the ones that died right? Did they come from the riot at the prison?"

"I don't know Nic. What the hell difference does it make anyway?"

"I'm not sure, but I think it makes all the difference in the world."

Confused, Vivian decided to change the topic as she and Nicole finished eating their lunches.

Once back on her unit, Nicole checked to see if anything had changed with her patients while she was gone. After checking in on them, Nicole went to the computer terminal away from the nurse's station. Knowing what she was about to do could cost her her license, she did it anyway. Quickly she pulled up the CCU census and scanned the names quickly. She couldn't explain why she was doing it, but just knew something was compelling her to do it. As she ran down the list, she slammed her fist down on the table.

The remainder of the day passed slowly for Nicole. As she neared the end of her shift, she taped report as Heather entered the room carrying large white box with a big yellow bow on it. Puzzled, and a little annoyed at being interrupted, Nicole looked at her with a somewhat drab expression.

"Hey, they're for you," Heather said. "But if you don't want to see what's inside or who they're from, I'll be more than happy to keep them. Do you know the last time I got flowers from anyone? I think I was in high school and had just had my appendix removed. Even then, the flowers were from my parents and I'm guessing these aren't from your parents. Jimmy doesn't believe in sending me flowers; thinks that would indicate he's whipped. I think he's just cheap" Heather said with a grin as she laid the long box in front of Nicole. "Go on, open it up. I'm not leaving here until I at least get to see them. I might as well enjoy someone else's flowers if I can't enjoy my own." Realizing that she wasn't going to leave until Nicole opened the box so she quickly pulled the bow off the box and lifted the lid. Inside, were two dozen gorgeous long stemmed yellow roses. Heather gasped as she admired the delicateness of their petals. Unable to resist, she carefully picked up one and brought it to her nostrils. The aroma was so sensuous, yet refined. Nicole opened the enclosed care and read it to herself. "I'll be there; wouldn't miss it for the world." Realizing that she must look ridiculous with her overt drooling over the flowers, Heather put the rose back and turned to leave.

"Take it," Nicole said before she left the room. Heather turned to face her. "I don't need two dozen roses, besides I don't have a vase big enough at home. Why don't you take some of them home and tell that husband of yours that a secret admirer gave them to you."

"No, I couldn't do that. He's got a jealous streak and might actually believe me. Don't need to do anything to set him off. Men are such jerks you know. He won't get me any; yet I'm afraid to bring one home. Go figure; relationships are so confusing! Oh, what the hell, if you don't mind parting with a few, I would love them."

Take as many as you want Heather."

"Thanks Nicki."

Nicole returned to the task of taping report. When she was finished, she made one last round to make sure everyone was settled. Glad the day was finally coming to an end, she decided to phone Gwen one last time to make sure the plans hadn't changed. Once Gwen confirmed, Nicole waited anxiously for the next shift to get out of report so she could leave. As she and her co-workers waited, Vivian got off the elevator to join them. She filled them in on her day.

"Are those guys still living Viv?" Heather asked nonchalantly.

"Last I knew. The last two guys went into surgery and were still in when I came down here. I know that the OR is swamped and they're waiting on anesthesia to start the last cases. One of the surgeons told one of them before the case was even started that he was going to lose his arm and from the way he looked, he probably won't even make it off the table. I can't imagine getting shot at point blank range."

"I can't imagine it. That's why I hate guns. Every day in the paper you read about someone getting killed, and in that guy's case, getting maimed by one. People are careless and innocent people lose their lives because of guns."

"Get off your soapbox Heather," Michele lashed out. "I for one, would like to keep my Second Amendment, and I have no intention of giving up my guns. Yes, there are idiots out there who have guns, but guess what; if the president and that crazy Bradford woman get their way and take the law abiding citizen's right to bear arms away from us, those idiots will still have their guns and we'll have absolutely no protection from them."

"That's what the police are for Michelle. Have you ever heard of calling them or 911 in case of an emergency?"

"Oh crap on that," Michelle sarcastically responded back at Heather, who by now was very into the debate. "If I had waited for the police when I lived in Dallas, I'd be dead by now. Do you know how many troopers are on patrol in your district during the night shift? Take that number, and then look at the square mileage they have to cover, and you tell me; if they're miles away, and someone is kicking in your door at 2am, and you have no protection, think you'll be okay until the police arrive 12 or 15 minutes later?"

Heather shrugged her shoulders but didn't respond; nor did Michelle let up.

"Think about what some guy who's high on drugs or crazy or just desperate could do to you or your kids in 12 minutes."

Obviously losing the debate, Heather quietly responded "But I've got two dogs at my house and I've always heard that a burglar will avoid your house and move on to your neighbors if you have a dog."

"And I've got an expensive security system," Sarah hesitantly offered.

Now really getting in to the dispute, Michelle turned toward Sarah as the elevator opened and shut again when no one got on it. "Does your expensive security system have a push button directly into the police station or does it just ring into the alarm company? And is your phone line buried?"

Sarah and Heather truly looked stumped by the questions that Michelle was firing at them.

"I don't know if it's a direct line to the police or not, and I don't think the line is buried, but I'm not sure. Why?"

"Because," Michele replied confidently, "By the time your alarm company calls you back and then calls the police, it could be too late. And if your phone line isn't buried, a burglar can deactivate your system by simply cutting the right wires." Sarah's face paled as she listened in horror. Seeing that she was really spooking the young single woman, Nicole finally spoke up.

"You've made your point Michelle. But one thing you must emphasize when you're plugging guns is that a gun is only an effective weapon if, and only if, you know how to use it properly. To be competent in defending oneself requires constant practice. You have to shoot regularly, and be very comfortable in the safe handling of a gun. And you have to be psychologically prepared to shoot to kill; otherwise it can be used against you. Now, we've already let three elevators go by, can we please drop the subject and get on this one. I, for one have things to do and would like to go home."

"Thanks for shutting her up," Vivian whispered in Nicki's ear as they entered the elevator. "She was really getting on my nerves."

The group rode the elevator in silence down to the lobby. Quickly they made their way outside and to the open air parking lot. The warm spring air was invigorating. Everyone said their good byes and headed in separate directions. Once in view of her car, Nicole quickened her pace, knowing that their little discussion had cost her precious time.

Pulling out of the parking lot, Nicki tried to phone Gwen to let her know that she was running a few minutes late. When she didn't answer, she tried to phone Jared, but he too, was not answering. Frustrated, Nicole accelerated and sped towards the lake. "This whole day stunk," she thought to herself. "Hope the evening at the lake goes well..."

The traffic was heavy on the freeway as Nicole cruised along, nearing her exit. Her mind kept wandering back to last night's news report and the riot occurring at the prison. She couldn't help but think about the men who were brought in to the hospital. Nicole had always kidded Jared about his boring job, but suddenly she was very happy that he did have a boring but very safe job. She tried to imagine what must have been going through the heads of the injured, and their spouses. Even the inmates might have family and people who love them. She couldn't imagine what it must be like to see a loved one clinging to life. She experienced death at the hospital but it wasn't usually due to violence, but to illness. The whole riot seemed stupid to her as she exited the highway and exited onto Birch Ave. With Poplar Street just a few blocks away, she reached for her lip gloss inside her purse. As she turned off Poplar and onto Sycamore Lane, her heart started pounding with excitement. She couldn't wait to be inside her new home. Suddenly, the events of the day seemed very distant and insignificant. All that mattered now was seeing her new house. She pulled into the drive to find Jared and Gwen coming around from the front of the house. Jared smiled as he saw Nicole walking toward them.

"Hey Nicki! I'm going to go open up and leave you two lovebirds alone for a minute ok?" Gwen shouted as she made her way toward the house. Hearing no response, she opened the door and went inside to turn lights on.

Jared and Nicole met at his car to retrieve her change of clothes. After thanking him for the roses, they stood momentarily making small talk when they heard a scream from within the house. They looked at each other and rushed toward the house, not sure what was happening inside. Before they got to the front door, Gwen came bolting out of it. Obviously terribly shaken up about something, they tried to calm her down so that she could tell them what was wrong. Gwen was hyperventilating and unable to talk. Nicole motioned for her to sit on the step and put her head between her knees to catch her breathe. Jared stood at Gwen's side as she tried to catch her breath, and didn't notice that Nicole had slipped away. When he realized that she wasn't standing beside him, he called out her name but she was already out of range.

Nicole made her way through the first floor and when she didn't see anything out of order, she raced up the stairs to the second floor. Unsure of what to expect, she cautiously made her way from room to room. When she entered the Master bedroom, she noticed that the shade was up and the window was ajar. The wind was blowing the faded and torn remnants of a curtain into the air. Nicole walked over, shut and latched the window, then proceeded down the hall, searching the other bedrooms. When she stood at the entrance of to what must have been a little girl's room, she saw that that window was open also. The wind was blowing off the lake so hard and coming in through the window that it was making the cradle on the floor sway back and forth. Nicole entered the room and sat down in the rocking chair beside the cradle to catch her own breathe from racing around. The room was comforting to the eye with its pastel colors and its' simplicity. Suddenly, she felt overwhelmingly cold and reached over to shut the window. She rubbed her arms to rid herself of her sudden chill and called out when she heard footsteps on the stairs heading in her direction. Gwen and Jared appeared in the hallway and as soon as Gwen saw what room Nicole was in, she practically screamed "Get out of that room Nicki. Get out now!"

"What are you yelling about?" Nicki asked as she walked towards them. "What's going on Gwen?"

"That room and that chair" she shrieked as the pointed at the rocking chair, "are possessed! When I unlocked the door, I distinctly heard a noise coming from upstairs, so like a fool, I came up here to check it out. When I entered that room, the cradle and rocker were rocking wildly back and forth in sync. Scared the shit out of me. It was like someone was sitting in the chair, rocking the cradle with their foot or hand. It was so freaking spooky!"

"I did see it, or at least the cradle rocking," Nicole answered back. By now Jared was looking very confused and a little spooked himself. "What I mean is, yes, the cradle was rocking, but the window was wide open and so was the one in the other bedroom. With such a strong wind coming off the lake, it's not surprising that it was moving."

"Well, what about the rocker? It was rocking too," Gwen protested, both waiting for and wanting a feasible explanation.

"I'm sure the wind was blowing in a different direction when you came in. Anyway, the wind is dying down now, so everything should stop moving. Let's close up all the windows now so you don't have to worry about anything moving" Nicole chuckled, poking fun at her best friend.

Not quite sure if she bought the simple explanation or not, Gwen shook her head as she stared at the now motionless locker perched beside the cradle.

Jared, Nicole and Gwen started moving furniture out of the master bedroom to get the room ready for painting. Dusk was quickly approaching and the air was beginning to cool off as they carried the few remaining pieces of furniture to the attic. Still a little shaken up by the evening's events, Gwen stuck close to Nicole for the duration of their stay. They were finishing up in the master bedroom when they heard a noise emitting from below. The voice was gruff and loud, and one they had never heard before. Gwen gasped as the voice grew louder and nearer. She looked for something to hide behind but found nothing since the room was now vacant. Quickly, Gwen made her way into the closet just as the voice rounded the corner and entered the room.

"Evening, just wanted to make sure you had business being in this house," the husky voice barked.

"Yes actually we do," Nicole spoke up as she straightened her stance in defense. "We're the new owners, I'm Nicole Brentwood and this is my husband Jared. And you are?"

"The name's Betty; Betty Langhorne, and I'm your closest neighbor. I live over yonder, just over the bluff," she said as she motioned over her shoulder. "Didn't mean to bother you, but this place still attracts busy-bodies, even after all these years. Just wanted to make sure you folks had reason to be in here. I'll be going on now, sorry for interrupting, oh and by the way, make sure you shut the lights off when you leave; some were left on last time someone left."

With that, the woman turned and left. Gwen slowly opened the closet door and peeked outside. When she saw that the intruder was gone, she once again joined her friends in the bedroom.

"Was she a gruff, amazon looking thing or what?" Gwen commented as she brushed the dust from the closet off herself.

"Yes she was" Jared replied back. "Bet she doesn't go around hiding in closet at the drop of a hat like you did," he remarked, laughing.

"Oh drop dead would you!" Gwen flippantly replied back in an exasperated voice.

"Not unless you push me off the cliff outside honey," Jared retorted back, again laughing.

"Stop it both of you. You two fight like sibling, are you sure you're not related?" Nicole asked; a little tired of their constant bickering. She made her way back into the hallway before either had a chance to respond to her question. Jared and Gwen stood looking at each other briefly before Gwen made a face at Jared and then scurried off to catch up with Nicole.

Nicole made her way downstairs and went outside onto the patio. The wind was blowing hard off the lake, and it felt crisp yet refreshing. A few black clouds were rolling in and Nicole thought to herself that she should go to her car and close the windows before the rain hit; but she remained stationary, lost in thought. She looked over the bluff to her left and saw the remnants of an old footpath between the Harteman and Langhorne's home. Nicole stood wondering if the path had been used by the family's children in happier times or if it was just a path worn down by the wind and possibly grazing deer. She stared at it for a brief moment, and as she squinted to see, she could make out the colors of Betty's clothing moving away from her. Nicole deduced that it was indeed the shortest route between the two homes. Both driveways were long and winding and there was a thicket of trees in between the homes. Neither home was in direct view of the other, so the two families probably used the pathway for convenience. Nicole stood watching her as she disappeared out of sight, not quite sure what to make of her. Southern in dialect, the woman seemed very protective of the house and its former occupants. Nicole couldn't pinpoint it, but there was something unusual about this woman. Her husband appeared so gentile and sincere. On the surface this woman was friendly, yet Nicole got vibes from her that were cold, that made her feel unwelcome. And why had she reminded them to turn out the lights when they left. To the best of her knowledge, they had turned all of them off when they left last time and there certainly weren't any on when they arrived today.

"Oh well, I'm not going to let Gwen's paranoia get to me too" she thought to herself before responding when she heard her name being called.

"Jared, I'm down here; out on the patio honey."

Nicole waited for Jared to make his way outside. She sat down on the much rusted but still somewhat sturdy rout iron loveseat. The wind, though moderately intensified, was soothing to listen to, and the spring breeze made it comfortable even in short sleeves. Nicole thought it hypnotic watching the waves and listening to the wind while waiting for Jared to join her.

Chapter 18

Over at the Langhorne's home, Bart found his wife sitting on their screen porch, rocking in her favorite wicker chair, sipping sweet tea.

"Where'd you go Betty? I came outside looking for you and you had disappeared."

"I went over to the house to see who was snooping around at this hour," she replied nonchalantly.

"They say their name's Brentwood. They're a young couple, and I didn't see any kids running around. Probably the professional type by the looks of the fancy vehicles they're driving. That house needs the laughter of children again, not some stuffy suits that work all day and will neglect the house," she huffed.

"I thought they were a very nice couple. The misses is a pretty young thing, obviously well-bred by her appearance and mannerisms. And the lad appears to be from good stock as well. Don't discredit them too quickly Betty, I think they're exactly what Rachel's house needs, and they'll be good neighbors too.

"When exactly did you meet them Bart?" Betty asked suspiciously.

"Don't you remember? I met them the night we were planting your shrubs and got rained on real bad. I saw her near the edge of the bluff and walked over to warn her not to get to close," Bart responded in defense of himself.

"She looks so familiar to me, did you by any chance ask her if she works and if so, where? Or ask where she's from?" he asked his wife innocently.

"No, I didn't get her life story, but I'll have them over sometime for brunch once they've moved in and you can quiz her yourself Bart" she replied with a hint of sarcasm in her voice.

"You don't have to get nasty. I just thought that maybe you might have recognized her from somewhere. For all we know, she could be one of the kid's friends; she's young enough to be." Bart decided to drop the topic and went inside to close the windows before the storm blew in.

Jared joined his wife outside on the patio with Gwen right behind him. Explaining that she had a big presentation in the morning to prepare for, she said good night and departed for her car. Once she was gone, Nicole turned to face Jared and took his hand in hers.

"I absolutely love it here Jared. I want to fix this place up just like it was when it was first built. I want to recapture the splendor hidden inside the house and make it beautiful once again."

"You really do like it here, don't you love? I haven't seen you this excited about anything in a long time. But before you get all carried away, don't you think we should leave the past alone; let's decorate this place differently than the previous life this home led, let's put our stamp on it and make it beautiful for us. I want to leave the past in the past."

"What do you think will happen Jared," Nicole asked, somewhat confused. The past is the past and is dead and gone. The past cannot and will not come back to haunt us."

"I know that. I just don't want to tempt fate, that's all."

"Oh honey, you always were too superstitious for your own good. Do you want to tempt fate right now by getting naked and fooling around right here on the patio?" Nicole kidded.

"Nicole Rose!" Jared laughed as he rose to leave. "You're too much I swear. Hold that thought while I lock up and we get home."

Nicole smiled as she stood up from the swing. She tossed Jared the key ring and headed back inside to make sure the windows were all shut and the lights turned off. When she was finished, she met Jared on the front step and they locked the house up together. Jared offered to lead the way to a new delicatessen that had just opened. More thirsty than hungry, Nicole agreed and they set off towards their cars just as the sun went down.

When the wind started whipping fiercely, and the sun had finally disappeared over the horizon, Betty decided it was time to retreat inside. As she made her way inside, she heard her flag being beaten in the wind. Not wanting the relatively new one to be torn as the previous flags had been, she decided to take it down quickly before the storm blew in. Slowly she started toward the edge of the bluff where the flagpole stood. When she reached the pole, she untied the knot and lowered the flag into her arms. Within a second of doing so, a burst of wind caught the flag and blew it up over her face. The sudden blindness cause instant vertigo and she started stumbling, attempting to regain her balance. Seeing what was happening from the upstairs bedroom, Bart screamed.

"Don't move Betty, you're going to fall" he yelled as he raced down the stairs and outside as fast as he could, knowing full well that there was nothing he could do to reach her in time. Betty flailed her arms wildly trying to free the flag from her face but only seemed to tangle it up further. Her knees buckled under her as she stepped on the uneven ground below. Afraid of tripping herself, she took a quick step backward to prevent herself from falling. When she did, the earth below her crumbled and she lost her footing. As she fell, the flag was lifted from her face with another gust of wind and right away Betty realized what grave danger she was in. Frantically she tried to grab hold of anything as she slid over the edge of the embankment. Bart ran out of the house just as he saw her going over. Racing as fast as his arthritic bones would carry him, he saw her look of horror as his true love dropped out of sight, screaming at the top of her lungs.

Nicole stood next to her car kissing her husband good bye when she paused. Unsure what possessed her to stop; Jared looked at Nicki with a puzzled look on his face.

"Did you just hear something Jar?" Nicky asked, straining to hear the sound again.

"Do you mean something other than the wind?"

"Yeah, I swear that I heard a man shouting. There! Did you hear it that time?" she asked as she starting walking toward the side of the house where they had been sitting.

"Nicki, I didn't hear a thing," he said as he quickened his pace to catch up to her.

When he rounded the corner, he caught a glimpse of her running off toward the bluff.

She heard Jared call for her but never broke stride as she raced down the footpath.

"Help Jared, something's terribly wrong" she shouted back at him as she disappeared into the darkness. Without thinking, Jared raced back to the car, grabbed his cell phone and flashlight and set off to find his wife.

As her eyes adjusted to the dimming light, Nicole ran as fast as she dared along the dirt path paralleling the lake. The wind was relentless and now turning cold. Several times the spray off the lake pierced her skin and stung her face. Every time she considered slowing her pace, she heard her new neighbor's voice crying out and knew that he needed her desperately. Jared, trailing behind was able to make up a little time as he had the flashlight to illuminate the trail. Just as Nicole reached the Langhorne's back yard, Jared had caught up to her side.

"Over here! Dear God please help me! We're over here!

Jared and Nicole raced to Bart's side. Both dropped to their knees beside the badly shaken man. They peered over the edge to find Betty pinned against the cliff's edge. She appeared completely still, as if in shock, standing on one leg. Her left leg was drawn up towards her hip in a peculiar angle and was apparent that it was fractured. She had both arms raised above her head holding Bart's outstretched arm. Jared quickly reached down to grab her other arm. Once his grip was secure, Jared instructed Bart to pull on the count of three. Nicole watched as the two men attempted to lift the woman to safety. Just as they started to lift her, her pant leg became snagged on a jagged edge of rock. Betty screamed out, both out of fright and because of the severe pain. Becoming aware of what appeared to be her imminent demise, she searched the water below, trying to determine if she should just jump and be done with it.

Almost reading her mind, Nicole shouted "No wait Betty, I'm coming down"

Jared looked at his wife with a look of disbelief and knew without conveying a word, knew that she wouldn't be stopped.

"Here, first wrap this around your wrist first" Jared motioned as he quickly pulled off his belt and wrapped it around her wrist. "It's better than nothing and all we've got."

"Thanks! Call 911 and get us help Jared" were her only words as she slowly lowered herself over the cliff's edge. All color drained from the men's faces as Nicki looked at them and forced a smile.

As Nicole lowered herself down towards Betty, the older woman remained frozen against the cliff's edge. All color was gone from her dirt covered face and her expression indicated that shock was quickly setting in. As Nicole made her way to the woman's side, she smile and spoke as if they were relaxing having tea together.

"Mrs. Langhorne, its Nicole. I'm here to help you, but you've got to help me first.

As Nicole began speaking with the woman; Jared frantically dialed 911 to summon help. Nicole continued talking to the woman in a soothing, almost monotone voice.

"I need you to promise to hold on, and do not under any circumstances, look down again. We've got help on the way and we're not going to let anything happen to you."

Betty glanced over at the young woman holding on beside her.

"I can't hold on much longer," she whispered. "The lake's calling me; just like it called her" she continued. "Look, don't you see her down there?" she asked as she glanced down at the waves crashing below.

Nicole responded in a stern, formal voice.

"Mrs. Langhorne, I am risking my neck to save you so damn it, hold on and do not look down again! There is no one down there; just the waves and very cold water."

Betty turned to her young neighbor and smiled.

"Yes dear."

Jared perked up when he heard the sounds of the approaching rescue units. He reached over and grabbed Betty's other arm that Bart was holding and after securing it, instructed Bart to go out and flag down the men. Bart hesitated briefly, looking down at his wife, then quickly did as Jared requested. Within a minute, four men joined Jared as they rushed to the scene with ropes, and tools in hand. Quickly two dropped to the ground beside Jared and peered over the cliff's edge. Nicole looked up and flashed a bright smile in spite of her predicament.

"Hi guys. It would be great if you could give me a hand down here. We've got a compound fracture, shock with delirium setting in."

One of the paramedics started passing a rope down to her and as he did asked "How do you know what her injuries are mam and what are you doing down there too?"

"I'm an avid rock climber sir and thought tonight's a perfect night to be scaling this cliff" she sarcastically replied. "No seriously, I'm a nurse in a trauma unit, and regardless, her injuries are quite apparent. I'm down here because I wasn't going to let my new next door neighbor fall without trying to save her," she meekly answered, trying to sound more polite than her previous comments.

"That's it!" Betty exclaimed. Bart said there was something familiar about you. Were you employed there back in 04?" Betty asked with the first sign of spirit since Nicole had joined her on the cliff.

"Yes, I was employed there in 2004 but worked on a different unit. Why?" Nicole asked as she tied the paramedic's rope around the woman's chest, just under her armpits.

"Because I had cancer and was a patient there for quite a spell," she exclaimed, smiling.

Nicole smiled back as she tightened the rope and gave the men a thumbs up signal. By now, the third paramedic was sending Nicole a rope for herself. Nicole looked back at Betty who was studying her face.

"The men are going to pull you up now Betty. It's probably going to hurt like hell but you'll be safe in no time and they'll get you to the hospital and get you the help that you need."

"What about you Nicole" the woman asked, who suddenly was sounding completely lucid.

"Oh, I'm going to be fine too honey, don't you worry."

With that, the men above started hoisting Betty Langhorne to safety.

Both Bart and Jared watched nervously as the rescue team went into action slowly hoisting Betty as she screamed in pain. Once her upper torso was up over the cliff, the men mobilized her leg as they completed the rescue. Bart dropped down beside his wife, tears welling up in his eyes. Jared smiled once Betty was safe but couldn't relax until his wife was also out of harm's way. The men turned their attention to Nicole once Betty was on solid ground and being attended to by the paramedics.

Nicole didn't move an inch until she was hooked into the harness. Two of the rescue squad started lifting her up and the other two men attended to Betty's injuries. Bart kneeled at her head, patting her forehead, and brushing her hair out of her eyes.

"Rest now dear; we're going to get that leg taken care of soon" he said as he continued to stroke her head.

"Did you hear her?" Betty asked quietly.

"Hear who Betty? You mean Nicole. That angel risked her neck to climb down there and help you. I don't know how I'll ever repay her for saving your life. I told you I knew you were wrong about her" Bart whispered into his wife's ear. "Now quiet yourself and rest while the men fix you up."

"No, I have to know," Betty exclaimed as she tried to sit up but collapsed back down again. "Did you hear Rachel calling to me?"

Before Bart could answer, Nicole, now on top of the bluff raced over to Betty and knelt beside her, grasping her hand. Bart looked at his wife's guardian angel and made direct eye contact with her.

"Thank you from the bottom of my heart." The tears openly flowed from his eyes. "She wouldn't have made it if it weren't for you and I don't know how I'll ever repay you."

Nicole spontaneously hugged Mr. Langhorne as he knelt beside his wife. When he regained his composure, he again started speaking to Nicole, but his eyes remained fixed upon his wife.

"She," he said as he nodded down at Betty, "keeps asking if I heard someone talking to her and I keep explaining that you were down there with her. But she keeps saying that it wasn't you that she heard. Did you hear anything down there or did she hit her head?" he asked with pleading bloodshot eyes.

"Oh Mr. Langhorne," Nicole responded reassuringly; "I think she's going to be fine. She must have hit her head and has a slight concussion. That or the mere shock of the accident and extreme fear would be enough to make her a little disoriented and think she's hearing things that aren't really there. It's not uncommon for people to think they're seeing long lost relatives or loved ones when they're placed in life threatening situations" Nicole said reassuringly to the visibly shaken man.

"So you didn't hear anything while down there on the ledge?" he asked once again.

"Just my heart pounding out of my chest," she responded, smiling lovingly at the couple beside her.

Jared stood silently at her side, not sure whether to hug her or yell at her for the fear that she had caused. Nicole, he realized had always been one to follow her gut instincts but she usually didn't put herself directly in harm's way. He stared down at this wife who was oblivious to how dangerous her act truly had been.

The rescue squad finished stabilizing Betty's leg and started loading her into their unit for transport. Bart, Jared and Nicole stood as the men lifted the stretcher up and wheeled her away. Nicole stepped away from Jared and conversed briefly with one of the men. Upon her return, she explained to Bart that Betty was being transported to United Medical Center and would be seen by an orthopedic specialist upon arrival. Bart thanked the young couple again, and then scampered off to join his wife.

"Now that the excitement is over, do you think we can go home now Nicole," Jared asked taking her into his arms, afraid to let go.

"We are home Jared."

"You know what I mean Nicki."

"Hey Nicole, Jared" Bart hollered from the side of the rescue unit. "Betty said to tell you to make sure you cut off the upstairs bedroom light. You left it on again."

"Thanks Bart, we will" Jared replied back as he retrieved his flashlight and wife's hand.

"Jared, she must have hit her head harder than I thought because I know we didn't leave any lights on inside" Nicole responded as they made their way along the path toward their home.

"Well, the house is significantly larger than what we're used to. Maybe you forgot one in our haste to get home" he offered.

As the approached their yard, the moon was shining through the clouds overhead illuminating the house slightly.

"See," Nicole said as she gestured toward it. "I knew I didn't leave any lights on."

"You right. And now that we've gotten back to where we started over an hour ago, let's get out of here before something else happens" Jared said as he opened Nicole's car door.

"Deal. Thank you," she said as she slid down into the driver's seat. "Let's skip dinner, go home and shower, and work on dessert," she winked as she shut the door and started the engine. "I can think of a few ways to burn off this adrenaline rush," she all but purred.

Chapter 19

The evening shift in the ICU was beginning to wind down. Already after ten o'clock, the nurses finished their last med pass to administer the few remaining meds to those who needed them. Upon completing their rounding, they started culminating around the nurse's station to start their charting. Meanwhile, just a few steps away, Marian Danbarry sat nervously in the surgical waiting room, impatiently waiting for her husband's return from surgery. It had seemed like hours had passed since she had received the call from the prison and the nightmare had started.

Her husband had been employed within the correctional department for over twenty-five years, and had never sustained even an abrasion from any altercations; and now he lay in surgery fighting for his life. Her mind raced. She thought of burying their first born son, of how she'd tell their girls if their father didn't pull through, and lastly, she tried to comprehend why this had to happen to Gary. She sat upright in her straight back chair, feverishly working her well-worn ivory rosary. A priest, a family friend had given them to her, when their son had first become ill. Many a night was spent sitting at his bedside, saying the rosary and praying for a miracle, just as she was doing right now for her husband. Marian, though only three years Gary's senior, looked ten years older. Her premature gray remained uncolored and pulled tightly into a bun, and her facial features, though plain, remained dormant without even a hint of makeup to brighten her overall bland appearance. Her clothes were outdated and appeared to be from thinner days, but were clean and coordinated. Everything about Marian Danbarry was simple, understated, and earthy.

Heidi, a relatively new graduate nurse came into the waiting room, finally breaking the silence. The smile on her face relieved any uncertainty Marian had been feeling prior.

"Mrs. Danbarry," she spoke softly but quickly, and right to the point. "Your husband is in Recovery. He's quite sedated and will be for a while but he's out of surgery and going to be ok. Dr. Menotta will be in to see you very shortly but said to make sure to tell you that your husband will be doing the shag in no time, whatever that means" the young nurse said with a somewhat confused look on her face.

Mrs. Danbarry blushed slight as the tears started to flow down her cheeks and she flashed a broad smile, revealing nearly all of her slight crooked teeth.

"It's a good thing darling; it's a kind of dance."

"Oh. Well, I've got a few things to do before my shift ends so if you'll excuse me; doctor should be with you shortly."

"Thank you miss," Marian responded and returned to rubbing her rosary and the tears continued to flow.

"Where am I" the guard asked as he opened his eyes slightly and scanned the room. "My throat, oh" he groaned as his hand went to his abdomen, "and my side are killing me."

"You're in the recovery room Mr. Danbarry," a grumpy stern looking nurse responded. "You," she said as she pushed her glasses up the bridge of her nose, "have got to just lie still for a while."

A woman in her late forties, Mary Tomkins had lost all sympathy for her patient's years before. She, though only five foot two, sounded like a giant as she barked off orders to the men and women in her care throughout her shifts. Reprimanded by Nursing Administration on more than one occasion, Mary remained defiant and set in her stubborn ways. She didn't believe in pampering drugged up patients that she believed wouldn't even remember their stay with her anyways.

"You're in the Recovery Room. You were stabbed remember?" she said curtly.

"Stabbed? No, I don't know. What happened?" he asked, half awake.

"I don't know buddy. I don't have time to read everyone's chart you know. Are you in a gang or running drugs? If so, then I would guess that's why you got sliced up" she responded derogatorily.

"Hey look lady," Danbarry responded, now awake and very irritated by her insults and accusations, "I happen to be a happily married correctional officer at Danville Prison, not some deviant who was cut up on the street peddling drugs!"

"Were you working yesterday when the riot broke out?" she asked in a less accusing manner.

"Yes, I was working yesterday, I think. But I don't remember any riot, or at least I don't think I remember any riot."

"From the size of the goose-egg on your head, you're lucky you can remember your name. You probably got whacked pretty hard by whoever stabbed you," she said as she charted the numbers appearing on the monitor in front of her.

"I know you're busy and all, but do you know if anyone else was hurt?" Gary asked in a soft-spoken voice as he felt the bump on his forehead.

"All I know is that they patched a bunch of people up in the ED and that several died at the prison and some died here but I have no idea how many. I know that one of the prisoners is still in surgery right now and he won't be rioting anymore once they cut his arm off," she said with a snicker.

"They ought to let him bleed out if he was in on the rioting" Gary responded, having no idea that the man lying on the operating table at that very moment was none other than the man who had played an integral part in saving his life.

The phone rang at the Drake's residence shortly after ten o'clock. Clarissa had retired earlier than usual that evening trying to ignore the frustration and fear that had haunted her all day. Richard had tried unsuccessfully all day to obtain information about the status of the riot and the father-in-law. He even went as far as to pull some strings within the judicial system, and got a friend of a friend to get ahold of the Danville Prison Warden himself. Unfortunately the only news the warden or the media was able to release was that several guards and inmates had been killed and several were injured.

The uncertainty of her father's fate was too much for Claire to bare. Feeling that she needed to turn towards her salvation in a bottle, she decided to go to bed instead. Richard declined her invitation to join her and chose to stay up to watch the eleven o'clock news instead. He sat silently in their library, reading when he heard Rosa jump from her chair in the kitchen to answer the phone.

"Hello, Drake residence." "Si, senior, Mrs. Drake has retired for the evening but 'I'll get Mr. Drake for you. Un momento please.'"

"Rosa, I'll take it in the library," Richard called out as he heard her scampering feet approaching the room.

"Hurry Senior Drake, it's the police. I don't remember his name but he sounds important."

"Thank you Rosa," he said as he picked up the receiver and listened for her to hang up her end before he spoke.

"Hello. This is Richard Drake."

"Mr. Drake, this is Sargent Stan Wilkes of the Danville Correctional Facility. I wanted to phone you myself, instead of some state trooper who doesn't know your father-in-law.

"Yes, yes. Excuse me, but get to the point. My father-in-law wasn't directly involved in the riot was he?" Richard asked quickly, trying not to sound too impatient or impolite.

"Well, yes sir, he was involved, but not in a negative way. Your father-in-law risked his neck, along with another inmate, to get myself and several other officers rescued. One, in particular, a dear friend of mine, would be dead right now if it weren't for Henry's heroics. But sir, I'm very sorry to have to be the one to tell you that Henry was critically injured during our rescue. He was taken to United Medical Center and I'm sorry, but I don't have any other information. He was alive when I saw him last and one of my officers heard that he'd been taken into surgery. I just thought that you'd want to know; since your wife's his only living relative."

Richard remained silent on the other end of the line, trying to absorb what he had just heard. He could feel the lump in his throat as he tried to speak.

"You're telling me Sargent Wilkes that my father-in-law saved several guards, and then got shot himself. By whom? If he was helping you, why would you shoot him?" Richard asked, still in shock.

"We didn't shoot him. As he was coming back to the cell we were locked up in, another prisoner tried to get to us first, and Henry jumped him. The guy turned on Henry and shot him point blank. Hey, look, I'm really sorry to be the one to tell you, but I thought you should know as soon as possible. And I really am sorry and hope he pulls through."

"Thank you officer; I appreciate you taking the time to phone yourself."

"Mr. Drake," Sargent Wilkes added, "I want you to know that if Henry pulls through this, the other guards and I will see to it that Henry gets another chance at being paroled. In view of the circumstances, he should definitely have a better chance of obtaining his freedom; that is if he makes it. I just thought you'd want to know that. Oh, and I arranged to have only specific guards stand watch outside his room, once he's out of surgery. It's the least I can do."

"Thank you Sargent Wilkes. Your thoughtfulness is appreciated. Good night."

Richard replaced the receiver and sat silently in the library. Unsure of how Claire would react to the news, he sat momentarily reviewing his options. If this call had come just one week prior, his job would have been made easier. But now that his wife was finally beginning to forgive her father, how could he tell her that it might already be too late to tell him in person. Claire had been given several tough breaks throughout her life, but losing her father again might make her go over the edge, he decided. After gathering his remaining strength, Richard got up from his chair and slowly proceeded toward the staircase leading to their bedroom.

"Mr. Drake, is it the children? Dear Jesus, tell me nothing's happened to the children. The policeman sounded very serious on the phone," Rosa stammered as she caught Richard in the foyer. Her face revealed concern as she stood staring at her employer and friend. Rosa knew that late night calls form the police only meant trouble for either Mr. or Mrs. Drake. With the children teenagers, Rosa immediately assumed the worst, that one of them had been hurt, and now even after all her years of employment with the Drakes, she still had that look of dread when the phone calls came in at this late hour.

"No Rosa, the kids are fine. It's nothing. Why don't you go to bed, it's late. Claire and I will be stepping out this evening and might not be in until sometime tomorrow." Before she could respond, Richard turned and proceeded up the stairs to awaken Claire.

"Oh something bad has happened," Rosa said under her breathe as she headed back into the kitchen. "Something very bad."

Claire lay asleep in their bed as Richard made his way into the room. He studied her face, trying to determine how she would react to the news. Cautiously he sat down beside her, and to his surprise she rolled over toward him and opened her eyes.

"Hi" she said sleepily. "I thought I heard you tip toeing around in here. Did I just hear the phone, or was I dreaming?"

"No honey, you weren't dreaming. The phone did ring. It," he said hesitantly, "Was a Sargent Wilkes from the prison."

"The prison," she repeated, now immediately awake and bolting upright in bed. "What did he want? Is it about my father? Oh my God, what's wrong Richard? I can see it in your eyes, what's happened?" she begged. "What time is it anyway?" she asked; her mind racing.

"Claire," Richard said softly. "I want you to listen to what I'm saying." He looked directly into her eyes before proceeding. Claire looked back at her husband with pleading eyes, begging him to fill her in on whatever news he had just heard. "Your father was involved in the riot, which thank God is now over. But, he was only involved in a positive way. He, and some other inmate, according to this Wilkes fellow, was solely responsible for saving numerous inmates and guard's lives. The officer said they were ultimately responsible to assisting the rescue teams in locating the guards and squelching the riot. You should be very proud of what he did," Richard added quietly.

Claire sat silently as she heard her husband tell of her father's heroics. Never had she envisioned her father as being one to take risks, let alone a hero of sorts. Claire couldn't fathom how a man who committed a murder against someone he supposedly loved, would then risk his own neck for others. Maybe, Claire thought, there were a lot of things she didn't really know about her father at all.

"Claire," Richard said softly as she sat in silence, still absorbing the news. "There's something else that you should know." Richard took a deep breath, and then proceeded. "Claire, Henry was shot during the riot, and is in surgery right now. The officer said that it's a serious gunshot wound, and that we might want to get over to the hospital as soon as possible."

Richard watched the color drain from his wife's face as she started to get out of bed.

"Yes, I think the officer is right. Maybe we should get over there. And Richard," she said in a near whisper, "Would you be kind enough to phone Jessica and Justin and tell them to meet us there. Maybe it's time that they meet their grandfather; if we're not too late."

As if in a trance, Claire got up and walked into her changing room. Richard stood staring at the door that Claire had just walked through. Unable to determine what she was thinking, he quickly did what she asked and phoned their children, telling them that it was imperative that they meet them at the hospital. Both agreed without question.

After a few moments, Claire came out of her closet fully dressed in a simple, yet refined pantsuit; the pale color of the linen gave her olive skin a rich tone, and set off her brown hair perfectly. She looked approvingly at what Richard had put on and then proceeded into the bathroom to apply her make up. Richard paced impatiently as she methodically put on her makeup. Unsure if she was stalling out of fear, or denial, Richard tried to expedite the process by offering to bring the car around front.

"That's ok Richard. I'll be ready in just a moment. I just thought I would like to look presentable for my father."

"Claire, please, your father won't care what you have on. He'll just be happy to see you. So please hurry, before it's maybe too late." Richard, aware of the critical nature of the whole situation didn't want to push his wife too hard, but he also didn't want to get there too late. For all they knew, Henry could already be dead.

Officer Danbarry, now fully conscious waited patiently for Mary to finish her paperwork so that he could return back to his hospital bed. The stabbing pain in his side was only intermittent, yet very intense when he tried to reposition himself in bed. His head pounded and his eyes were tired, but his pain seemed trivial when he thought of his co-workers who had died. Gary slowly started piecing the events of the last day together, but the overall riot still remained a blur within his mind. He tried, as he lay motionless in the sterile looking room to remember who he had been confined with, who had died, and how he ended up in the hospital.

Setting his telemetry monitor off, Mary stormed into Gary's room, obviously annoyed at the inconvenience. "What seems to be the problem?" she asked sarcastically. "I told you before, you need to lie still and relax so I can finish up your paperwork and get you upstairs."

"Are you always this pleasant or were you saving it all for me?" Gary flippantly replied back."

"Very funny. Now if you don't mind," the crude nurse responded, never taking her eyes off the computer screen in front of her.

"Maybe I do mind. You know, you're not the most pleasant thing to be around right after surgery. In fact, your mannerisms suck! Maybe you've been doing this too long, or maybe you're always a bitch, but one thing's for certain; lady, you need a new job!"

"Is that so," Mary responded back, now ready for a fight. "Well Mr. Perfect, why don't you put yourself in my shoes for a moment? Day in and day out I take care of you idiots as you come out of anesthesia. I get puked on, spit on, and kicked. I have to clean your asses when you're incontinent of stool and urine, not to mention what it's like when one of you have a laryngospasm and suddenly

BITTERSWEET JUSTICE

can't breathe. Everyday I'm saving someone's life and for what? No one remembers being down here and knows how much we do for them. Everyone sends letters to fucking administration praising the glorious ICU nurses or the peon staff nurse who discharged them. Well," she said as she rose, stood, and stared him directly in the eyes, "I'm sick of taking care of drug addicts, child abusers, derelicts and welfare abusers who don't give a damn about themselves, let alone everyone else. I'm sick of my tax dollars going toward keeping people like that prisoner who's in surgery right now, alive. Maybe you're right; maybe I do need another job, one where I'd get a little respect."

By now, Mary's glasses were practically off her nose as her nostrils flared, and Gary suddenly felt very sorry for the woman staring down at him. She probably started out enthusiastic and kind, ready to save the world. But, like many nurses, the long hours and the stress of dealing with other people's lives had gotten to her. Now, she categorized everyone as unappreciative and cold. The years had tainted her opinion of the general public and she looked at everyone in the same derogatory way. None-the-less, he still felt that she didn't have a right to think that everyone who came through the doors was evil, and Gary intended to tell her so.

"Hey, look, I'm sure we could keep this pissing match up for hours, but I would like to go see my wife now, and I'm sure you've got other patients to see, so why don't we call it a truce and get me out of here okay?" Gary looked at her, waiting for her response. When he saw a smirk come over her face, he realized that the battle was over and in her feeble mind. May had thought that she had won. He was now too tired to care, and just wanted to get out of her path. As she unhooked his cardiac monitor, he offered her one last word of advice.

-118-

"I know you think you're not appreciated because no one tells you that you are, but at least in here they don't shoot at you. Think about that for a few moments. I too, take care of the public. Yes, they're locked up for whatever crime, but they are people who did come from the public sector. I see those derelicts, child abusers, and drug addicts on a daily basis too. The only difference between us in, in here, they probably don't want to kill you. If it weren't for those lovely members of society, I wouldn't be in here right now, remember? Keep that in mind the next time you're feeling sorry for yourself."

With that, Gary Danbarry was whisked away to a different unit by the transport nurse. Mary stood silently watching him leave, realizing that, though she didn't want to admit it, he was right. They're jobs were in fact very similar; both thankless jobs.

Marian Danbarry had finally started to drift off when she heard the automatic doors opening. She opened her bloodshot eyes to find her husband being rolled up beside her. Their eyes met and tears welled in Marian's as she finally saw that her beloved Gary was alright. Gary gave her a wry smile and reached for her hand. Heidi the transport nurse grinned as she viewed the love these two people had for one another. Once alone in his room, she went to his side and kissed him tenderly on his cheek.

"I'm a pretty sad sight for sore eyes aren't I" he asked jokingly.

"No, you're the best sight I've seen in quite a while," Marian responded back as the tears once again welled up in her eyes. She squeezed his hand and smiled her crooked smile; "The absolute best sight."

Chapter 20

The parking lot at the hospital was practically empty when Claire and Richard pulled in. Except for a few scattered cars, they appeared to be alone; thou Claire searched it looking for her daughter and son's cars. Realizing that they had arrived at the hospital first, she quickly got out and locked her door. Richard came around to her side and reached for both of her arms.

"Claire, no matter what happens, or already happened tonight, I just want you to know that I love you and we'll work through this."

"He's not dead Richard," she whispered, as if he could read his mind. "Come one, I think my father needs me," Claire said as she loosened his hold and started toward the entrance.

Henry lay unconscious on the operating table as the surgeons tried to reattach his arm. From viewing the x-ray's and upon visual examination, the neurosurgeon and orthopedist had both agreed to attempt to save the extremity since most of the damage had been muscular. Their first intent had been a simpler approach which would have been to simply remove the inmate's arm, but after the warden and the officers at the prison made their appeals on behalf of this man whose life lay in their hands, both doctors agreed to give it their best shot and attempt to save what was left of his arm. The surgery was actually going much better than either doctor had expected or though that had only been operating for four hours; they had most of the vessels reattached. The surgeons worked diligently on the patient in front of them, discarding the fact that he was a prisoner; to them, he was just a patient. All had been informed of his heroics, and each wondered to himself what could have transpired to have made a prisoner become a hero. Each had their own theory, but right now, they were all too busy trying to save the man's life and his arm.

Claire and Richard obtained directions to the surgical waiting room and quickly made their way to the somber looking room. Their son and daughter simultaneously walked in and impulsively hugged their visibly distraught mother. Both remained unsure of how to interpret their mother's sudden interest in her long forgotten parent, but neither cared at the moment. Clarissa Drake appeared to be, once again, the caring and sensitive mother that they both had once loved with all their heart. As young children, they had once asked Claire why they only had one set of grandparents. Claire at the time tried to explain to them that her parents were dead. It wasn't until much later in life that they discovered the truth. When Richard was up for reelection, an unscrupulous reporter decided to once again dig up the past regarding the Harteman murder. The young reporter took pleasure in describing Claire's father as not only a murderer, but also a child and wife abuser. When Justin relayed the horrifying information to Jessica, both decided to confront their mother to find out the truth. Claire, caught off guard, flew into a fit, screaming at them, demanding that they never mention his name or the murder again. Confused, and scared, Justin and Jessica vowed to one another to forget their mother's secrets of her childhood. Now, years, later, they were once again forced to remember their mother's dreadful past.

"Hello children, I'm so glad you came on such short notice," Claire said, breaking the silence.

"Hello mother, father. Would either of you mind filling us in on what's going on" Justin asked.

"Dad called and only said that something terrible had happened to your father. I didn't even know that your father was still living or that you had any contact with him," he continued.

"Yeah mom, since when do you care what happens to him anyway?" Jessica added sarcastically.

"I've cared ever since I started believing that he didn't kill my mother. And furthermore, the man lying in there fighting for his life is, and will always be your grandfather. And that same man risked his life tonight to save several others. Now, I realize," Claire said softly, wiping a tear from her eye, "that I have forced both of you to forget you even had another grandfather, and for that I'm truly sorry. Right now, he really needs all of our prayers." Emotionally drained, Claire hung her head and wept.

"Dad," Jessica whispered, almost embarrassed by her earlier sarcasm. "What happened to him?"

"There was a riot at the prison where Henry is incarcerated. From what we're told, Henry and another inmate were trying to assist the injured guards and he was shot in the chest by another inmate. He's been in surgery for hours now."

"Damn, you think he's really got a chance in hell of making it?" Justin asked innocently.

"Of course he does," Claire snapped. "He's a fighter, and he will make it. He's been in prison and has survived. If he has made it this long, he is going to make it through surgery!"

Unsure of what to do, both children nodded silently in agreement.

Gary dozed on and off for several minutes, then awakened to see Marian resting quietly at his bedside. "Are you sleeping?" he asked in a voice not much louder than a whisper.

"No, but you should be."

"I've got to know how I ended up in this hospital, and how I got out of that damn prison. Everything seems fuzzy, like it was a bad dream. Did Ron tell you what happened in there?"

"Quiet yourself dear. We'll discuss it in the morning. Right now you need to rest."

"No, Marian, I need to remember so please tell me what you know; now, not tomorrow."

"Maybe it's God's way of protecting you. Maybe he doesn't want you to know or doesn't think you should know. Please let it go Gary," she pleaded.

"Marian, I can't let it go. Just tell me what you know."

After slowly nodding, she met his eyes. "Ron said," She replied hesitantly, "that you and the other men were being held hostage in solitary and that being locked up is what probably saved you. He said that several guards were killed when the riot first broke out, but that he assumes you and the other officers were put in there for safe keeping to be used later as pawns, for negotiating or possibly as human shields. We'll never know what their true intentions were but he said that two inmates actually were instrumental in saving you. He said they were able to secure a cell phone that ultimately got help in to you. He didn't' give me details but," wiping her eyes, "he said that you wouldn't have made it out alive if they hadn't risked their lives to save yours. Ron said that you were bleeding to death in front of them."

"Oh my God," Gary said as he tried to sit up, "Henry."

"What is it Gary? Please calm yourself," she said as her eyes darted to the alarming monitors beside her husband's bed. "Who is Henry?"

"Henry Harteman, Marian. He's the one that saved me. He's the one I told you about! Remember I told you that I was going to have my nephew review his case because I don't honestly think he killed his wife? Oh my God, it's coming back to me. He's the one that rescued us!"

"Oh my," Marian replied out loud, though she thought she had said it to myself.

"What do you know about Henry that you're not telling me?"

"Please Gary," she said, begging him to drop the subject. Let it go until the morning. You've been thru enough tonight."

"I need to know Marian. Please; he saved my life."

"Gary," she said as she cleared her throat, trying to think of the right words to say. "The other inmate, Mac, I believe they said his name is, is fine and being guarded in a secure location away from the prison. Henry, Ron said, wasn't quite as lucky. He was shot by another prisoner as he was rescuing you."

She sat back, trying to read her husband's expression. Marian Danbarry knew that she was married to one tough man, but she also knew that deep down he really cared for this Henry fellow, prisoner and all. Gary lay motionless in his hospital bed, absorbing what his wife had just told him. He could not remember the shooting, nor seeing Henry return with the phone. His mind wandered, trying to determine just where and how Henry could have possibly gotten shot. Beads of perspiration formed on his forehead as his wife watched helplessly, observing the increase in his heart rate on the monitor. Again setting off the alarms, Holly immediately entered the room when the alarms didn't reset.

"What's wrong Mr. Danbarry? Are you in pain?" she asked as she observed his drastic change in heart rate.

"No, I'm not in any severe pain. Well, maybe just a little but I'm okay."

"Ok, well, then what's wrong sir? Your blood pressure and heart rate jumped up a lot. Would you like something to help you sleep?"

"Maybe I should go honey," Marian said as she picked herself up out of the chair. "I told you not to get yourself all worked up about this Henry fellow. I probably should never have told you."

"No Marian, I'm thankful you did. Now why don't you go home and get some rest. But please, please pray for Henry."

Holly remained in attendance, messing with the monitor. She listened with interest as he spoke about someone who obviously meant a great deal to him.

"Are you talking about the inmate?"

"Yes!" Gary replied, as his eyes lit up. "Do you know anything about how's he's doing. Please. It's very important that I know how he is. He saved my life and I need to now that he's ok."

"To be honest with you Mr. Danbarry, I don't know details but know that he's in surgery and probably doesn't have a good chance of making it. From what I'm heard, they're doing everything they can to save him but he isn't expected to make it off the operating table. I'm sorry."

Gary Danbarry was an individual who thrived on control. He couldn't help but shrivel up inside his hospital bed when he heard about Henry's demise. Fear, anger, and frustration at not being able to help, nor control the situation, ate at him as he tried to remember what had gone so terribly wrong during their rescue. He couldn't fathom why Henry, who was only trying to help spare needless bloodshed, was now fighting for his life, or already dead.

In surgery, they continued to work on reattaching the patient's arm. When they were finally closing the last part of the incision, the neurosurgeon left the room, discarded his surgical wraps and mentally prepared a statement for not only the press, but also for his patient's family. Unsure if the circulation would be sufficient enough to save his arm, the physician wanted to be as optimistic as possible during his speech, but also knew he needed to be conservative just in case the outcome wasn't what he predicted. When he made his way, he immediately was greeted by the Drake's, who all stood as he entered the room.

Dr. Wei explained in layman's terms what had happened to Henry and the extent of his injuries. Claire sank into her husband's arms upon hearing that he had in fact made it through the surgery. Justin drilled the doctor with a barrage of questions as Claire wept silently, thanking God for the chance to make amends with her father,

Chapter 21

The next three weeks passed like a whirlwind. They finally got their commitment letter and before they knew it, they were cleared to close and a closing date was set. Nicole and Jared spent nearly every evening in their new home, painting, refinishing floors and stripping long outdated wallpaper. The home's charm and character was once again restored, thanks in part to fresh paint and Nicole's flair for fashion. The rooms came to life with vivid colors and charisma. She decided to paint the entrance foyer a deep but very rich sandstone color and carried the theme into the adjacent dining room to offset the vibrant burgundy walls. Jared had painstakingly spent an entire weekend in the enormous dining room as he refinished the wainscoting and crown molding. He was truly exhausted by Sunday night but kept working alongside Nicole as she finished the last of her painting. The room's focal point though, was the new crystal chandelier that lit up the room revealing its grandeur. Even Jared was taken back by the room's elegance as he stood in awe. Nicole stood by her husband, hand in his, closing her eyes and trying to envision what the room must have looked like in its original splendor, but quickly decided that even in it's prime, it couldn't have looked any better than it did right now. With the closing just a day away, the young couple was simply overjoyed with their new home. As they finished up for the evening, Jared excused himself and headed out to their car. Nicole stood cleaning their paintbrushes as she watched her husband reenter the room. He was carrying something obviously delicate, for it was wrapped in tissue paper and he kept his eyes on it as he walked toward her. Nicole dried her hands and smiled at the thought of a present.

"Now that the closing is tomorrow, I thought it only right to give our new home a gift."

"You mean that gift isn't for me?" she teased.

"No, for once, it isn't. Well, actually it is. I already give it to you quite some time ago and now it's time for you to give it to the house."

"Indian giver," she teased as she unwrapped the tissue paper.

Inside lie the wind chimes that Jared had purchased when they first found out that their offer on the house had been accepted. Nicole smiled in delight as she held the chime up, allowing what little daylight was still able to peak through the clouds to reflect off it.

"Oh Jared, this is almost too beautiful to hang outside. What if the wind destroys it? Remember how strong the wind was just a few weeks ago."

"Nicki, it's called a wind chime. It's supposed to be blown around by the wind. Besides, the angels are our good luck charms, remember?

"Okay, Okay. Where should we hang it? She asked enthusiastically.

"How about on the back veranda; like we discussed before?"

"Awesome! I'll bring it around back and you go get a nail and hammer and meet me there."

"Alright, I'll be right out," he said as he made his way inside.

Nicole looked once more at the still filthy paintbrushes lying in the utility sink, but decided they could wait until later to be cleaned. With the delicate chimes in hand, she shut off the garage light and made her way around the side of the house toward the veranda. By the time she got there, Jared, anxious to get home, was already standing there waiting for her with nail and hammer in hand. She smiled when she saw him and quickened her pace to join him.

Within a minute, Jared had the chime fastened to a bracket on the wall. The air was relatively still that evening, but the angels danced in midair regardless. Nicole and Jared watched their whimsical dance for a moment, and then decided to pack it up for the evening. Just as they started to leave the patio, Nicole noticed that the upstairs light was still on. Positive that she hadn't left any lights on, she summoned Jared over to where she was standing.

"Look at the chime Jared. Do you notice anything unusual about it?" she asked inquisitively.

"No, what should I see?"

"Don't you notice how detailed their faces are now?"

"Yes, I guess so. Come on Nicki, let's go; I'm exhausted."

"No. Look. Just a moment ago, you couldn't make out any minute detailing; now you can see every curve in their delicate faces."

"That's probably because the moon just came out from behind a cloud honey. Look at how it lights up the sky."

"I don't think it's the moon that's causing the chime to be so illuminated. It's that," she said as she pointed directly at the upstairs bedroom.

"Okay, so you're probably right. The light from the room is quite bright. I'll run upstairs and turn it off,"

"It's not that the light is on," Nicole contended, growing impatient with Jared. "It's how it got on in the first place that bothers me."

"What's the big deal? I'm sure we must have left it on when we were cleaning. No big deal, I'll go get it now. Before Jared could take a step, she snapped.

"It wasn't on a moment ago Jared! Don't you get it; I think it came on by itself or with someone's help."

Taken back, "Do you think someone is in the house right now Nicki? Jared asked, thinking she mean an intruder.

"Someone or something."

"What are you talking about Nicole?" he asked, not quite sure he knew or wanted to know where this line of conversation aw going.

"I'm not sure Jared," she responded in a serious tone.

"It's just that sometimes things seem to happen when we're here; silly, uneventful things really. Frequently, I've dismissed them as coincidence, yet sometimes I feel that maybe we're not alone in the house. I can't pinpoint it, and I'm not scared or intimidated by the feeling, but sometimes I really think that someone else is present in here when we're working."

Feeling the hairs on his arms rise as he listened to his wife speak, he understood what she was talking about, yet refused to buy into it. He too, had noticed a few peculiar things around their new home, but his logical side had simply dismissed them the way Nicole had. Still, there were a few events that were more than mere coincidence. The most memorable event that came to mind was centered on them picking out the paint colors for the rooms. Initially, Nicole had her heart set on very warm, soft shades for the rooms. She had even brought home samples that she had showed to him. Upon agreeing with her choices, he tucked the samples into his wallet and had every intention of purchasing the paint the following evening after work. He no sooner got to work in the morning when Nicole phoned him stating that all the colors were wrong and she knew exactly what the house needed. Somehow in the course of less than twenty-four hours, she had changed her mind one hundred and eighty degrees. Even she couldn't explain it, but knew that her decision was right. Then there was the episode of the nursery furniture. Nicole had helped Jared rearrange the small nursery to make room for their computer equipment since they didn't anticipate having children in the near future. The completely rearranged the room, tucking the majority of the antique furniture safely away in the attic. The following morning, Nicole woke up in a deep sweat explaining to Jared, that it was all wrong. She was so insistent that they rearrange it back to its' original state, that she insisted that he meet her there during his lunch hour. Realizing that arguing with her was futile; he gave in and did what she asked. He had questioned her as to why they were doing it and she again, could not give a local answer, just knew that it was the right thing to do.

"What are you thinking Nicki? I'm sure that I simply forgot to turn the light off."

"Honey, she said almost pleadingly, "I walked around the side of the house to meet you, remember? The path was very dark. Now look at it; it's well lit from the light shining out through the window."

"If you're implying that the light wasn't on just a few minutes ago, then how to you explain it being on now?"

"I know you won't believe me, and I'm not sure I believe it myself, but sometimes I really feel that Rachel is here, still, in this house. Sometimes I think that she's trying to communicate with us, and through me. Please don't look at me like I'm crazy, but isn't it possible that she has never been able to rest, knowing that her husband is rotting away in prison for her murder, a murder that he didn't commit."

"I'm not going to tell you that you're sounding a lot like your lunatic friend Gwen, but I would like you to listen to yourself and what you're saying. You're talking about ghosts, and in particular, you're saying that our new home is haunted with the ghost of a murdered woman."

Unable to comprehend such an illogical theory, he started to turn as if to leave the area.

"Why would it be so hard for you to accept the fact that not everyone goes directly to heaven or hell? As a Christian," she protested, "you believe in purgatory right? Then why can't you fathom the thought that some souls get caught in between life on earth and the afterworld, sort of like purgatory on Earth. I've always told you that my grandmother didn't go right up to heaven. She was always here to take care of me while I was growing up and then she died unexpectedly from a damn blood clot in her fractured arm. I know without a doubt that she hung around until she was certain that I was going to be okay. So why is this any different? Rachel fell or was pushed off a cliff and died a horrible death. Then they prosecute her beloved husband and split her family up even further; Christ, if I was her, I would have stuck around too if I could, to rectify the situation!"

Jared stood motionless; listening to Nicole's very convincing speech. He also realized that though she was trying to give him the hard sell, she didn't have to, for he had sensed her presence also. Although against his better judgment, he too, had come to accept the possibility of some kind of apparition still resided in their home.

"So, what do we do now Nicki? It's not her house anymore, and what can we do to rectify her situation? I really don't want to share my new house with a ghost, spirit or whatever you want to call it. You don't think she minds us being here, do you?" he asked, starting to develop his usual paranoia again.

"How would I know? It's not like we're on a first name basis here" she gave her husband a sarcastic look and grin, then continued. "In all honestly Jared, I don't think she minds us being here because she can sense how much we love this place.

"Nicole, I don't know if I can deal with having some kind of ghost living in my house. We need to do something to get her or whatever it is in this house out."

"I agree with you honey," she said compassionately, "and I know how we can do it."

Startled and still a little bewildered, Jared look at his wife with questioning eyes, wondering what she was thinking. Before he had a chance to ask any further questions, Nicole told him of her plan.

"I believe in my heart that what we've been experiencing is a direct result of Rachel. If I'm right, then the only way to allow her peace is to prove once and for all that her husband wasn't her killer."

"And just how do you propose to solve a thirty year old murder Nicole? You're a nurse, not a detective."

"I haven't figured that part out yet, but you can bet we need to start by talking to Rachel's husband."

The words had no sooner left Nicole's lips when the upstairs bedroom light flickered off. Both Jared and Nicole stood in silent agreement. The only way the house on Sycamore Lane would ever become theirs would be when Henry Harteman was cleared of murder.

Claire sat silently at her father's bedside, half dozing as he slept in the hospital bed beside her. She couldn't believe that it had already been three weeks since the shooting and subsequent reunion with her estranged father. The first few days following the surgery had been hell for everyone. Henry lay unconscious hooked up to a ventilator and in a medically induced coma; while Claire kept vigil at his bedside morning and night. Neither her husband, nor the nurses could get her to leave his side for much longer than the time it took her to shower and freshen up daily. She refused to eat her meals in the cafeteria, let alone go home for a night's sleep. Claire simply explained that she had rejected her father for more than half of her life and wanted to be the first person he saw when he woke. She theorized that she had a lot of lost time to make up for and wanted to start making amends as soon as her father was conscious.

When her father finally regained consciousness, four days after the operation, he slowly came out of his stupor to find his only daughter weeping softly at his side. Since he was unsure if it was a dream or not, Henry closed his eyes again and tried to focus more clearly. Their subsequent reunion was filled with many more tears being shed by Henry, Claire and practically all of the nursing staff. Before regaining consciousness, Claire had discretely explained the situation that had caused such hatred between she and her father; and before any of the staff could draw any conclusions, she went on to explain that she was only a child when it happened and now as an adult, was going to have his case looked into for she no longer felt that he was the individual that harmed her mother. Stoically professing her belief in her father, Claire championed the staff of nurses and physicians to see Henry not as a murderer but as a father, and hero who saved countless lives during the riot.

While Claire kept her bedside vigil; her husband expedited a formal parole hearing on both Henry and Mac's behalf. With numerous officer's testimonies, along with the warden's recommendations; not only were they officially released from prison for the crimes they had been convicted of so many years ago, but both were pardoned and now free men.

Claire broke the news to her father on the same day that his best friend from the prison, Gary Danbarry, was released from the hospital. Prior to discharge, Gary insisted on visiting Henry. Tears flowed from the middle-aged officer's eyes when he heard the good news, but even then, he vowed to find Rachel's real killer. He promised Henry, that even though he was now a free man, he wouldn't rest until the right person paid for what they did to Rachel, and subsequently to Henry and his children. Henry smiled at his friend as he was wheeled out of the room and closed his eyes and thought of his only love. Visions of Rachel filled his memory, of the good times they shared, of the birth of the children, and of the precious love they felt for one another. Realizing that it was a lifetime ago, Henry opened his eyes and saw his wife's image in his daughter's face. Although Rachel was gone; he still had Clarissa.

Reconciliation between the two had come unexpectedly easy. When Henry first saw his daughter and recognized who it was, he was overcome with joy. The years of bitterness and anger quickly faded from both their memories. Claire tried as best she could to explain why she couldn't face him after the murder. Henry didn't care the reason, he just felt blessed that she was here now and felt his heart was finally healed. The rest of his body was taking longer to heal though, due to his injuries. Always a fighter, the chest tubes and other medical equipment that had been vital in his recovery were slowly removed one by one. Even the neurologist was astonished at how well his injured arm was healing. He confided in Henry and Clarissa that he hadn't expected it to take but now three weeks out, it appeared that it was healing better than anyone expected or anticipated. Henry was making great progress but both he and Claire realized that it was going to take months of physical and occupational therapy in order for him to regain use of his injured extremity. Before she even spoke with her husband of father, Claire started making arrangements with a home care agency to come out to her home and provide the necessary therapies at their home. Driven by guilt and remorse, she wanted only the best for her only living parent.

Claire's decision to have Henry move in with them came as a shock to Richard. Normally a very private person, Claire was now inviting a practical stranger into their home, but he chose not to mention his reluctance to his wife. The transition in her, from a bitter, revengeful, near alcoholic; to once again being the caring woman that he fell in love with was welcomed. Still, he was leery about having her father live in their home. How would this poor man feel and how would he react if he ever found out that his own daughter's hatred and son-in-law were what had kept him incarcerated in the first place. Richard knew that he and Claire were going to have to face the fact that Henry's blood was essentially, on their hands for they were the reason that he was still in prison at the time of the riot. Maybe, Richard speculated that his wife was already keenly aware of that fact and that was the driving force behind her present actions. One thing Richard knew for sure, Clarissa was a different person now and he welcomed the change.

Chapter 22

As Henry's discharge day neared, everyone hustled to get the Drake household in order. The staff straightened and cleaned the already immaculate house in preparation for Henry's arrival. Claire had the library converted into a guestroom so that Henry wouldn't have to climb stairs.

Meanwhile, Nicole and Jared were also busy. With the closing of their home scheduled for the following morning, both Nicole and Jared couldn't concentrate on anything but moving into their new home. Unbeknownst to Henry, his house that he shared with Rachel had been in the family until just a few months prior to his release. With the riot, Henry's surgery and subsequent release from prison, neither Claire nor Richard had given much thought to the house, but knew through their attorney that the closing would be taking place any day. While Claire and Henry had all but forgotten about the home, Henry sat in his hospital room wondering when he would ever have a place to call home again. His mind wandered back to a happier time. His wedding day, the day they moved into Sycamore Lane, the day the children were born and many other wonderful memories from his past life. Many long lost memories came rushing back. For years, Henry had repressed those very memories as they were too painful to relive. He now welcomed them, for they were his past, and his only future was with his daughter. Henry thought of those bittersweet memories as he sat in his hospital bed and drifted slowly off to sleep.

Chapter 23

Gary Danbarry had only been home from the hospital for less than a week and he was already acting like nothing had happened. Against his wife's advice, he had started making phone calls the moment that he was released from his physician's care. His first contact was with his nephew in Syracuse, explaining to him the importance of reexamining Henry's case. He explained that even though the man had been paroled, his name still needed to be cleared. Although reluctant, his nephew agreed to at least review the case and see what new angles could be explored. With phase one of his plans accomplished, Gary set forth on obtaining any pertinent information that he could about the three decade old murder. Driven by a need to know, and a desire to help, the man was unstoppable. Only when the pain became unbearable and he found it hard to breathe, did Gary take a break. Marian Danbarry knew her husband's motivation and determination, yet she couldn't help but worry about his endurance. He wouldn't admit how severe his internal injuries had been and dismissed the notion that he should relax more in order to heal. Marian prayed silently that he had the strength to accomplish his goal and not jeopardize himself in the process.

Once Dot, a pleasant petite woman in her early seventies agreed to help Gary look up the court transcripts and police reports, thanks in part to his nephew and a phone call placed by the warden, his plan was initiated. The file clerk had taken it upon herself to look up the case on the station's computer system, a task that would have taken the officer weeks to figure out. When he made it into the station four days after his discharge, she not only had the court records, and police reports, but also the autopsy report and various newspaper accounts of the murder. Gary was astonished that in such a short time, this wonderful woman that he didn't even know had been able to dig up such a vast amount of information on a case that had taken place so long ago. Now it was up to him to look for anything that might help exonerate Henry. Gary felt confident that within his stack of papers that now cluttered his kitchen table, lay the information to clear Henry once and for all. And he prayed that he could find it...

Chapter 24

After an extremely restless night, both Jared and Nicole woke to find a beautiful sunrise. Once fully awake, Jared realized that in a few hours, he would officially be a homeowner. Fear, joy and anxiety filled his mind when he thought of the tremendous responsibility that he and Nicole were about to undertake. He also couldn't help but think of their conversations regarding the house. Up until this point, he had been about to rationalize every unusual event that had occurred within and around the house, but now he was beginning to think that maybe Nicole was right. Maybe something or someone else did in fact, reside in what was about to become their new home. And that thought was not only unsettling; it absolutely terrified him.

"Good morning honey," Nicole chirped from the bathroom once she realized that Jared was awake. "Do you know what today is?" she added cheerfully.

"Hump day?" he teased as he stretched in bed.

"Very funny," she responded back, with her mouth full of toothpaste.

Once finished in the bathroom, she noted that Jared was still in bed, checking his emails on his phone and not paying attention to her. She quickly approached her unsuspecting husband, grabbed a pillow and blasted him upside the head with it.

"There" she said as she removed the pillow from the side of his head. "Did that remind you of what today is silly?" she said laughing.

He didn't answer but grabbed the pillow still in her hand and pulled her onto the bed.

Quickly he flipped her onto her back and pinned her to the bed. Before she had time to react, he kissed her fast and fiercely. Surprised, it nearly took her breath away, though she didn't seem to mind. So often, she had to be the aggressive one within their relationship, so when her husband made any sexual advance, she received them openly. When he finally pulled his mouth away from her, he softly responded to her question.

"Of course I remember what day it is Nicole. Today is the start of a whole new chapter in our lives. Today will be the first day in our new home."

"I can't wait Jared! Thank you for believing in me and in this house. I love you" she whispered as tears started to well up within her eyes.

"I love you too Nicole Rose," he responded sincerely. "Now, unless you want to be late for our closing, we had better get going or we're going to miss it."

With that, both Nicole and Jared jumped out of bed and made their way toward the bathroom to get ready. The morning dew was still present outside when Nicole stepped into the shower and Jared stood at the sink shaving. Early morning fog still lingered as the sun started its' slow ascent into the sky and with the window ajar, Jared could hear the sounds of robins chirping as they gathered worms. There were several things about the townhouse that both he and Nicole were going to miss, but the time had definitely come for them to move on. Jared glanced at his watch and realized that in less than two hours he was going to own a real home. He stopped momentarily as he looked around, reminiscing and trying to absorb all the happy memories that he and Nicole had shared within those tiny walls. As he stood there, staring off into space, Nicole exited the shower and almost instinctively knew what her husband was daydreaming about. She embraced him from behind with a bear hug and smiled.

"I have wonderful memories of this place too Jared, but we're going to make new memories that we can share with our kids in the new house. It's time for us to move on."

Jared turned and smiled in response to her simple statement.

"I know Nicki, but this will always be someplace special to me. It holds a lot of memories, a lot of firsts for us."

"It's special to me as well. But I'm ready to move on, really I am. I want to start a family and I want it to be in our new home. That home needs our love and we somehow need that home."

"Come on honey. Don't go and get all weird on me again okay," Jared responded as he pulled away. It's a house. It has no feeling, therefore it doesn't need us and we can't need it. It might need someone to fix it up and we might want a new house, but the house doesn't specifically need us and only us."

"Yes Jared, it does!" Nicole responded adamantly. "It is our destiny to own that house, whether you believe it or not. That house needs love. It needs to hear laughter again. It needs to hear the little footsteps of children running up and down the hallways and staircases. It needs to realize that happiness and love exist again within its' walls. And when we close on it this morning, we will be one step closer to achieving that goal. Now, before I start freaking you out as I usually do, let's change the subject and get ready; deal?"

"Deal;" Jared quickly undressed and stepped into the still running shower. Before he shut the door, he turned back to his almost dressed wife and smiled. "You sure are a strange one Mrs. Brentwood, a strange one."

Nicole smiled as the shower door shut. "I know Mr. Brentwood. But I love you too."

Henry lay awake in his hospital bed as the day shift nurse entered the room. Her greeting was warm and friendly, as everyone's had become over the course of his hospitalization. He wasn't used to people treating him as an individual, let alone, a decent human being. His recuperation had been a long process, but with such support around him, he had found strength in their genuine caring and concern. Now, he was being forced out into the cold cruel judgmental world where he, ultimately was going to be on his own. The thought terrified him as he watched the young nurse scurry around the room. Though he was going to initially be discharged to his daughter's home, which he assumed was going to be extravagant, he also realized that eventually he would have to find a home of his own. Though they were blood related, Henry was well aware that he was a stranger to his own daughter and that his welcome would fade away quickly. He wanted to maintain a relationship with his only daughter, but also wasn't quite ready for how quickly everything was happening. Just one month earlier, he had been prisoner number 905941. Now people were congenial and treating him like some kind of celebrity. The riot, subsequent shooting, hospitalization and reunion with his family were beginning to take its' toll on him mentally. The anxiety and fear that Henry was feeling began to escalate as the nurse turned to address him.

"How are you feeling today? You must be so excited about busting out of here today!" As soon as the words left her lips, the young nurse realized that the way she had phrased the statement had come out totally inappropriately. Her face blushed and she tried to retract the sentence immediately.

"Oh Mr. Harteman, I didn't mean it the way it sounded. I just meant that you must be excited to be leaving the hospital finally. You know, with bad food and all. I swear I didn't mean to say anything to offend you. I'm sorry."

"No offence taken Jane" Henry replied back, smiling. "Would you be kind enough to get me a glass of orange juice when you have a moment? I'm extremely dry this morning."

"I'll go get you one right now," the young nurse volunteered, seeing this as a great opportunity to leave the room and collect her composure. She exited Henry's room before he had a chance to respond.

"Yup, I'm breaking out of here alright. But here hasn't been such a bad place to be," he thought silently to himself as he sighed. "I'd rather be in there than out there," he thought as he glanced out the window.

Henry sat quietly in his private hospital room waiting for the nurse's return. Within a few moments he heard her footsteps coming back down the corridor towards his room. As the door started to open, he turned to retrieve his juice and to his surprise he saw his daughter entering the room, with juice in hand.

"Good morning Henry," Claire exclaimed, "Your cute little nurse told me that you wanted this," she said as she extended her hand containing the orange juice. "She sure is a pretty little thing. That must be enough to get all the men's blood pumping when she enters the room," she continued with a smile on her face.

"Clarissa, what are you doing here so early?" her father asked, completely surprised. "It's barely eight am."

"I'm here to check you out of this place."

"Yes, today is the big day; I just didn't expect you to come so early. I didn't even know if the doctor has filled out the discharge paperwork yet. He's probably not even here yet."

"Would you stop worrying Henry; I've met with the social workers, and your doctors. Everything has been taken care of, and once you've finished your breakfast, you are officially discharged from the hospital. So just relax and let me take care of everything."

"Guess I have no choice" he thought to himself as he just sipped on his orange juice and smiled.

As Henry sat in his hospital room, Gary Danbarry also sat quietly at his kitchen table. Unable to rid the case from his mind, he had been getting up at four in the morning ever since he had obtained the files from the clerk. He threw himself into every account of the murder and subsequent investigation. His wife had already begun to worry about him as if an unseen force seemed to be driving him on. She tried to talk to him about pacing himself and taking it easy, but after the first few days, realized that her words were fell on deaf ears. He was determined to pay back the debt that he thought he owed to Henry by clearing his name once and for all. Now, nearly eight o'clock in the morning, and already four hours into the files, Gary reached for his third cup of coffee. Marian Danbarry stood a few feet away scrambling eggs for their morning meal, unaware that her frustration with her husband's drive was being taken out on the eggs within the bowl. She couldn't help but worry about his health, yet all he appeared to worry about was some convict that had already been paroled. She couldn't understand why her husband was so hell bent on pursuing a case, which in her mind, was already resolved. When Gary tried to explain that he needed to prove that Henry was innocent of the heinous crime in order to restore his good name; she had commented that he was already free so it didn't matter. That singular statement had caused them the biggest fight of their long marriage. To Gary Danbarry, it did matter. It mattered more than he was willing to admit.

"I spoke to the nurses at the hospital yesterday Gary about Mr. Harteman."

"You did?" What did you do that for without telling me?"

"Well you said that he should be getting out of the hospital soon and I thought that he might need a place to stay. I know that Agnes has a room available for rent in her apartment complex and I thought that he could rent it if he needed a cheap place to stay. I told Agnes to hold it as a favor to me," Marian replied as she poured the well-beaten eggs into a frying pain.

"She wasn't too keen on the idea at first but I told her that he was the man who saved your life and that brought her around fast enough."

"Well wasn't that mighty nice of her," he responded sarcastically. "And what did the nurses tell you about Henry?" Gary asked, now giving her his undivided attention.

"Well they didn't want to tell me anything at first, you know, patient confidentiality and all, but eventually the charge nurse who understood who you were and your bond with Henry got on the phone. She said that Henry is being discharged this morning and is going home with his daughter to Syracuse. From what Mrs. Adams said, his daughter has been at his side since he came in."

"Well it's about God damned time!"

"Gary!" Marian gasped. "I know that you're close with that man; but I will not have you taking the name of the Lord in vain in this house! I don't care if he saved your life or not. If it wasn't for God, Henry wouldn't have been able to do what he did," she exclaimed as she glared at her husband with piercing eyes. Marian Danbarry rarely raised her voice about anything, but cussing was against her innermost beliefs and she wouldn't tolerate it in her own home.

"Save me the sermons Marian. I'm sorry. I just don't like the woman that's all. The poor guy has been in prison for over half his life and she finally decided to be his daughter again after he nearly dies. There's just something phony about her. All this devotion to a man she hasn't gave a, oops-sorry, hasn't cared about, for all these years. Now she is doting all over him. It smells of some wrong doing."

"Maybe she's just trying to make up for lost time Gary. Did it ever occur to you that maybe she feels guilty that she hasn't been there for him until now?"

"I think you're right about the guilt part. I think she's guilty of something. I just have to figure out what."

"I think you're reading a lot into the fact that his daughter is trying to care about her long lost father. I think it's noble of her taking him in the way she is. Having a virtual stranger move into your house is a big endeavor and I admire her for that.

"Believe me Marian, they've got the money and I'm sure the house, to do it. Did you know that her husband is a big shot judge in the city? He's up there and I'm sure they're loaded. They've got money to burn and connections to everything."

Marian listened to her husband ramble on about the Drake's good fortune knowing that he was envious of their lifestyle. Since the injury, their income had become very limited. Barely making ends meet, she knew that Gary was bitter at anyone who was well off.

"Oh my God," he exclaimed, as Marian glared at him for taking God's name in vane again. "That's it," he shouted as he jumped from his chair and hugged his startled and slightly irritated wife. She finally moved when she realized that the eggs were starting to burn.

"What's it Gary? Please sit down and relax. You're going to hurt yourself jumping around like that," she fussed as she coaxed her husband back to his chair.

"Their connection Marian," he exclaimed. "I've always thought it odd that every time Henry went up in front of the parole board, the same few members refused to grant his freedom. I never quite understood it when they're allowing others far more dangerous out early. I always thought that there was more to it than met the eye. I think that somehow his denial is linked to his daughter. She's a bitch, and I tell you Marian, this new found love of her father isn't genuine. I think that she had some kind of vendetta against her father and used her title; or her husband's power and clout, to bride the parole board into denying his parole."

After making his declaration, Gary sipped on his now cold coffee and sat smugly at the table.

"Those accusations carry a lot of weight Gary. I wouldn't go around voicing your opinion very loudly. Right now you're on disability and if the prison got wind of your accusation, the warden might decide that he doesn't need you anymore and we need your income. We can't afford to have you lose your job because you've got a big mouth. Besides, what proof do you have to support any of it?"

"Well," he stammered, "I don't have any solid proof yet, but I think the answer to the whole truth lies somewhere within here," he responded as he patted the stack of court records spread across the table. "I think that we're going to find some of the answers right here, and the rest will fall into place," he replied confidently, trying to convince both his wife and himself. "I hope you're right Gary, but if you're not, you're not only going to cause some potentially irreparable problems between not only yourself and Henry, but between Henry and his daughter. What you're starting is a dangerous game and people's lives and reputations are at stake."

"Marian, Henry's reputation has already been destroyed. I'm trying to get it back for him. Don't you see? I'm not doing this for me; I'm doing it for Henry."

"I think you're doing this for yourself too Gary. I know how badly you wanted to become a cop and how devastated you were when they denied your admission to the academy just because of your bad back. Don't you think that maybe you're so driven to prove Henry innocent just so that you can prove to yourself that you would have been a great cop and an even better detective?"

Marian's words stung to the core, but Gary realized that there was no use arguing with the truth. He sat silently absorbing what she had said as she too felt his pain. When they had first started dating, Gary had boosted how he was going to one day be the best detective on the force. When he passed the admission; he was on his way to fulfilling his lifelong dream. Then Gary went for the pre admission academy physical and everything changed within the hour. The physician conducting the physicals refused to sign off on Gary because of his scoliosis of the spine. Back in the eighties when Gary first applied to the academy, the curvature of his spine didn't have a definitive name and there was no cure. They flatly denied his admission even though Gary had proven that he was physically fit. Devastated, he trained to become a corrections officer not out of desire but out of necessity.

"Maybe part of me wants to prove to the world that I'm more than just a peace officer at a stinking prison. But I gave up the dream of being a real cop a long time ago Marian. That dream was from another lifetime. I just want to prove Henry's innocence."

"Just be careful Gary," she warned. "I think that Clare Drake is someone you don't want to mess with and whether you have all good intentions or not, you don't want to rub her the wrong way. We don't need any more complications in our life right now."

"Don't worry Marian, Clare Drake is going to get only what is coming to her. Good or bad, that bitch is going to get what she deserves!"

Marian plopped the now cold eggs onto her husband's plate and sat down. She changed the subject of conversation but her mind continued to center on the court records in front of her. There would be no stopping her husband until he resolved his inner conflict and solved this case and she could do nothing but sit back and pray that he was wrong.

Gary, too, sat in silence eating his cold eggs and pondering on the prospect of Clare Drake bribing judges and lawyers. The thought excited him and gave him the determination to move forward. He decided that he would devote the entire day to reading the court manuscript prior to reading the interrogation transcript. With his adrenaline now up, Gary devoured his dry toast and eggs quickly, washing them down with what was left of his coffee.

"I will learn the truth soon my friend" he thought to himself as he finished his meal in silence.

Henry was finishing his breakfast when Dr. Wei entered the room. After a brief exchange, Henry stood and shook the young doctor's hand with his good arm. The doctor bid him farewell and with that, swiftly turned and left the room. Henry and his daughter sat silently for a moment, both trying to absorb the finality of the doctor's words. Henry was officially discharged from the hospital and could leave once the paperwork was signed. Claire pondered momentarily at the thought of bringing this practical stranger, that she had once called her father, into her home. At first, it appeared to be the only logical answer since Henry had nowhere else to go and no money; but now Claire was getting apprehensive about the whole concept. Henry seemed to pick up on her doubts and spoke softly to her.

"I know that this whole situation has been overwhelming for you Clarissa. Why don't you let me make some other arrangements? You and your husband don't need me moving in with you and disrupting your life. I'm sure I can find someplace else to live. You've already done enough for me."

"Nonsense! I won't hear of it. You're family and you need me right now; so it's settled. You're welcome in our home for as long as you would like to stay. And you will have full access to whatever we have. So come on, let's get you packed up and get out of here," she smiled as she stood.

"If you're sure Clarissa, then let's go."

"I'm sure father."

Realizing what she had just called him, both Henry and Claire smiled in agreement. Henry was going home.

Chapter 25

Nicole and Jared dressed in silence, while listening to her favorite Barry White CD. Both heard his soulful voice in the background but neither paid much attention as their minds wondered. Nicole, still picking out colors for furniture and décor in her mind had forgotten about their earlier conversations. Jared on the other hand could not rid his mind of the possibility of a spirit lingering in their new home. Logically, he dismissed the whole idea as ludicrous but his inner voice told him that Nicole was right; something or someone did still reside in their home. And that thought still terrified him and left him very unsettled.

They left their townhouse and headed for the lawyer's office before heavy rush hour. They rode in silence, thinking about their future in their home. As they neared the city limits, Nicole's excitement became more and more evident. They had always talked about someday owning a grand house, big enough to house a dozen children, and for Nicole, today her dream was coming true. Being an only child, Jared didn't fully understand the dynamics behind a big family, but he saw how happy she was amongst her siblings during family gatherings. Somehow over the course of time, he too, had decided that they should have a big family. Now, with the closing just minutes away, the time had finally come to start that family. By now, even Jared was getting excited, putting all negative thoughts out of his mind as they pulled into the attorney's parking lot.

The closing was uneventful for all parties involved. The Drake's has already pre-signed the documents and weren't present for the closing, which irritated Nicole. She had desperately wanted to meet Claire Drake face to face. She couldn't explain it to Jared, but felt that she had to meet Rachel's daughter before she moved into her home. Maybe she just wanted to see what she looked like, maybe she wanted to thank her for selling them the house; she wasn't sure, but one thing she did know was that she had a tie with the family that wasn't going to go away. Regardless of her frustration, the closing proceeded without any hitches and within an hour, the house on Sycamore Lane was transferred from the Drakes to the Brentwood's. Upon completion of closing, Nicole struck up a conversation with the attorney representing the Drake family. She was a young woman who didn't look more than 26 or 27, and Nicole couldn't help but be curious as to how she had become appointed to represent the family. The woman appeared to be very shy but quickly warmed up to Nicole's charm. After a brief exchange, she explained that she was fairly new to the law firm that the Drakes used as council. She went on to say that her father also worked in the firm and since he was Richard Drake's Saturday golf partner, she had grown up knowing the Drake's since childhood. When asked about the Drake's, the young attorney explained that Claire was an excellent attorney and ruthless in the courtroom. Nicole thanked the young attorney for her time and with Jared at her side, exited the office, heading toward their car. Jared carried the closing papers under his arm and before they reached their car, extended his free arm to Nicole. Dangling from his fingers was the key to their new home. Nicole's eyes lit up as she reached for the key ring. Her dream had finally come true; they now had a home of their own.

"Let's go there right now Jared."

"But Nicole, we've got so much to organize at the townhouse before everybody arrives in the morning. They're going to be there in the morning to pack up our things. We'll be in the house soon enough. Let's just go home and finish getting things ready, okay?" he bargained. From the look on her face, he know it was useless to attempt to change her mind.

"Okay, we'll go by the house; but just for a minute."

She leaned over and kissed him on the cheek, leaving her coral-toned lipstick on his face.

"Thanks Jared. I swear we'll just stay a minute; I promise."

With that said, he started the engine and they left for Oneida Lake.

Henry packed the few personal effects that he had in silence. Claire studied the middle-aged man inquisitively. Unable to determine what he was feeling or thinking, she tried to pry as delicately as she knew how.

"It's going to be a beautiful day out Henry. The air smells like spring and you might want to wear that running jacket that Justin bought you because there's still a briskness to the air."

"I had completely forgotten about how beautiful the flowers are at this time of year. Remember how beautiful your mother used to have the gardens around the house?"

Suddenly a flood of emotions opened up for Henry while his daughter sat helplessly.

"She was a good woman, your mother; and I swear to you Clarissa, I didn't hurt her."

The tears welled up in both of their eyes as he spoke.

"I now know that Henry. I just wished that I had known that a long time ago. Please forgive me Henry. I was so young when it happened," she sobbed, "And everyone said that you did it."

"Oh Claire, I never blamed you. You were still just a child. My friends and family even doubted my innocence; so how could I blame you for doubting me? I just wish that we could turn back time."

"Me too; but now it's time to move on, so let's dry those tears and let's say we get out of here before I have to eat another hospital meal okay?" he replied with a half grin; trying desperately to change the subject.

"Sounds good to me; let's go home."

"Yes, let's go. Do you think," Henry asked hesitantly, "if it's not too far out of the way, do you think that we could drive by Sycamore Lane; just this one time since no one is living there now? I will never ask again; I just need to see it this one last time."

Unable to get herself to tell him the truth about their former home, Claire just smiled and calmly replied, "Sure Henry, we can drive by the house if you want."

"I'd like that very much Clarissa. More than you know. Thank you."

Nicole and Jared pulled into the drive of their new home and quickly exited the car. Nearly noon, the sun was directly overhead without a cloud in the sky. The house sparkled in the intense sunlight and was a welcome sight. Nicole, with key still clenched tightly in her hand, bounded toward the front door, full of excitement. Even Jared stood back looking at the house, impressed with how all their hard work had paid off; the house looked magnificent. The last six weeks had been grueling for them, between working full time and then spending numerous hours making repairs and painting, but their time had been worth it. The house looked like something out of a magazine. Before Nicole stepped into the foyer, she felt a tug on her sleeve. Turning, she met Jared who had snuck up on her, standing at her side.

"What do you think you're doing young lady?" he teased, wrapping his arms around her.

"I'm going inside."

"Not before I get a kiss to seal the deal," Nicole smiled and moved her body closer to his. Just as she started to kiss her husband, she let out a gasp as Jared swept her off her feet and into his arms. Their embrace was intense and hot. As he kissed her, he reached for the door handle and opened their front door. Hearing the noise, Nicole pulled away to see what he was doing.

"Isn't the groom supposed to carry the bride over the threshold of their new home?" he asked innocently.

"Oh Jared, you're too much. That's only when you're first married," Nicole laughed. "Besides I weigh a little more now than I did when we were first married and you might hurt yourself if you try that."

Teasing, Jared allowed his knees to buckle. "You're right; you are becoming a fat ass!"

"Fat ass my butt. I'll have you know that I've only gained five pounds since we were married," she replied somewhat indignant.

"Oh, you know I'm just kidding" he continued as his lips met hers again. "Come on, let's take this inside. Once inside, Jared kissed his wife passionately and deeply, scooping her up in his arms and carrying her up the stairs leading to their bedroom. Nicole, meanwhile, was oblivious to the movement as she caressed his neck and unbuttoned his shirt. Once inside their bedroom, which still lacked furniture, he lay down on a blanket that they had used as a drop cloth while painting. Nicole didn't seem to mind that she was now lying on the hard floor, on a dirty blanket with a designer suit on. Jared finished unbuttoning his shirt and bent down toward his wife, who was waiting patiently for his embrace. He leaned in toward her and while she was still sitting upright, moved around to her back side. Puzzled by what he was doing, she remained motionless, waiting for his next move. Before touching her, he leaned backward and flipped on the radio that they had left in the room. The music was softly playing as he leaned back toward her. Suddenly she could feel his strong hands touching her neck and shoulders. They felt so good; thou she didn't realize how tense she had been during the closing.

"Relax honey, let me help you unwind," he whispered as he worked his way across her shoulders.

"Jared that feels so good," she moaned softly.

"Good. I'm glad. Why don't you take off your blouse so that I don't wrinkle it any more than it already is."

Quickly she complied. As soon as the last button was undone, she removed her blouse revealing her best assets. Jared tried to keep his libido contained as his had once again started massaging her shoulders. As his hands caressed her soft skin, she started getting that special warm feeling both inside and out. Slowly she reached her arms behind her and as Jared watched, unsnapped her bra, allowing her breasts their freedom. Now, unable to contain himself, his hands worked their way around to her chest, quickly making contact with her already erect nipples. Her body responded by sending quivers to her toes, as his touch grew more intense. Nicole loved the way he touched her, so softly yet forcefully. As her body yearned for his, she reached toward his pants. Quickly she found what she was after. Gently at first, she started stroking him through his trousers, and then increased her rhythm and intensity. She turned to face him and slowly stood up, allowing her breasts to brush against his face as she did so. Jared sat silently as he watched her step out of her pumps, one by one, then methodically unzip her, by now, very wrinkled slacks. Once unzipped, they quickly slid to the ground revealing how truly excited she was. Unbeknownst to Jared, his wife had gone to the closing sans underwear. Now seeing her before him this way was more than he could take. He almost exploded right then as she moved closer to him to stand beside her. Once standing, it was her turn to kneel. As she did, her hands went to his belt, which by now was being pushed in a precarious angle by his excitement. As she unbuttoned his pants, she kissed his abdomen making his body spasm with delight. As his pants dropped into a pile on the floor beside her clothes, he knelt down beside her. Now flesh to flesh, their body heat intensified as their mouths once again made contact. Their hands caressed and moved over the other's body, as their embrace grew hotter. Nicole wanted him and wanted him at that moment. Her rhythm never slowed as she slowly pushed him back onto the blanket and moved on top of him. Now oblivious to the music playing in the background, their bodies swayed to their own rhythm as they reached ecstasy in each other's arms as they came to a climax in their sexual dance. Still in an interlocked embrace, they collapsed in each other's arms on the blanket.

"Wow! I like out new house already!" Jared whispered.

"So do I," Nicole laughingly replied. "So do I."

Though content to spend the rest of the day in each other's arms, Nicole and Jared jumped up simultaneously when they heard a noise coming from outside the house. Scampering for their clothes, they watched a silver Escalade approach and park in their circular driveway. Unaware of whom the occupants were, both dressed as quickly as they could, fearing they might ring the doorbell. Inside the car, Henry stared at his former home in disbelief, unable to fathom the idea that the house looked exactly the same as it had thirty years before. Even Claire was awestruck at the similarity to her childhood home. The last time Claire had been near the house was just prior to her Aunt's death, which had only been a few months ago. The house had been dark, dingy and cold, and looked tired and rundown. Now it sparkled with life, and warmth. The yard was meticulously mowed, the hedges were trimmed with precision and the flowerbeds once again sparkled with an assortment of tulips and daffodils. The shutters had been freshly painted and the windows were spotless. Tears wells up within Henry's eyes when he looked at his former home and remembered what life had been like there.

"I can't believe you've kept the house up this way Claire. It looks as beautiful as it did when your mother was living."

Tears now filled Claire's eyes as well when she saw the pride her father still had for the house. Unsure how to break the news to her father; she simply blurted the words out.

"I didn't keep the house up Henry. I visited the house maybe a half-dozen times over the last thirty years. I couldn't bear to come here; I hated this house. It hurt too much. I wanted to bury the memories of this place, the same way we had to bury her. It's about time I told you the truth about this place."

Henry took out the handkerchief that Justin had given him while in the hospital and wiped his eyes, looking at his daughter, somewhat confused. He wasn't sure what she was about to say, and he felt his chest tighten while he waited.

"When Auntie passed away, I put the house on the market. I didn't have the time or the desire to take care of it, so I sold it ASAP. A young couple fell in love with it instantly, or so my agent told me, and they brought it the same day that they looked at it. They closed on the house today," she said, wiping a tear from her eye. "That's probably their car in the driveway right now."

Henry looked at the car and then again at the house that had once been his. It seemed so unfair that everything that he loved had been so easily taken away from him. A great feeling of despair came over him as she continued.

"If I had known that you'd be out of prison, or that you would have ever wanted to see the house again, I swear to you, I wouldn't have sold it. I just thought that the sooner we ridded ourselves of the last tie to mother's death, the faster we could move on. We all need closure Henry."

"I won't have peace and I won't have closure Clarissa until your mother's murderer is found."

Claire nodded silently as she heard her father's proclamation.

"I swear, with God as my witness, I will find out what really happened that night. And only then will your mother and the rest of us finally find peace."

As the words left his mouth, the front door opened and Nicole stepped out. Henry signaled for Richard to stop the car and he stepped out the face the woman staring into their SUV. He tried to feel hatred toward her, simply for the fact that she had something that was rightfully his, but when Nicole approached him, hand outstretched and smiling, any animosity that he had felt melted away. Looking at the young vibrant woman standing before him was like looking at his own wife. Her eyes sparkled in the bright afternoon light and her smile was genuine.

"Good afternoon, I'm Nicole Brentwood. Is there something that I can do for you?"

Henry took the outstretched hand and shook it, remaining silent and mesmerized by the woman. Feeling awkward by the way this man was staring at his wife, Jared stepped forward and introduced himself to the elderly man.

"And I'm Jared Brentwood, Nicole's husband."

Henry quickly came out of his spell that Nicole had put him in, and regained his composure as he shook Jared's hand.

"Hello, my name is Henry, and I'm very sorry to bother you folks. I was just interested in seeing the Harteman residence one last time. You see," Henry stammered, "I haven't seen it in quite some time and it used to be very special to me."

Sensing his uneasiness, Nicole quickly spoke up.

"Mr. Harteman, you're not bothering us in the least. You're welcome to come inside or simply look around the grounds; after all, this was your house."

"You're the Henry Harteman," Jared intervened; "The hero from the prison riot?"

"Jared!" Nicole snapped. "Mr. Harteman's been through enough. I'm sure he would just like to see the house. Come on sir, let me show you around."

Before Nicole could get Henry to move, the rear door of the Escalade opened and Clarissa Drake appeared from within. Both Nicole and Jared remained stationary as she walked toward them. Once within speaking distance, she cut right to the point.

"Jared and Nicole Brentwood I presume," she said in a monotone, almost rude tone.

Instantly Nicole didn't like the woman.

"Correct, and I assume you're Clare Drake, though I wouldn't' know since you didn't grace us with your presence at the closing," she sarcastically responded. "I just invited your father to look around; feel free to join us if you'd like," she continued as she turned away, allowing her voice to soften just a little.

"We don't have time to be wandering around, dredging up old forgotten memories father. Besides, we don't want to disturb these people on their first day in their new home," Claire retorted as she continued to stare at the house.

"Where do I have to be Claire?" her father asked innocently. "I've been tied up for thirty years so I don't think ten more minutes will kill me. Besides, I would like to walk out back and simply look at the water."

Horrified at the prospect of going to the bluff, Claire insisted that they really needed to leave. Finally, Richard who had been a silent observer up until this point stepped in.

"Leave him be Claire. Maybe he needs to see the bluff again. Maybe it's part of the healing process," he whispered as he placed his arm on hers. Seizing the moment, Nicole spoke up as she turned back toward the house.

"Come on Mr. Harteman, I'll show you around." Taking his arm in hers, she smiled and turned back toward her new home. Unsure of what to do or say, Jared followed behind as Richard and Claire remained frozen by their car.

"You've done a lot of work around here already. My daughter told me that my sister-in-law really let the place get run down as she got up there in years. I'm sure it was too much for her to try and keep up," he said trying to maintain his composure as they rounded the corner, making their way towards the veranda. Once in the back yard, Henry looked out at the water. Suddenly feeling faint, he quickly made his way over to the loveseat a few feet away and sat down. Sensing his anguish, Nicole sat down beside him, without saying a word. Jared stared out at the water helplessly, unsure if he should break the silence or not, and if so, not quite sure of what to say. Nicole looked at the elderly man who was softly crying beside her. With his arm still wrapped up and in a sling, he looked so pitiful. She could only imagine how much pain he was in at that moment, both physically and mentally. As she stared at the man who was her father's age, she could feel his agony and despair as he tried to regain his composure.

"You still miss her don't you Mr. Harteman? She asked softly.

"Oh miss, I've missed her every day of the last 30 years. She and the children were my life."

"It must be very hard trying to move forward with your new life now, but at least you have your children here to help you."

"I have Clarissa, that's true, but she's a very important, very busy woman and I can't impose on her family forever, and my son, my poor son," he said as his voice trailed off, "I don't even know how to find him. Claire said that she would fill me in on the past when we got home. Up until this point, she's refused to tell me anything about what has become of Robert; she said I'd been through enough."

Confused by his statement, Nicole sat in silence as Henry looked out at the water once more. The lake was calm as a few birds hovered by the shoreline. The blue-green hue of the water was beautiful as the water lily's cast their reflections upon it, and the air smelled fresh and clean. Henry watched the bird's movements as they circled above the water and then got up, and started toward the edge of the bluff. As he neared the edge of the embankment overlooking the water, something made him freeze in his tracks.

Quickly Henry turned to find the source of the noise, which was coming from the veranda where he had just been sitting. Both Nicole and Jared turned and looked back as well, as they made their way to the visibly distraught man. All three looked in amazement as Nicole's wind chime started blowing in the breeze. The chime seemed to dance in the wind as if someone was orchestrating its moves. As the chime continued swaying in the wind, the three could feel the warm air as it moved up the bluff and onto their faces. Finally dismissing the noise, Henry turned to Nicole and smiled.

"I see the wind can still come up pretty quickly around here."

"Yes, and storms really roll in very unexpectedly we've found."

"I'm going to go inside and make sure all the windows are latched," Jared remarked as he excused himself.

Nicole turned to look at her visitor and new friend standing beside her.

"Mr. Harteman, may I ask you something?" she said gingerly.

"Sure," he said turning to make direct eye contact with the woman standing beside him.

"I know you didn't do anything to hurt your wife, and I know that Rachel knows that too. Do you believe in the afterlife?" Nicole blurted out looking directly at Henry.

Before Henry could answer, Nicole tried to explain herself.

"Henry, I know you don't know me from Adam, and I promise you that I'm not some lunatic who just purchased your house, but I firmly believe that Rachel is still present in this house and she wants me to help prove that you didn't hurt her."

As she spoke, the wind's intensity increased significantly, so much so that she and Henry made their way back toward the house. As they walked towards the house, Henry glanced up at the upstairs window as the light turned on.

"That," he said gesturing towards the lighted bedroom, "was Rachel's favorite room in the house. She used to sit by the window in her grandmother's rocking chair and knit for hours. She said that she had the best view of the water from up there."

Henry stopped talking and glanced again up at the window. Unsure of what he saw, or thought he saw; Henry once again addressed Nicole.

"Mrs. Brentwood, I don't think you're crazy. And I think that Rachel won't rest until our family is whole again, that is, as whole as I can make it without her around. And I could see why Rachel would connect with you, if that's possible. You seem to love this house as much as she did."

"Please call me Nicole. And yes, I love this home more than I can express. Something drew me to it, and once we saw the house, I knew it was what I've been waiting for all my life. Would you like to see the inside?" she asked as she stepped onto the veranda. "And did you say that the bedroom with the light on was your wife's favorite?" Nicole asked, for Jared's benefit since he had just rejoined them.

"Well, yes, it was," Henry fidgeted, "I probably should get back to Claire. She's probably wondering where I am by now."

"I'm sure that if she wanted to leave right away, she'd have come to find you. Come on it, if you feel up to it, and I'll show you around."

Not giving him a chance to say no, Nicole opened up the atrium door leading into the study. Henry gasped as he stood in a room that hadn't changed in the last thirty years. The shelves were dusty for Nicole hadn't had a chance to concentrate on the tiny room yet, and the books were disorganized, but the room was virtually unchanged since the time when Henry used to call it home.

Nicole paused a moment, then continued into the kitchen. It too, looked the same except for the fresh coat of paint, and new stainless appliances. Nicole had also put up a glass tile backsplash to accentuate the cherry cabinets. Even the kitchen table and chairs that Nicole had purchased for the breakfast area were similar to what Rachel had picked out so long ago. The room sparkled with sunlight and Henry was again forced to recall a happier time in his life. Feeling increasingly uncomfortable with the whole situation, Jared spoke up, breaking the silence by encouraging Nicole to show their unexpected guest the more formal rooms in the front of the house. Nicole obliged as she and Henry made their way down the hallway. Once out of sight, Jared hustled up the back stairs to pick up the drop clothes that were still lying in the master bedroom. Jared noticed that she spare bedroom's light had yet again been left on; flicked it off and raced to the master bedroom as he heard Nicole leading Henry up the front staircase. They toured the second floor quickly and were going back down the front staircase when the doorbell rang. Opening the door, Nicole was face to face with Claire. After a brief exchange in which Claire refused to go inside the house, Nicole motioned for Henry to come to the door. Once in view, Claire commented to her father that they had overstayed their welcome and that they needed to get to the pharmacy before continuing home. Henry thanked his hosts and abruptly left, with Claire already waiting by the car. Nicole and Jared stood on the front landing as they drove off, their car kicking up dust the entire length of the driveway.

"Well, that was an interesting visit," Jared commented, once they were out of sight.

"Yes it was."

"Nicole. I know that look. What are you thinking?"

"Nothing, except that I told you before that that man was incapable of killing his wife, and now I believe it 100%; but that daughter of his, now she's one cold bitch. I wouldn't be surprised what she's capable of."

"Leave it alone Nicole, I'm warning you. You're going to get yourself into something over your head. And I'm afraid that if you go after Claire Drake, you're going to come out on the losing end."

"Then you underestimate me Jared. I'm not going after anyone per say. I'm going after the truth and the truth lies within this house and the Harteman family. And no district attorney, or her husband whether he's a judge or not, is going to stop me from learning the truth. Now, let's lock up and go to the townhouse. We've got a lot of packing to do still," she said as she dismissed her husband's warnings.

Deciding that he could try to speak with her about it once they got home, Jared decided not to push the issue any more, but knew that he had to convince Nicole to drop it before anyone got hurt, especially them. He reached for the keys that were lying on the table in the foyer and locked the front door. Not sure if Nicole locked the atrium doors to the veranda, Jared offered to run around back to double check. Nicole started in that direction instructing Jared to start the car and wait for her there. He shrugged and headed toward their car, and Nicole stepped out of sight. Once on the veranda, Nicole paused for a moment, looking out at the water that had so mesmerized Henry. Unable to fathom how hard the day must have been for him, Nicole checked the lock on the door and headed back toward the car. As Nicole rounded the side of the house, she didn't look back to notice that the bedroom light turned on.

Henry was silent during their thirty minute drive back towards the city. Both Richard and Claire were curious to know what was going through his head after seeing the house again. Unbeknownst to Claire, the visit had actually been therapeutic for him, and was a means towards closure of a terrible part of his life. For Claire, it was just the opposite. Seeing the house again made her relive the long suppressed memories of the day her family was shattered. While there, the memories came back stronger and stronger with every step she took in the house's direction. The late night visitor's when her father was away, the nights of listening to her mother crying, hours of taking care of her brother day in and out, and the woman who lived next door who had always been so mean to both she and her mother. "Oh yes, the bitch next door— bet she's dead by now, hopefully," Claire thought to herself as she stared back towards the gathering of trees separating the two houses. Claire felt the hatred grow inside her as she waited for

Henry to walk to the car. As a child, she had never understood why Mrs. Langhorne, who had once been so friendly to her family, had grown to dislike them so much, when her husband had always remained pleasant. While he went out of his way to be congenial and a good neighbor, she hardly ever allowed her boys to play with Claire and her brother, and when they did, she was always nearby to monitor the activity. On rare occasions, the two families did appear to get along fairly well. Once or twice a summer, the families would get together for a barbecue or picnic lunch but the air was always tense, or so it had seemed to Claire. Though only thirteen the last time the families had done anything together, Claire could remember the day as if it had been yesterday as she stood frozen in time. It had been a hot August day the day Mr. Langhorne had come up with the idea, and much to his wife's reluctance, had invited her family over for the day. The air had been calm and the sky clear as they packed up their picnic basket and set out through the well-worn path connecting the two homes. Rachel had baked a fresh apple pie that morning and Claire could still smell the aroma in her nostrils as she reminisced for a moment. The day had been great fun as everyone laughed and ate, and the children swam and played. Even Betty had appeared to relax a little as the afternoon wore on.

Claire was lost in thought as Richard drove in silence on their way back to Syracuse. He knew that today was going to have an enormous impact on both Claire and Henry's lives and whether it was good or bad; both were going to have to deal with their emotional baggage of their past. Richard only hoped that his wife could handle it without the help of the bottle. He said a silent prayer that she was strong enough to make it through this chapter of her life.

Chapter 26

The rest of the afternoon and evening passed quickly for Nicole and Jared. The following morning they were met early by two of Nicole's brothers and Gwen. Everyone worked diligently throughout the day packing up boxes and furniture, stuffing all into the two rental trucks that Jared had secured. By late evening, everything was packed into the trucks and all that was left in the now vacant townhouse were sleeping bags and a few personal possessions that they'd need to spend the night. Before Nicole's two brothers, Neil and Aaron left, they agreed to meet them at the new house at 9am. Gwen sighed at hearing that she'd be up early again the following morning. Before she left for the evening, Jared kidded her by telling her to get all the beauty sleep she could; with Gwen promptly instructing him where to go and how to get there. After everyone departed and they shared a quick bite, both collapsed in their respective sleeping bags and were asleep within minutes. Even though it was a quick night's sleep, both woke revitalized when the alarm sounded at 7am. With nothing left in the townhouse to eat for breakfast, Jared quickly showered and ran to the store, arriving with fresh coffee and bagels just as Nicole was finally up and moving. With coffee in hand, both made their way out of the city and toward the lake.

Surprised she had woke up before her alarm sounded, Gwen was also dressed and on her way to help. She wasn't sure why, but she was anxious to get back to their new home and snoop around. She had offered to go with them right after closing, but both Nicole and Jared had insisted on going alone once it was officially theirs. Sometimes she just didn't understand her best friend, but then again, sometimes she just didn't understand married people in general. Regardless, she was once again going to be in their house and wanted to dispel any irrational fears that she had had in her previous exposures. After all, she thought to herself, it's only a house and now it was her friend's home. Gwen made her way along Route 196 feeling better and munching on her Danish.

Jared pulled into the drive nearly fifteen minutes ahead of schedule with Nicole right behind him. Nicole stretched as she slid out of Jared's truck, and walked over to meet him. The morning was brisk with a slight wind coming off the lake, but the sun was already warm and there wasn't a cloud in the sky--- a picture perfect day for a move.

Upon entering the front door, even though they had scrubbed and cleaned majority of the rooms and painted many, the home still had an odor so Nicole set out to open windows. The musty odor dissipated quickly as the brisk fresh air filtered in. Nicole made her way upstairs ahead of Jared who was starting to unload the U-Haul. The rooms were so bright and sunny and she didn't notice at first that the light was on in the former nursery. Once she realized it, being energy conscious, chastised herself for yet again, leaving a light on all night and wasting energy and money.

Lost in thought, she jumped when the front door bell rang. Expecting it to be her brothers, she was shocked to see not only Gwen but all five of her brothers and three of her sister-in-laws. Tears welled up in her eyes when she saw that even Jimmy, her estranged brother had shown up to help. Pushing everyone aside, she quickly made her way to him as the tears flowed down her face. He looked at her shyly, not making eye contact as she got within touching distance. Years of tension and anger between them seemed to melt away as she gently lifted his chin and looked him in the eye.

"Thank you Jimmy," Nicole mouthed unable to say the audible words.

"Hey, I wasn't going to let my kid sister down, again," he said as he hugged his only sister. "I've changed Nicki; I've really changed."

"Hey, I know that this is a Hallmark moment and all," Gwen chirped, breaking the tension of the moment, "But I got out of bed way too early on a Saturday morning to help you move in, so let's get a move on!"

Jimmy laughed as he stepped away from Nicole's embrace and smirked as he addressed Gwen. "I've changed a lot Gwen; glad to see you haven't changed a bit. You're as abrasive as ever."

Before she could reply, everyone broke out in laughter. Even Gwen had to laugh at his rude but appropriate response. Now that the ice was broken, everyone mingled for a brief moment before one of Nicole's sister-in-laws asked if she could look around before they started moving everything in. Jared offered to show everyone around, as Nicole watched her entire family pile into her new home. Only Gwen and Nicole remained outside as the group went inside.

"It's good to see Jimmy again Nicole. Bet you were surprised?"

"Gwen I haven't spoken to him in nearly five years. I can't believe that he's here, and that he's sober. Mom told me that he'd cleaned up after Jean left him, but I guess I was still so mad at him for all the pain and hurt that he'd caused in the past, that I never tried to make amends.

"Well he certainly looks good now," Gwen commented. "And you say his wife left him?"

"They never got married. She left him just before the wedding," Nicole responded.

"Never married huh; even better!"

"Gwen, no; don't tell me you're interested."

"Well, some old habits die hard. You know what a crush I had on him when we were young."

"Yeah, but Gwen, that was years ago."

"Hey sweetie, I'm not getting any younger and we did have a few fun nights together way back then. And damn it, I haven't gotten laid in freaking forever!"

"Gwen, you're incorrigible!"

"No, I'm just horny."

Both women laughed as one of Nicole's brothers exited the house.

"You've got a pretty big place here sis. Hope you and Jared plan on having lots of babies to fill up those rooms pretty soon."

"I'll start having them as soon as you and Marcia start" Nicole joked back.

"Well, we're going through the motions if you know what I mean. Mom expects lots of grandchildren so we all better start giving them to her pretty soon."

"Well, why don't you let us at least get settled for a week or two before you expect me start producing mom's grandbabies okay?"

By now, most of the moving crew was back out on the front steps and lawn, anxious to get started. The men jumped right in to start unloading the boxes and the women started talking amongst themselves to see what they could do first to help Nicole. Nicole caught Gwen staring at her big brother and wasn't sure how she felt about it but quickly decided that maybe it wouldn't be so terrible if the two of them found each other again. Once in the kitchen, the women started unpacking and laughing as her favorite sister-in-law was already pouring them glasses of wine to commemorate the occasion. Before long, the house was full with the sounds of music, laughter, and multiple sets of work boots stomping across the hard wood floors.

Chapter 27

Betty was sitting in her chair tending to one of her many flower gardens when her husband came out of the garage with a shovel and hoe in hand. She wiped her forehead with her sleeve as she looked up at him towering above her. Bart stood silently looking at the dirt surrounding his wife and the weeds scattered throughout the bed. Practically every morning they went through the same ritual of having coffee, putting the flag up the flagpole and setting forth on one of Betty's landscaping challenges. To the naked eye, their yard looked like something out of Better Homes and Gardens, but to the homeowners who maintained its upkeep, it was like having a full time job. The two of them spent every morning hoeing and spading the dirt and mulch, pulling weeds and dead blooms. Today was no exception. Betty had been outside since before eight am working on the flowerbed. She had explained to her husband that since they had to leave home by noon, she wanted to get a few hours in before midmorning. Aware that protesting would be useless; he had staggered reluctantly out of bed and 6am when he first heard her footsteps on the hardwood floor.

"It's after 10am Betty, do you think we should call it quits for the day? After all, we've got to freshen up a bit before we head into town."

"We don't have to be at my therapy session until 1pm," she responded, somewhat frustrated. "But I might as well quit. Can't hear myself think with that racket anyway," she retorted, shrugging her shoulders towards the old Harteman estate. "Sure hope those kids aren't planning on playing that crap every day or we'll be having a little neighborly chat."

"Don't get yourself in an uproar Betty. They're moving in today, remember? They're bound to be a little noisy; just give them a chance. I think they're going to be good neighbors."

"You're just saying that because you think the misses is an attractive young thing" Betty snapped, with a half grin on her face.

"Not nearly as fine as you dear," he winked back.

With Betty blushing, but still a little perturbed, Bart helped her brush the dirt from her slacks, gather up her tools and head towards their greenhouse. As she neared the boundary closest to the Brentwood's new home, she paused briefly, not to listen to the noise emitting from their property but to absorb the laughter. Unable to get a clear picture of how many people were involved in the move, Betty could only surmise that the group was not only big, but also in good spirits. The laughter resonated from the property and the air was filled with happiness and for one brief moment, her hard shell was permeated.

"Sounds like they're having a hoot over there, doesn't it?" Bart asked nonchalantly.

Now that her trance was broken, Betty replied back in her usual drone tone.

"Yeah, and it better be over with by the time we get back tonight."

"Oh lighten up Betty. They're just having fun for Christ's sake. Leave them be."

"Fine; I won't say another word," she snapped as she dropped the gardening supplies onto the floor and stepped over them, heading toward the house.

"Oh, here we go again," Bart mouthed as he started off to catch up with his now disgruntled spouse.

By the time supper rolled around, Nicole and Jared's new home was taking shape. With majority of their furniture unloaded off the rental truck, they finished up as Nicole made a pizza run. Once back with pizza and wings, the group converged on the veranda and dove into the hot food and cold beer. Most of them were silent as they inhaled the food and absorbed what was left of the warm daylight air. There was a slight breeze coming off the lake and Nicole's wind chime bounced gleefully as the group ate.

"That's an absolutely gorgeous wind chime Nicole," Valerie commented.

"Don't get any ideas honey" Nicole's brother commented. "We're not the rich ones of the family, remember? We don't have a fancy house like this to hang one at, even if we could afford it," he teased. "It's probably Lenox or Tiffany."

"Would you shut up," his wife of seven years shouted back.

"Yeah, shut up Neil," Nicole teased back, seconding her sister-in-law.

Deciding to change the subject, Jared took his knife and started tapping on his beer bottle to get everyone's attention. Once everyone was silent, he stood up on one of their patio chairs and proposed a toast, holding up his half empty Corona.

"Now that I have your attention, I would lie to propose a toast," he said as he tried to maintain his balance. "I would first of all like to thank each and every one of you for making this day a truly special and memorable one for Nicole and me. And a sincere thank you for those who put forth that extra effort to make this day fantastic for my wife," he said as he looked over at Jimmy, who was standing apart from the group. "We all know how much today has meant to her. And now, before I totally bore you, I'd like to propose a toast to our new home. I hope that this house can bring us years of happiness and warm memories, and provide us with a loving environment in which to raise our kids." With bottle raised, Jared shouted "To our new house and those who visit us within it's' walls."

In unison, Nicole's family and Gwen shouted back "To the new house!"

After the clanging of the bottles waned and their laughter died down, the group went back to eating what was left of the pizza. Just as they were finishing up, a familiar noise captured their attention. Everyone turned toward the source, and Nicole gasped when she saw her mother and father rounding the corner, coming towards them. Betsy Flanahan smiled at her family as she slowly made her way towards them. Arms laden down with deserts, two of Nicole's brothers instinctively moved towards her and eased the delicacies from her arms. Nicole and Jared rushed over to their unexpected guests. Tears streamed down Nicole's face for the second time that day. Having spoken with them earlier in the week, she never dreamt that they'd journey this far away from their farm, especially in the middle of haying season. Though semi-retired, her father still worked the farm every day, just like he had done when she was growing up. Having five older brothers, Nicole hadn't been forced to help out much with the manual labor involved in maintaining a working farm, but she was aware of the long hours needed daily to maintain it. Nicole's role had been to help her mother can and pickle every fall. Though Nicole loved nature and healthy home grown foods, after canning what seemed like hundreds of vegetables and fruits every year for almost two decades, Nicole vowed that she would never plant a garden of her own. Once her arms were free, Nicole's mother gave her only daughter a giant bear hug, which practically took her breath away. Betsy Flanahan was a stocky woman of fifty nine, though she barely looked to be in her late forties. She had worked hard all of her life, but thanks in part to her Irish ancestry, her complexion had maintained its milky white texture. Short in stature compared to her children, Betsy was able to instill fear in them by simply raising her husky voice up an octave. But today was a day of celebration and she continued to hug her daughter and everyone who came over to greet her.

Nicole and her mother had always had a special bond that went beyond just mother and daughter. They had been friends, confidants and buddies growing up. Nicole had been the answer to Betsy's dreams. They had adopted Nicole as an infant after Betsy's friend Meghan had given birth and decided to give her infant daughter up for adoption. Betsy had dedicated herself to ensuring that Nicole had everything that a little girl should have, while growing up in a house full of boys. Nicole's brothers never exhibited any jealousy over their mother's affection towards her; mostly in part because she had always been there for them too. Growing up, Betsy had been the den mother for Boy Scouts, score keeper for the baseball teams, and was even known to play pickup football right alongside her boys. Both of Nicole's parents had always been there for them then, and as usual, were here for her now.

"Well, I didn't drive all afternoon just to stand outside. Let me see this mansion," James Flanahan proclaimed as he winked at his son-in-law.

"Oh Daddy, I'm so glad to see you both. You and everybody else" she said as she looked out at her family, "Have made me so happy." "Well good," her mother exclaimed. "Now why don't you show us around a little bit and then we'll have some dessert. It's not much, but it's you and your brother's favorite.

"Oh mama, it's wonderful. Thank You!"

Nicole took her mother's hand and proceeded to head into the study from the veranda. Jared followed in behind his father-in-law, who was touching the woodwork as he walked into the room. As Nicole and Jared started to show their new house to her parents, the rest of the group huddled around the picnic baskets of goodies that their parents had brought. Even Gwen forgot about flirting with Jimmy for a brief moment when she inhaled some of the aroma radiating from the basket at her side.

"Lord if I had grown up in your family, I would have weighted twice as much as I do already," Gwen proclaimed as her mouth watered.

"I," Jimmy said meekly, "think you look just fine the way you are right now."

"You always know how to impress a lady, don't you Jimmy?"

"Nah Gwen, on the contrary, I used to turn them off. You know, with my drinking and all."

"Yeah, but that's the past," Gwen was quick to intercede "And this is the present, and I'm impressed," Gwen said, trying to make her voice sound husky and seductive, as she moved closer to Nicole's brother.

"You mean it?" Jimmy asked, almost shocked by her declaration.

"Yes Jimmy, I mean it," Gwen responded, blushing for the first time in years.

"Do you think that maybe we could go get a coffee after we finish up here?" he asked, building up his courage again.

"Sure, I'd like that Jimmy."

"Hey, are you going to stand around all day chatting or are you going to help us with passing out some of Ma's cheesecake?"

"Yeah, be right there Aaron."

After helping distribute the desserts quickly, Jimmy and Gwen said their goodbyes and made a hasty exit. Nicole was just coming back outside with her mother on her arm as Gwen got up into her brother's truck.

"God, I hope she knows what she's getting in to," she thought to herself as they drove off toward the now setting sun.

The rest of Nicole's family sat around the veranda drinking coffee, and gorging themselves on Betsy's desserts. She had brought not only a huge cheery cheesecake, but also chocolate chip cookies, with morsels the size of miniature boulders. The sun set over the water's edge as they ate, laughed and caught up on the gossip. When they final decided that they were through working for the night, everyone parted ways, leaving Jared and Nicole alone at last in their new home. She had offered to give up her bed to her parents, but they had already made arrangement to stay with Tom and Kathy, Nicole's second oldest brother. Upon Nicole's insistence, everyone had agreed to meet back at their house for a country breakfast the following morning. Once everyone was gone, their new house seemed mysteriously quiet and empty. Nicole commented to her husband as they picked up the remaining dishes about how much the day had meant to her. With the house now dark, Nicole stepped out onto the veranda again and sat to reflect on the day. The lake was peaceful and dead calm as she glanced out at the water.

"Beautiful isn't it?" a voice whispered from behind her.

Unable to scream, Nicole whipped around to see the shadow of a man standing just feet from her. Unsure of what to do, she bolted from her seat and instinctively stepped back toward the atrium door. The stranger didn't say a word as his lips formed an eerie smile as he took a step toward her. Nicole braced herself for whatever confrontation was about to occur as the adrenaline rush almost took her breath away. She strained in the darkening night to make visual contact with the man who was approaching her. Sensing her fear, he made one large step toward her and stepped into the light, stopping just inches from her body.

"Oh my God," she shrieked as she looked at the gray haired man's face. "Mr. Langhorne, you nearly scared me half to death," Nicole said as she put her hand to her chest, trying to calm herself down.

"Oh, I'm sorry miss; truly I am. I was just out for a walk this evening along the bluff and saw you sitting there. I just thought that since it's your first night in the house and all," he stammered, "I just wanted to give you our number in case you and your husband needed anything."

Mad at herself for letting her imagination get so carried away, Nicole smiled and gladly accepted the old man's number. Mr. Langhorne smiled, and left as quickly as he had appeared.

"You looked just like her you know. She loved to sit out on her veranda and look at the water."

Unsure of what to make of her conversation with the elderly man, she sat back down for a moment to gather her composure before heading inside to join Jared. The last thing she needed was to make him paranoid about their next door neighbor. Still, there was something peculiar about Mr. Langhorne and something just didn't feel right Nicole concluded.

"Maybe I'm the one who's getting a little paranoid," she thought to herself. "After all, he only stopped by to offer us his number in case of an emergency. Christ Nicole, "she thought to herself, "He's only being neighborly." And with that, she made her way inside.

Bart Langhorne remained motionless in the shadows as she turned her back to where he was standing. He watched her silently as her footsteps echoed on the slate veranda's floor. Once she was inside, he knew it was time for him to hurry home before Betty got suspicious over his whereabouts.

"Good night my love" he whispered as he blew a silent kiss in Nicole's direction. "I knew you'd return to me someday."

Chapter 28

Sleep came easily for the exhausted couple and before either was ready, the alarm clock was blasting. Jared reluctantly rolled over and shut the siren like noise off as Nicole started to stretch. She didn't open her eyes and spring out of bed in her usual manner, partly due to fatigue and mainly because of her desire to continue the dream that she was in the middle of when the alarm went off. The details of the dream that had seemed so real just moments earlier now were fading into a distant memory but as she woke, but she remembered most of it. She tried to make sense of what it meant as her husband leaned over and kissed her.

"Good morning Nic" he said as he smiled down at her. "Are you ready for round two of unpacking?"

"Ah, it's gone now," she said as she put her pillow over her face.

"What's gone Nicole?" Jared asked, somewhat confused.

Removing the pillow, she opened her eyes and smiled. "Nothing honey, nothing. I was just having a dream, that's all," she said reassuringly.

"Come on, you invited your entire family over here for brunch so we had better get moving if you're planning on feeding that army!"

"I hear ya. That's what they looked like when they were all here yesterday didn't they? Come on, I'll race you to the shower."

Before he knew what hit him, Jared was pushed out of the way as Nicole sprang to her feet and ran toward the shower. He smiled as he rose from their bed and looked around their new bedroom.

Henry woke in his new home well rested and in good spirits. Much to his surprise, he fell rapidly to sleep after getting settled into his daughter's home. The Drake staff had been at his every beck and call throughout the afternoon and evening and when he had finally been alone, he realized how physically and emotionally tired he truly was. Now, awake and alert, he lay in bed thinking about the events of the day before. Though it came as a shock to see someone else in his home, he wasn't upset or surprised. He had immediately liked the young couple and smiled when he thought of how much Mrs. Brentwood had reminded him of his late wife.

"They'll take good care of the house for you Rachel," he thought to himself as he reminisced about his lost love. He thought back to all of the wonderful memories that they had had in their home there on Sycamore Lane. The laughter, tears and love they shared within the confine of the walls; the places they had thrown caution to the wind and made love in, like the veranda and in the old boathouse. He thought of how many times they'd slipped their shoes off and danced on that very same veranda under the stars while he sang to her. He realized too that nobody knew just how much he loved his wife, even though she had been unfaithful to him. She and the children had been his life and now two of the three were gone. His thoughts quickly drifted back to Robert. Claire hadn't ever answered his question when he had asked about his only son while he was in the hospital, and he had failed to force her response last night when he moved into her home for fear of upsetting her and being thrown out of the only place he had to go. Almost afraid to find out the answer, Henry decided as he lay in his bed that today would be the day to get all of his questions answered. All of them, except the most important question he'd wanted answered for thirty years; who killed his wife.

Claire too was awake and had been since long before dawn. After tossing and turning for hours, she silently slipped out of their bed as Richard lay sleeping and made her way to one of the spare bedrooms. She tried to read a few depositions, but couldn't concentrate. Her mind kept returning to her childhood home. Though she wanted to remain indifferent towards them, she was forced to admit to herself that the Brentwoods appeared to be decent people who were right for the house. She realized that they would fix it up and take care of the house the way it was meant to be taken care of, not the way her aunt had done. The reunion with her father too, had taken its' emotional toll. She sat at the burrow trying to rationalize her feelings but slipped deeper and deeper into despair over the loss of her mother and the breakup of her family. Then she thought of Robert. How was she going to tell her father that she hadn't seen her only brother in nearly twenty years? She sat in silence wondering how she had let her ambition and reputation alienate her from her only remaining family. Yes, he was different and a little slow, but he was her only sibling and she had severed that relationship as easily as she had the one with her father. Robert hadn't done anything wrong and for all she knew, it could be too late for them too. She knew he was alive and residing in a residential home for the mentally disabled but other than that, she had had her aunt manage any contact with the facility. Suddenly feeling ashamed of her vanity, she grabbed the phone directory and knew what had to be done.

"Oh there you are. Good Morning Claire. Did you sleep well?" he asked as he winced in the bright daylight.

"Yes Richard, Good morning. I slept fine, and you?"

"Have you checked in on your father yet?"

"No. I'd thought I'd let him sleep in for a bit. It was probably his first night of true uninterrupted sleep that he's had in a while."

"I know. I just hope that yesterday wasn't too much for him to take."

She remained silent for a brief second then looked up at her husband and with saddened eyes blurted out "I have a brother Richard."

"Excuse me?"

"I said; I have a brother. His name is Robert and I haven't seen him in over twenty years. He has some "issues" and I withheld telling you about him because I was afraid of any negative press it might generate when I knew you had set your aspirations on running for Supreme Court someday."

Richard sat down in disbelief but focused in on his wife asking her to explain what she had meant by that statement and the secret she had kept from him for their entire marriage.

"When we first started dating, I sincerely wanted to tell you the truth about my entire family but was embarrassed by all of them. My father was in prison, my mother had been murdered, I had been raised by a very unstable aunt who shipped me off to boarding school as soon as I was old enough to go, and my only other living relative was a handicapped baby brother."

Having said it, Claire took a deep breath and continued on. "My brother was only seven when my mother died. He was too much for my aunt to handle and even with me taking care of him most of the time; she chose to have him institutionalized. Maybe if she hadn't sent me away, I could have kept raising him but she didn't give me the option. So when I left for boarding school, I let the memory of ever having a family die."

Not really listening to what she was saying anymore, Richard asked coldly "How could you not tell me about your brother? Your fucking flesh and blood for Christ sake! I don't care if he's retarded, has a deadly disease, can't walk or has two fucking heads; he's your brother!!!"

Now suddenly feeling the need to defend herself, Claire retaliated quickly. "When I first met you, you were living in a glass bubble. Everything about you was being scrutinized, from where you lived to whom you associated yourself with. Remember that you were up for election and your entire life was for public viewing. I didn't think it would have been beneficial to you to have my family brought out into the lime light do you?"

"Claire, I wouldn't have gave a shit if I had been up for election to Congress; you have a brother and I had a right to know," he snarled. You kept first your father, and now your brother from me. So where is he now Claire and when is the last time your brother was graced with a visit from you?"

"I don't know the last time I saw him; before the kids were born I guess. He's still at Brymore. I let that part of my life die and I'm sorry I didn't tell you sooner."

"Would you have told me if your father wasn't out of prison? And are there any more family secrets I need to know about Claire? "

"No Richard. I'm sorry. I just did what I thought was best for everyone."

"You mean, best for you Claire. How could abandoning your brother be best for him?"

"Richard, you have to understand; he's been living there for so long now, he doesn't know any other life. Certainly removing him from that setting would have been traumatic for him."

"If you haven't spoken to him in twenty some odd years, I don't think you have a right to decide what's best for him, do you?"

"Point taken; but I did what I did for us."

"No Claire, you did it for yourself. You did it to save the embarrassment and you did it to forget your past. I don't think I can just write this one off Claire. You've pushed me way too far this time!"

Before she should say another work, Richard looked sullenly at her and calmly said one last thing before exiting the room.

"You're going to tell your father what has happened to his son and you're going to tell him today. Then, if he's up to it, we're going to go see your brother this afternoon."

With that said, Richard left the room allowing Claire to wallow in her anguish.

Chapter 29

Once they were both showered and dressed, Nicole and Jared made their way to the kitchen to start breakfast before the onslaught of company. The coffee was perking as Jared left on a bagel run. She raced around frantically picking up and heard the doorbell chime just as she washed the last dish. Expecting it to be her mother or one of her brothers, she quickly made her way to the front foyer.

"Good morning Nicole. I can call you Nicole can't I?"

Startled, Nicole replied hesitantly, "Why good morning Mr. Langhorne. And yes, you can call me Nicole."

"I've bought you something," he said as he handed her a wicker basket with a towel covering its contents."

"Your wife didn't need to do this," she said as she pulled back the towel, revealing freshly baked muffins.

"She didn't. I got up and made them for you Rachel; I mean Nicole."

"That was very kind of you Mr. Langhorne. Thank you," Nicole replied as she reached out and squeezed the older man's hand. "You're a wonderful neighbor."

"That's what Rachel used to always say" he thought to himself as he stood silently smiling at Nicole. The moment of silence drew awkward and Nicole started feeling uncomfortable at the way her elderly neighbor kept staring at her.

Instinctively she asked, "What is it Mr. Langhorne? You look like you're a million miles away."

"No, just thirty; I'm sorry," he replied now that his trance like state was finally broken. "You just look remarkably like someone I knew a long time ago, that's all.

Dismissing the statement, Nicole smiled, now feeling more comfortable with his bazaar, but harmless behavior.

"Everyone tells me that I look like somebody they know. Guess I just have one of those faces."

"No, you have the face of an angel."

Feeling embarrassed for openly expressing his innermost thoughts regarding his new neighbor, he promptly excused himself and headed home.

Nicole stood transfixed on the little man as he scurried back toward the hedge of hemlocks separating their properties. His pace was brisk and he never slowed until he was through the opening and almost out of sight. She wondered if her new neighbor was just eccentric or possibly a little demented. Dismissing the later, she concluded that he was just being friendly and was excited at the thought of having a new neighbor. He was no sooner out of sight when she heard the sound of her parent ancient Volvo coming up the drive.

"Hi guys," she squealed with her face radiating and flashing her bright smile. After the car came to a complete stop, her mother squeezed herself out of the front seat and stood up to hug her baby girl. Nicole towered over her by nearly six inches when they stood next to one another, but to Betsy, Nicole would always be her little girl.

"How'd my baby sleep in her new house last night?"

"Oh mama, we slept great. And waking up this morning to the smell of the fresh air and breeze off the lake, it was so wonderful."

"Well come on girl, help me with this stuff," her mother coaxed as she opened the rear door, revealing baskets full of goodies.

"What'd you do mama, rob a bakery this morning?" Turning to her father, she smiled.

"Daddy, what the hell time did she get you up this morning to make all of this?"

"Three am baby girl" he replied, deliberately yawning just to get under his wife's skin.

"And it didn't hurt you one bit old man. Our girl deserves to be treated like a queen sometimes."

As they were unloading the car, Jared pulled in behind them. He evaluated the situation and seeing their hands full with assorted pasties, muffins and fruit; tucked the bagels he had just purchased under the seat and out of sight. Once the engine was off, he jumped out to help carry in the food, as his nostrils took in the wonderful aroma of home cooking.

It wasn't long after the arrival of her parents that her brothers started trickling in one by one. Most of them looked refreshed as they had slept in and skipped church, a fact that they didn't point out to their mother. Though there were all grown adults, their mother still scolded them for not honoring the Sabbath. Nicole was starting to get nervous when she saw that Jimmy hadn't arrived yet, but realized that Gwen too, was also missing. Fearing the worst, she was greatly relieved when she saw his pick up pulling into the drive. Surprised but not shocked when she saw Gwen step out of the passenger side, she quickly made her way to greet them.

"Hi you two; I wasn't sure if you were going to make it or not."

"Free food. Of course we'd come," hugging her best friend. As she drew closer to Nicole, she whispered, "Yup, he's still got it."

"Yuck Gwen- he's my brother!"

"Hey, what are you two talking about?" Jimmy asked as he made his way over to their side of truck.

"Nothing," they both responded simultaneously.

"Nothing my ass. I know what you two are like when you're together."

"Yeah, well, big brother; I now know what you two are like when you're together," she retorted back, casting a big smile at her brother.

"Geez," was his only response as his face turned the same red shade as his truck.

Chapter 30

Gary Danbarry sat at his kitchen table absorbed in the court records, documenting Henry's trial and testimony. Henry's account of what happened was essentially verbatim to what he had told Gary prior to the riot. None of his testimony was surprising different, nor did it reveal any new light on the case. The officer was becoming increasingly discouraged with the case, for he had thought by now he'd have found some smoking gun but unfortunately all the evidence still pointed to Henry Harteman. Still, in his heart he knew that Henry was incapable of this type of crime. He continued to skim the documents feeling that there was something that he was missing, something that would shed new light on the case or at least blow it wide open.

"Gary, "his wife asked gingerly, "Maybe you should give it up. Maybe you can't find anything because there's nothing to find. Maybe Henry really is guilty."

"No Marian. The answer is here. I just have to find it."

"You've already helped him gain his freedom, that's enough."

"No, it's not. He has lost thirty years of his life, and his good name. I, and the state of New York owe it to him to find his wife's killer."

"But"

"No buts about it Marian; I'm not giving up so don't waste your breathe."

"Well if I can't talk to you logically, then I can at least help you can't I?"

His eyes looked up at his wife standing beside him and without saying a word, pulled out the chair beside him. She smiled as she removed her apron and sat down.

Pushing the glasses up on her nose, she focused on the notepad she had been carrying. "Okay, what you got so far?"

He again smiled, then went to work showing her the notes that he had accumulated and the names that had been mentioned during the trial. The list included friends, family, former employers and neighbors. She read the depositions and the names. Gary studied her face as she read feeling thankful that he did indeed have a very understanding and compassionate wife. He knew that he had put her through hell and back recently, still she was willing to assist him without even having to ask. She remained silent for what seemed like eternity and after a few minutes, he returned to his pile of documents to read. The only sound that could be heard was the dull ticking of their kitchen clock. Just as Gary was about to get another cup of coffee his wife sat up straight in her chair.

"Oh my gosh, you didn't tell me that!"

"Tell you what Marian?" he asked, giving his wife his full attention.

"You never said anything about Mr. Harteman being under the employ of Nicolas Carelli."

"It didn't mean anything to me. He's a union rep for one of the local CSEA's right?"

"Gary," she exclaimed, somewhat frustrated with her husband's obvious ignorance; "Everyone knows that that's just a front. He's one of the biggest mobsters in Central New York with ties to the city.

"Where'd you hear that?"

"I read the paper and watch the news you know. Maybe you should sometime. In fact, he and his son were just arrested a few years back on racketeering charges. I don't recall if they were convicted or not."

He studied her face as she smugly continued on.

"You know, if Henry was working for a man like that; there's no telling what he was capable of."

"Marian, Henry was not involved in anything illegal. I'd stake my life on it."

"You start messing with those kinds of people and you might be doing just that."

Marian got up from her chair as she let her husband stew on what she had just told him for a moment, and then she got him another cup of coffee as he sat silently.

"Why don't you invite Henry over for supper sometime when he's feeling better and ask him about his relationship with Mr. Carelli. Maybe it was innocent."

"It says right here," he said as he pointed to the court document, "that he simply ran errands and delivered packages for Carelli as a part time job on the side. He had nothing but good things to say about the man. Says here that Carelli was the one who gave him the down payment for their first home as a Christmas bonus."

"A person like Nicolas Carelli doesn't give someone enough money to cover a down payment on a house and not expect payback. What did he get in return?" she asked as she continued to study the list of names.

"I don't know. Henry never mentioned any of it to me before. Maybe he had worked out some sort of payment plan with the guy."

"Carelli's type doesn't work out payment plans, they enforce them and they take whatever they want. I watched Soprano's you know; I know the type," she said with a smile.

"Yeah but Marian, Henry was a simple hardworking middle class man trying to support a family. He wouldn't have had anything other than money to offer a guy like Carelli.

"Would seem that way; but since you're the one playing detective, it's up to you to find out."

Marian planted herself back in her seat and resumed her reading. When she had completed the list of names, she arbitrarily grabbed another document, which happened to be Rachel's autopsy report. Realizing that the graphic description of the state her body was in might be too much for his wife to handle, he reached over and grabbed the paper from her.

"You shouldn't read that honey. It's pretty descriptive and gory."

"I can handle it Gary. So if you want my help, let go of the paper and let me read it."

"Okay."

"Thank you."

"You're welcome, but be forewarned."

"Gary," she replied, somewhat exasperated, "I'm a big girl now and if I kept it together seeing you lying there in that bed bleeding to death, surely I can read a report on a woman I never met, who, let me point out, has been dead for thirty years."

"Point taken," he quietly replied and went back to his reading.

Marian studied the report silently, absorbing the details. Though she didn't have a medical background, nothing stood out as unusual. Wiping away a few tears, she turned to address her husband.

"That poor thing was too young to die such a violent death, especially being with child."

"She was pregnant with someone else's child and that was what the jury used as their rationale for Henry's motive to kill her."

"Then we need to find out who the father of her child was" she said excitedly; "And add them to the list of suspects!"

"But we can't find someone who might have been her lover; that was thirty years ago. There's no way to know."

"Yes there is."
"How?"

"Ask Henry."

"No."

"Yes, you've got to if you want to add to your list of who might want her dead. Call his daughter's house today and invite him over for dinner this week, tell him Wednesday or Thursday would be great."

"Alright," he replied hesitantly; "I'll call him a little later this morning."

Marian smiled and while looking at her husband lovingly, thought to herself that Henry had the biggest motive to want his wife dead. Knowing her husband would never buy into his guilt, she kept her opinion to herself but also knew that many had murdered for much less.

Gary's mind was also spinning wildly at the moment. He wasn't thinking along the same line as his wife but he was definitely thinking about Henry as well. He tried to imagine the thoughts that went through the poor man's mind when his beloved wife told him that she was pregnant. He couldn't imagine what pain, anguish and rage Henry must have felt. Gary wondered if Henry had any idea who his wife was involved with but didn't know how he was going to broach the subject. He decided to reread the court testimony to see if Henry, Rachel's sister or the neighbor's statement alluded to her lover. He fumbled through the stacks of papers now covering the majority of their table until he found what he was looking for and started rereading it for the third time.

Both husband and wife remained transfixed on the documents for nearly two hours. Both took notes but kept their comments to themselves. Finally Gary set the paperwork down, removed his glasses and looked over at this wife.

"So my dear, who do you think did it?"

"You know what I think Gary, but if you want to know who else had motive, I'd say no one."

"What do you mean no one?"

"Well," Marian started, "Everyone seemed to love Rachel. Her sister spoke of her as being a devote Christian, good mother, and wonderful sister. The neighbors all seemed to love her too. The immediate next door neighbor, a Bart Langhorne went on and on during the trial about what a nice person she was; a great neighbor, mother and close personal friend. And even the few members of their former parish who testified on Henry's behalf all said that they were a couple completely devoted to one another and to their children. They went on to say that she was always volunteering at the church and always doing something for someone else."

"Yeah, she was doing something to someone else, and that's how she got knocked up."

"Gary!"

"Well, it's true. I like Henry and it makes me sick to think that his wife was a tramp."

"I'm only going to warn you one time Gary. You'll never be able to view this case objectively if you bring it to a person level."

"It's already personal. That man saved my life and that makes it very personal!"

"Yes," she said cautiously, "And for that I am eternally grateful but that has no bearing on what transpired thirty years ago. He could still be the cold blooded killer they made him out to be."

"Or he could have been railroaded and an easy scapegoat to close the case and appease the public. I think we need to talk to his old employer like you mentioned."

"He's still in prison I believe Gary. But if I recall, he has or had a wife when I read an article about him a year or so ago. She might know something but how would you ever get close enough to ask her. And it's not like you can walk up to her, introduce yourself, and ask her what her husband's dealing with Mr. Harteman was."

"I know," Gary agreed. "But I could ask her if he was a loan shark couldn't I?"

Marian gave her husband an evil glare and he just smiled.

"Just kidding."

"I'd stay completely clear of Mrs. Carelli if I were you. Her husband might be locked up but you can be assured that he still runs business from the inside. Please don't mess with a person like that Gary."

Deciding to drop the subject all together, Gary stood up from his chair, stretched and looked at his concerned wife with a loving smile. "Come on," he said as he hugged her, "Let's get cleaned up and go for a ride on this gorgeous morning."

"Where we going and what are you up to?" she asked accusingly.

"We're not going anywhere in particular and I'm not up to anything. Now come on, let's go for a ride, it's beautiful out. Put on one of your fancy dresses and I'll take you out to lunch."

Before she could answer, he started picking up the stack of files and documents on the table and started whistling his favorite tune.

Shaking her head in uncertainty, she headed off toward their bedroom to change as her husband requested. As soon as she was out of sight he searched through the pile of white papers and quickly stuffed a solitary piece into his trousers pocket.

"We'll go for a Sunday ride and if we happen to end up on Sycamore Lane, so be it. It can't hurt anything to drive into the neighborhood and possibly speak with the neighbors," he thought to himself as he headed toward their bedroom.

The Brentwood's new residence was alive with laughter again this morning. By ten, all of Nicole's brothers were present, along with her parents and Gwen. By eleven, everyone was busy rearranging furniture and unpacking boxes. Jared was outside with two of his brother-in-laws when he heard the sound of an approaching car. Glancing up, he realized that it was none other than his parents. Shocked that they had made the drive from their Long Island home, he rushed out to greet them. Once his father stepped out of the car, he smiled and gave him a firm handshake.

"Dad, it's so good to see you but what are you doing here? And how did you find your way here?"

Before the senior Brentwood could answer, his wife made her way around to her only son.

"Jared, it's so good to see you and look at your new house, it's absolutely lovely!"

Jared was so surprised to see his parents that he remained silent as he hugged his mother and gleamed with pride. His upbringing had been much more structured and disciplined compared to Nicole's and his family didn't ever have public displays of any type of emotion, but today he could tell how proud his

-199-

parents were of his accomplishments. Growing up, his greeting to his father had always been a formal handshake, not a hug or kiss like other families. To Nicole, it seemed so cold and distant but not all families interacted the way hers did. It had taken several exposures to her family for him to finally loosen up and realize that it was okay to show your emotions and openly express affection. But even after all the years of marriage to Nicole, Jared still remained formal in his greeting to his father.

Jared's mother finally broke the silence. "Nicole phoned us and gave us directions. We drove to Albany yesterday and visited your great Aunt Bernice and drove the rest of the way this morning. We couldn't wait until this summer to come visit so we decided to come out to help you get settled in. But, by the number of cars in your yard, it looks like you've got more than enough help," she smiled. "Maybe I can just sit back and look at my son's new house."

"Oh mother, you don't have to do any work. I'm just so glad you stopped by. Mom and Dad Flanahan are inside, along with Nicole's brothers and their families; and Nicole's girlfriend."

"The one that was in your wedding dear?"

"The one and only."

"Has she settled down a little? Or is she, heaven forbid, still as, shall we say; obnoxious?"

"She's still obnoxious mother, but she is the one who found this house for us so I have to give her a little credit where credit is due. And she is, after all, Nicole's best friend so watch what you say when you're inside."

"Watch what who says about what?" Nicole joked, having snuck up without anyone noticing.

"Hi honey," Jared stammered, "I was just warning Mom and Dad to watch what they say about how gorgeous the house is around your brothers and their wives. I wouldn't want anyone thinking we're boasting about how fortunate we are when I know that some of them aren't as fortunate as we have been."

Proud of his quick thinking, Jared smiled slyly at his wife.

Nicole appeared somewhat taken back by his comment.

"My brother's would never be jealous of what we have. They're not as superficial as you may think they are." Changing the topic, she turned to her in-laws.

"Mom, Dad Brentwood, so nice to see you" turning her attention to her company. "Come on inside and we'll show you around."

"Okay honey. And I'm sure Jared didn't mean it to come out the way it did honey."

With that they all headed toward the house and made their way inside. Once inside, they were greeted by Nicole's entire family and started catching up. Everyone was talking and before anyone realized it, it was late afternoon. The day had gone surprisingly fast and they had accomplished a lot. With the kitchen pretty well set up and the master bedroom organized, Nicole and Jared could easily finish the other rooms at their leisure. Most of her brothers decided to head back home, refusing to stay for dinner so when suppertime came around, it was just the six of them, Nicole and Jared and their parents. Both mothers were busy with aprons on, whopping up delicacies with whatever they could find in Nicole's pantry and still unpacked boxes. Nicole who had been kicked out of her own kitchen, was busy in the master bedroom, trying to finish emptying the last remaining boxes. She worked silently, listening to the soft music she could hear emitting from the radio. Jared, and their fathers were keeping themselves busy working outside. Unsure of what they were doing, she let the three men proceed without questioning their actions. Realizing that the bonding time was good, she smiled when she thought of how proud Jared had been showing them their new home. Their life was going really well and the only thing that could make it more complete, in her mind's eye, would be a child. She came to the last box that contained her socks. Unsure of where to put them, she decided to stuff them for the time being in a small borough that she had found in the attic. She was particularly taken to it because of its' ornate workmanship and delicate features. At first, she had planned on putting it in the guest bedroom but Jared had pointed out that it would be a good corner piece to take up some extra space in their sparsely furnished bedroom. The master bedroom was significantly larger in their new home compared to the one in the townhouse, and their furniture looked miniscule once placed in the new room. Jared had been right. The borough looked perfect in the room and did in fact; filled up the extra space nicely. She grabbed a handful of bandanas and socks and proceeded to stuff them into the drawer, pushing them in to make room for the remaining ones in the box. As she pushed them into the back of the drawer, her hand hit something. She pulled a few scarves back out in order to free her hands up and reached back in to retrieve the object. When she put her hands back in, she had to give it a tug to retrieve whatever was jammed into the back of the drawer. Her tug freed it from the wooden frame of the dresser and Nicole pulled it out. Much to her surprise, it was not a book as she had expected, but a dusty, well-worn journal. She brushed the dust off with one of the bandanas that was still sitting on the dresser and the cover revealed a black and white photo of a family in a formal pose. Her heart starting racing as she looked at the tethered photo, realizing that it was Henry

Harteman and his late wife Rachel. Nicole started at the photo for what seemed like hours, then opened the cover to reveal its' inscription:

For My Beloved Rachel,

I love you to the moon and back...

Forever yours,

Henry

For reasons even Nicole couldn't understand, her eyes welled up with tears as she stared at the inscription on the cover and then looked back at the photo. She saw pride in Henry's eyes and warmth and love in Rachel's. The only thought that came to mind when she studied the eyes of their daughter was hatred and selfishness. She had a sullen look on her face and her stance was rigid and the girl's half smile looked forced. Nicole's impression of the woman from whom they had just bought the house had been right all along; even as a child, this lady had been a bitch. Their son on the other hand looked jovial and content. His face radiated with a bright full smile and big dimples. Nicole smiled as she studied his face from which she estimated him to be about six or seven years old. Though she realized that the journal's contents were personal and were supposed to remain private; she Nicole turned the page to find the first entry and told herself that she'd only read one of Rachel's entrees and then put it back where she found it. Just as she was about to read the first inscription, she could hear her mother calling from the kitchen. Quickly she tucked the book back into the borough and rushed down to her.

As she bustled down the stairs, she thought of the date she had noticed on the first entry in the journal and realized that it had in fact been just four months before Rachel's death. She wondered how a man could murder his wife in cold blood such a short time after giving her a personal, heartfelt gift like that. The more she thought about it, the more it didn't make sense and now she was convinced more than ever that Henry Harteman was indeed, not a murderer.

"The answers to who the real killer is might be in that journal" she thought to herself as she entered the kitchen to find her mother and mother-in-law finishing up supper.

"What have you been doing up there for so long child? You look like you're in another world."

"No mom. I'm just a little tired that's all. I was finishing up the boxes in our bedroom. Boy, something smells good!"

"Well, it's just about ready so why don't you gather up the men and I'll set the table. Remind them to wash up before they step foot in this kitchen."

"Yes mother Brentwood. I'll go get them but leave the table, I'll set it when I come in. You've done enough."

"I'm fine. Now hurry on."

Nicole stepped out onto the back veranda still fixated on the journal. She knew that if indeed Rachel did have a lover, the name of that lover could very well be within the contents of those pages. Nicole felt a little guilty about her burning desire to read someone else's personal thoughts but she only wanted to help Mr. Harteman and if somehow there was something in the journal that could exonerate him, then it would justify her reading the journal in the first place. As she looked over at her husband, she quickly decided that she could keep the journal a secret, at least for the time being.

She didn't want him criticize her for reading it, nor did she want to go against his wishes, so she decided that what he didn't know, wouldn't hurt him.

"Hi guys, are you ready to eat?"

"Absolutely!" Everyone hustled into the kitchen and quickly filled their plates and took a seat at the table. For majority of the meal, they ate in silence as everyone was famished. As they stated to finish up, Nicole's mother broke the silence.

"So tell me about the woman who was murdered in the house honey?"

Nicole almost choked on her mouthful of food and Jared practically spit out his wine as he heard his mother-in-law's question.

"What? What murder?" his mother shrieked. "You never told me someone was murdered in your house. Oh my God, when did it happen? How? Who?"

"Oops. Guess I brought up a bad topic," her mother whispered to Nicole's father.

Trying to regain their composure, Nicole glared at her mother with an extremely serious expression on her face.

"Who told you about that mom?"
"Why Gwen did dear."

"Figures."

"Jared, please. What did she say to you mom?"

"I just told her that I couldn't believe that my baby was living in such a mansion and she said that you got it for a song because it was an estate and because someone had been murdered here. So tell me, who was killed?"

"Jared, I think I'm done with dinner. If you would please excuse me."

"No mother, please sit back down. Nobody was murdered in this house; isn't that right Nicole?" he said through clenched teeth.

"Yes, Jared is telling you the truth. No one was murdered in this house."

Jared's mother breathed a sigh of relief before Nicole continued her explanation.

"Actually, she was killed outside in the lake."

Jared's mother gasped and Nicole's mother's eyes lit up with curiosity.

"So someone really was murdered here?"

"Well, they called it murder; but it could have simply been a horrible accident."

"Besides," Jared interceded, "It happened over thirty years ago."

Nicole continued where her husband left off. "A woman was thrown, or pushed off the cliff overlooking the lake and drown. She was supposedly murdered by her husband."

"Oh my!"

"Yeah, well I honestly don't believe he did it but back then, he was the easiest suspect."

"What do you mean Nicole," the senior Brentwood asked.

"Just what I said Dad Brentwood, I think Henry Harteman, the supposed murderer was set up. He was the easiest person to convict at the time and of course was the natural prime suspect since he was home at the time of the murder and had just been made aware that his wife was pregnant with another man's child."

"How very interesting," Nicole's mother interjected. "How did you find all of this out honey?"

"Gwen told us about the house's history, and I went to the library and was it was big news back then, it was easy to find articles in the archives. As a matter of fact, there was a prison riot recently, at the very prison where her husband is incarcerated. From what they said on the news, several of the guards and inmates perished.

"That is just dreadful; yes we had heard briefly about it on our news" Mrs. Brentwood said as she attempted to excuse herself again.

"Mother, relax would you. It was so long ago and doesn't change anything about the house. Besides, all older homes have histories.

"Yeah," Nicole giggled, "Ours is just more interesting than others."

"Now that's an understatement if I've ever heard one," her father-in-law said as he winked at his daughter-in-law and smiled.

Nicole's parents remained intrigued by the house's history while Jared's mother got up from the table and left the room heading toward the kitchen. Jared decided that he had better go settle his mother down before she got herself all worked up and decided to leave. He suddenly realized where he got all of his paranoia from as he listened to her fret all the way to the kitchen. He excused himself as Nicole started telling the story of the murder in more detail. Once in the kitchen, he realized that she must have stepped out onto the veranda to get some fresh air, so he quickly made his way to the door. Just as he had deduced, he saw her sitting out on their patio looking out at the water. With her back to him, she didn't hear his approach until he was just a few feet away.

"Mother, there you are."

"Oh Jared, you startled me!"

"Well, who did you expect? A ghost?" he chuckled.

"That's not funny."

"I know. Sorry."

"Why didn't you tell me that your house was a scene of a crime? A murder no less?"

"Because I know how you are mother and I wanted you to love the house. You do love it, don't you? You have to admit, it's a great house."

"Yes but…"

Quick to cut her off, Jared intervened, "No mother, it's still the same house. The one you boasted about just a few short hours ago. Yes, something tragic happened here a long time ago but that doesn't affect the present."

"I hope you're right honey."

"Trust me," he replied as he hugged his nervous mother.

As they stood hugging on the veranda they noticed that now that the sun was setting, the wind had definitely picked up. Jared's mom turned when she heard a delicate noise coming from behind her. She turned to see Nicole's new wind chime dancing in the breeze. Taken by its' intricate beauty, she walked over to it and admired it up close.

"Beautiful isn't it?"

"Jared, it's exquisite. Did you buy it?"

"Yes, in a little boutique in Toronto when I was there on business recently. You know how Nicki's crazy about angels."

"It's perfect for out here on the veranda. It'll act like a guardian angel for you and Nicole."

"Mother, don't start that nonsense again okay? There's nothing that we need guarding from here so please don't start again. Come on," he said, changing the topic, "Let's go inside. It looks like everyone must be upstairs. See the bedroom lights are on. Come on," he said as he opened up the atrium door. His mother gave one last look at the dancing angels and hesitantly followed him inside.

"Take care of my baby," she prayed silently to the angels as she entered the house.

Chapter 31

Gary and Marian Danbarry enjoyed their day as they rode around the countryside. They had stopped at several antique shops along the way and had a wonderfully fattening Sunday brunch at a little inn. Though Gary had had a definite plan in mind, he enjoyed spending the day leisurely driving and talking with his wife. He realized as they made light conversation that he had been very unapproachable during the last few weeks. He had become so enmeshed in his desire to clear his longtime friend, that he had forgotten everything else that was important to him. As they drove silently, he reached over and squeezed his wife's hand.

"I love you lady."

Surprised by his spontaneous declaration of love, she looked over at her husband oddly.

"I love you too Gary." Still looking puzzled, he smiled and continued. "I know that I don't tell you enough, but I do in fact, love you with all my heart. And I know this whole thing hasn't been easy on you either and I wanted to say thanks for helping me out."

"That's what marriage is all about; for better or worse, in sickness and in health, remember?"

"Yeah, I know. But when we started out, who'd have thought I'd get knifed someday just trying to do my job."

"What matters now is that you're going to be okay Gary. You've been given another chance by God and he wants you to make the most of it."

"Yeah," he kidded, trying to lighten the topic, "Or the devil wasn't ready for me quite yet."

"Gary!"

"Just kidding honey; Say while we're in this neck of the woods, how about we take a drive out by the lake. Bet the flowers are beautiful out there in the spring."

"Gary," she said in a serious tone, "If you want to go by Henry's old house, just do it. Just don't eat up all of the gas in the tank pussy-footing around trying to figure out how to ask my permission."

"Thanks Marian, you truly are amazing; and very understanding. Oh, and cute," he winked as he turned off the state road and started toward Sycamore Lane.

Claire hadn't been prepared for her father's reaction when she told him about his son and his institutionalization. She had expected him to be furious with her as her husband had been, but instead he seemed to take it quite well. Indeed he wanted to immediately go see his only son and started making inquiries about how soon they could go; but he never placed blame on his deceased sister-in-law nor Clarissa for placing in a state run facility. His mind raced with the excitement of being reunited with his son, but then acute depression started to settle in at the prospect that his son might not even know who he is, let alone care. As he dialed the number listed in the directory, his hands started shaking as he held the received waiting for a voice to come on the other end.

"Hello. Brynmar Center. How may I direct your call?"

"Hello. Yes, how do I find out if you still have a relative of mine living there?"

"What is the client's name sir?"

"Robert. Robert Harteman mam."

"Just one moment please."

Henry's heart beat wildly as he waited for what seemed like eternity until the operator came back with the answer to his burning question.

"Yes sir. Mr. Harteman resides in our assisted living compound. Hold while I connect you to their reception desk."

Before Henry could respond to her voice, the operator had flipped the switch and Henry was again listening to their selected elevator music.

"Greenwood, how may I help you?"

"Ah, hi. My name is Henry and I'd like to inquire about one of your residents that you have living there. No, on second thought, could you please tell me how I would go about visiting one of the clients there? It's been a very long time since we've seen each other and I'm not sure how your facility runs."

"Sure. Does the person whom you'd like to visit reside within this compound?"

"I'm not sure. But the operator did switch me over to you."

"What's the name sir?"

"Robert. Robert Harteman."

"Yes, he does reside here. And I'm sure he'd love company. He's such a nice man," the energetic young voice replied.

"You mean you know him personally?" Henry asked with his voice trembling.

"Of course sir; Robert's been here as long as I've worked here. He's terrific. He practically runs this place when I'm too busy to do everything."

"Then he's okay?"

"Well, I don't know what your definition of okay is sir, but we all love him around here. He's an inspiration to several of the young kids we get in here. Do you want me to give him a message for you, or connect you to his room?"

Not ready for that yet, Henry quickly responded to her question.

"No man, no thank you. You could however possibly tell me what your visiting hours are?"

"Oh, that's easy. You can visit anytime from 10am to 10pm any day. And I'm sure Robert would love to have you come visit him sir. He's really a great person."

"Thank you."

"You're welcome sir. Have a great day and come visit us sometime."

"Thanks, I will," Henry said, hanging up and allowing the tears to stream down his face.

Henry desperately wanted to go there immediately and reclaim his long lost son, but after the initial jubilation of finding him wore off, he realized that he couldn't simply barge into this young man's life after all this time and pick up where they had left off. Henry wondered if Robert would even realize who he was and what he would say to Robert about this mother's death of so long ago. His mind raced when he thought of how to approach the entire reunion. As the questions kept racing through his mind, he heard a light tapping on his door.

"Come in."

"Henry, it's me Clarissa, may I come in?"

"Yes, of course, come in."

"Is everything okay in here?"

"Sit down Clarissa. I want to talk with you," he said as he padded the bed beside him.

"What? What is it? Is he?" she asked hesitantly, "Is he dead?"

"No Clarissa, "he smiled ecstatically, "He's not only alive, he's doing great."

Breathing a silent sign of relief, she smiled as the tears welled up in her strained eyes.

"Thank God. What did they say? Did you talk to him?"

"No. I couldn't just get on the phone after all this time. I thought it'd be better to see him in person. But, they said he's doing fine and would probably love some company. Will you come with me Claire? Will you bring me to see my boy?"

"Of course I will. When?"

"Now. As soon as you can get ready."

"Right now?"

"Yes."

"All right. Just give me a minute to freshen up and we'll go." As she turned to leave his room, she looked back at her father still sitting transfixed on the bed. "Father, please forgive me for not looking after him all these years."

"Already forgiven Claire. We've all made mistakes and you did what you did because you thought it was for the best. Now go get ready. We're going to go see your brother."

Claire smiled back at her father and left the room. She found her still disgruntled husband and explained her conversation with her father to him. Though still irritated with her, he quickly offered to drive them. He too was anxious to meet the brother-in-law he never knew existed.

Claire and Richard entered their bedroom and dressed in silence. Both had a magnitude of different thoughts and feeling racing through their heads yet neither wanted to share them. Once ready, they exited their master bedroom and met up with Henry who was pacing in the front foyer. He was smiling calmly as they came down the stairs but the expression in his eyes showed the extreme urgency that he felt. He had waited far too long to be reunited with his son and he wanted to get there as soon as possible. Richard stepped beside his visibly nervous father-in-law and retrieved the keys to the Escalade and proceeded to open the door for everyone.

"Rosa, Mrs. Drake, Henry and I are stepping out for a few hours. Don't wait up for us," he shouted in the direction of the kitchen."

"Okay Senior Drake. Drive carefully."

With that, he pulled the heavy oak door closed and they set off for their car.

Chapter 32

Marian Danbarry wasn't quite sure what she was feeling as they approached the end of paved road leading onto Sycamore Lane. Gary himself hadn't been aware that the house was situated on a dead end street. As he approached the house, he felt his stomach twist into knots. It was that same dreadful feeling that he had felt when the riot first broke out. Not quite sure of what to do, he kept driving toward the house but slowed his speed to a crawl.

"Gary, look, there it is," Marian exclaimed.

"And look at that, there's cars in the driveway," she said, pointing toward the house.

"I know Marian, I can see that."

"Well if course, someone's going to be there. Someone does live in the house now don't they?"

"Last I knew, Henry's sister-in-law lived there."

"Well maybe it's her birthday or something."

"Yeah maybe."

"Well come one. I want to meet Henry."

"What? He won't be there!"

"You heard me. I haven't ridden around with you all day long just to go home empty handed, except for a full gut. Let's go up to the door and ask to see Henry."

"We don't even know who owns the house anymore?"

"Well if the house isn't in Henry's family anymore, then nothings lost except for the brief moment it takes us to stop and ask. So come on," she said with her voice growing in intensity and filling with excitement.

"Well okay," he smiled as he turned into the long driveway just ahead of him and approached the luminous looking house dead ahead.

"You are something else Mrs. Danbarry."

"I know honey, I know."

Nicole was returning to the dining room to pick up the last few remaining dishes when she saw the flicker of headlights flash across the window. Thinking it was one of her brothers or possibly

Gwen returning, she didn't bother to find out their source. She carried the pile of plates and dirty silverware back to the kitchen and grabbed a wash cloth to wipe her table down with. As she reentered the dining room she glanced out to see who had come back. As she pulled the curtain back she looked out through the sheer, trying to make out the vehicle. Two middle-aged faces stared back at her from afar. A little disgruntled and moderately frustrated by the invasion of her privacy, she let loose of the curtain, allowing it to fall back into place and marched herself toward the front door, ready for a confrontation with the busy-bodies outside.

As she made her way outside, without the acknowledgement of her family or husband, two not so menacing looking people whom she guessed were close in age to her parents greeted her at the bottom of the landing.

"Good evening miss. My name is Gary Danbarry and I'm a friend of Henry Harteman. I sure am sorry to bother you," he stammered, "but could you tell me if Henry is available to see me for just a minute. I wanted to thank him for something in person."

Taken back by the man's mannerisms and politeness, Nicole allowed her guard down just a bit.

"Henry Harteman doesn't live here anymore. He's in prison and if you're a friend of his, you should know that too."

"Why yes mam, I know he was in prison, but he's out now. You see he saved my life while he was in there and I wanted to thank him again for it."

Thinking that the man standing in front of her was one of Henry's former cellmates or possibly one of his enemies, Nicole felt the hair on her arms stand on end.

"Yes, well that's nice and all, but his family doesn't own this house anymore and I have no idea how you can reach them so if you would excuse me," she said with a hint of annoyance in her voice.

Marian sat silently inside the car trying to figure out where she had seen this woman before. Thinking it was one of the Harteman's, she racked her brain trying to determine if it was from a newspaper clipping or possibly the TV. She studied the young woman's face and then it hit her when she looked down at Nicole's white Ann Taylor boat shoes.

"She's a nurse at the hospital."

"Miss, oh miss," she said as she made her way to a standing position beside their car just as Nicole was turning to go back inside. Nicole turned to see what the woman wanted, now quite irritated by the invasion of her privacy.

"Don't you work at the hospital?"

"Yes, I work at a hospital," Nicole replied coldly. "Why?"

"Yes, you work day shift don't you?" Marian exclaimed trying to prove her authenticity.

Now a little curious, Nicole turned to face the woman squarely and much to her surprise, Marian was already approaching her.

"Yes, I saw you almost every day at the hospital. Gary Danbarry, my husband, was knifed nearly to death during that terrible prison riot you probably heard of on the news. Well, he was in ICU then on 6North for nearly two weeks so I lived at the hospital for much of that time. If you don't mind me saying, you're so beautiful that once I saw you the first time, I remembered your face. I guess it just took me a minute to put the two together when I saw you standing here since I was expecting to see Henry's daughter or some other member of his family.

Still a little on the defensive, Nicole glanced over at Gary who was standing dumbfounded, surprised by his wife's conversation with this stranger.

"I know it's none of my business, but you are in fact at my house and on my property. If your husband was knifed during that riot, how come he's not back in prison since his injuries have obviously healed?" Nicole asked snidely, still not convinced of the woman's sincerity.

"Laughing, Marian exclaimed, "Because he was one of the guards, not one of the prisoners."

Breaking the tension, both Nicole and Gary burst out laughing along with Marian. Nicole's face turned as scarlet red as the blouse she was wearing as she tried to apologize. Gary stepped forward to where his wife was standing and extended his hand. "Let me formally introduce myself. I'm Captain Gary Danbarry, one of the good guys."

Somewhat embarrassed, Nicole reached out and shook the man's hand.

"Sorry. It's very nice to meet you."

"And this young lady is my wife Marian."

The two woman's eyes met and they exchanged warm glances. Somehow Nicole got the distinct feeling by looking into this woman's eyes, that the couple was sincere.

"It's very nice to meet you. But how can I help you? We, my husband and I only bought this house from Henry Harteman's daughter a few months ago and just closed on it. I have no idea how you could get in touch with him. And besides, I thought he was in prison still?"

"No," Gary responded quickly, "He's been pardoned and is free. You see, I'm trying to find Henry Harteman to thank him for saving my life," the man replied, his voice nearly breaking. "If it weren't for Henry, I wouldn't be here today."

"He saved your life? How?" Nicole inquired, somewhat curious.

"During the riot, I was knifed and was locked up along with several other guards, to be used as hostages I guess. Anyway, I was literally bleeding to death. Thanks to the quick actions of Henry and another inmate, the prison was infiltrated and they got me to surgery in time to stop the bleeding."

"And that's where I first saw you," Marian offered.

"I just want to thank Henry again and tell him that I'm going to see to it that his name gets cleared of the crime he was convicted of. You do know the story behind your house don't you?"

"Yes, I know about the murder of Rachel Harteman," Nicole said solemnly. I also know that her husband didn't do it," she responded off the cuff. Gary's eyes lit up as he looked up at the woman standing beside him.

"What did you say?"

"I said" Nicole responded as she cleared her throat, "that Henry Harteman didn't kill his wife. He was convicted on circumstantial evidence alone and if," her confidence now building, "if he were to go to trial today for the same offense, the judge would throw the whole thing out due to lack of evidence."

"What makes you so certain miss? I don't even know your name" Marian asked.

Nicole, Nicole Brentwood. I'm certain because I looked up the case when we were considering buying the house. I've always been intrigued by mysteries and it was a very unusual case. The more I read about it, the more convinced I became that Henry was the easiest scapegoat to be used to cover up a heinous crime, and calm the communities' nerves. And besides, he was the most logical suspect."

"See Marian," Gary said jubilantly, "It isn't just me who thinks Henry's innocent."

"How," Nicole said skeptically, "Do you plan on clearing Mr. Harteman?"

"I'm not quite sure yet, but I'm going to speak with my nephew who's a defense attorney locally."

"Well," Nicole said as she tried to end the conversation, realized that she'd been outside far too long, "If there's anything I can ever do to help you, please let me know."

"As a matter of fact, there is. If, while you're living here, Henry ever stops by, please give him my number and tell him I need to get in touch with him. Something tells me that he might be stopping by this house someday. He always spoke about how much he loved it out here."

Taking the piece of paper from Gary, Nicole smiled at the two of them and turned toward the house. "Why don't you just call him yourself?" Nicole offered.

"I don't think I can because he's currently residing with his daughter."

"Oh, ok, if I ever have the opportunity to meet Mr. Harteman, I certainly will give him your number."

"Thank you."

"You're welcome and good night."

"Good night Mrs. Brentwood."

With that, the Danbarrys turned and got into their car. Nicole watched them from the front stoop as they buckled up and drove off. She pondered whether or not she should have told them about her visit from Henry but decided that since she truly didn't know about their sincerity and motives, she had done the right thing in keeping silent. Glancing down at the scribbled name on the scrap piece of paper, she tucked it into her jean's pocket and went back inside.

"There you are. I was wondering where you had wandered off to. Was that a car I saw leaving?" Jared asked inquisitively.

"Sure was honey. It was just some old couple asking directions."

"Oh. Hey, your parents and mine are going to go out for a little ride since it's such a nice evening and want to know if we want to join them. I volunteered us to do the dishes and tidy up, if that's okay?"

"That's fine. I'm really tired and would definitely prefer to stay in this evening. I'd love to take a bath and just relax, then go to bed early."

"Am I invited?"

"In my bath or my bed?"

"Both."

"That depends."

"Depends on what?" Jared asked with a twinkle in his eyes.

"On whether or not you'll give me a back rub."

"I'll rub anything that needs it."

"Then you can join me," she whispered as she leaned over and nuzzled up against his neck."

"Okay, just give me a second to throw our parents out."

The two laughed and entered the family room where their respective parents were visiting. After a few moments, everyone stood to leave and Jared walked them to the front door. Nicole's parents said their good-byes as they anticipated spending the night with Nicole's older brother and the senior Brentwoods estimated they'd be gone anywhere from three to four hours. With that, their parents exited the house and drove off in their respective vehicles.

Desperately anxious to start reading the journal she had discovered Nicole asked Jared if he would mind cleaning up the dishes so that she could have a few minutes to soak in the tub alone. He happily obliged and she quickly made her way to their master bathroom. While the tub was filling, she undressed but not before retrieving the journal that she had tucked back into the borough. She clutched it tightly as she eased herself into the hot bubble filled tub. Once situated, she glanced once again at the cover and stared, transfixed on the portrait of Rachel. The woman's eyes were so expressive and seemed to reveal both joy and pain. Nicole reasoned with herself one last time about why it was okay for her to read someone else's personal and extremely private thoughts, and then she formulated the conclusion that she only wanted to help the deceased woman's family. At peace with the decision, took a deep breath and opened the journal.

May 13th

This is my first entry in the new journal that my beloved Henry has given me for mother's day. I am truly blessed to have such a loving husband and two beautiful children. Clarissa is anxiously awaiting the start of summer vacation and her numerous swim camps. I swear that girl is already a fish; she has no fear and I've even caught her swimming in the lake at night when the waves are much too rough. My Clarissa simply laughs and thinks I worry too much since I can't swim a bit. Robert, oh my beautiful Robert; he is so excited anxiously waiting for the return of our annual flock of geese. The spring flowers are lovely this time of year, with the Daffodils looking more splendid than usual. How I wish Henry allowed himself more time at home to enjoy the beauty around us.

May 16th

My dear friend Betty brought me over a delicious apple pie this morning, as I've been a little under the weather this week. Springtime, though beautiful, has always been a difficult time of year for my breathing but this spring pollen must be stronger, for

I have been not only with teary eyes and runny nose, but have been so sick to my stomach. Henry says that I look exhausted and should take more time to rest but the children need their mother and I have to be there for them. At least he's promised to ease up on his schedule soon. I pray that he'll do it and cut all ties with that evil man he works for. Henry doesn't know how I hate his employer and if he only knew the truth about that horrible man, he would be sick.

May 28th

He promised me that he wouldn't do it anymore, but as usual, the bastard lied. I don't know how much more I can take of this. It has got to stop, for if my Henry knew of it, he'd go mad and do something drastic. Every time he touches me, I want to die. Today, while he was here, Clarissa came home early from school. Thank the good Lord he was just leaving. But even so, she stared accusingly. Oh, how I wish I could talk to someone, someone who would understand what's going on here. I just want it all to end. Rape is rape but how do I get him to stop. This blackmailing has been going on for months now and I don't know how to end it. Betty phoned today and invited me over for tea tomorrow. Maybe I'll confide in her. For if I don't relieve myself of this heavy burden, I feel that I'll kill myself. Maybe, maybe if I didn't feel so ill all the time, I could think more logically and clearly. If I didn't know better, I'd swear that someone was poisoning me since I'm the only one sick in our home.

May 29th

I visited Betty this morning after Henry left for work. Betty and I had a nice conversation about the spring weather, the flowers, our gardens and such. I tried to tell her about my situation but didn't *know how to put it into words. How exactly does one tell her friend that her husband's employer is blackmailing her and forcing himself on her in exchange for not getting her husband arrested for the "favors" he's doing for his employer?*

Tears welled up in Nicole's eyes as she read the entries in the journal. She sensed the extreme desperation in the young mother's words. Nicole could only speculate how this woman got herself into the situation she was presumably in against her will. She quickly wiped her eyes as she heard her husband's light tap on the bathroom door. Before she said a word, she silently but quickly tucked the book under her bath towel and slid it out of direct view.

"Who is it?" she kidded.

"Just your friendly ghost," he joked back.

"Are you a good ghost or a bad ghost and are you a boy or girl ghost?"

"I'm a boy ghost and I'm very very bad."

"Well then, come on in. I've never seen a ghost before," she mused.

As he entered the bathroom, the room suddenly went completely dark. Stunned and surprised, they remained motionless momentarily, waiting for the lights to come back on. When the seconds passed and the lights remained off, Jared instructed Nicole to stay still and he would flip the circuit breakers downstairs; assuming that the increase in the intensity of the wind outside must have somehow tripped the breaker. Within a minute, he disappeared and Nicole stood up in the tub, uncomfortable with the thought of sitting in a tub full of water in the pitch black. Relaxing in the dark with candles glowing in the background and making love was one thing, but pitch black and in dead silence was another. As she stood, she realized that she inadvertently forgot to close the blinds. As she leaned over the edge of the tub toward the window, a flash of lightening lit up the entire sky. For the split second that the sky was bright Nicole glanced at the ground below.

"Couldn't be," she thought to herself as she strained her eyes in the darkness of the now black sky.

"Was someone out there in this? Or did I just see a tree?"

Not sure why she was doing it, she continued to stare out into the darkness and whispered, "Rachel, if you're here, I'm trying to help you. Please help me. Tell me who's spying on me."

Before the words lift her lips, the sky lit up again with a magnificent flash of lightening, Nicole, still naked, focused all her energy into staring out into the darkness and then she saw him. There was in fact someone out there, standing in the shadows of the trees. Unaware if he could see her or not, Nicole tried desperately to make out whom it was but before she could, he turned and disappeared off into the woods. Nicole lunged for her half hidden towel, and nearly tumbled out of the tub in the darkness. Losing her balance, she shrieked as she started to fall. Instantly she felt something or someone grab her arm and helped her regain her balance.

"What the hell!"

"Be careful Nicole. Everything is not what it seems. Be so careful," a voice in the dark whispered.

As quickly as the lights went off, then came back on and within seconds she heard the sound of her husband's footsteps on the stairs. Still shaken, she whipped around in the tiny bathroom searching for the source of the voice. Jared walked in to find his dripping wet wife spinning around in a circle looking into thin air.

"What are you doing Nicole? I told you I'd be right back."

"I know," she stammered, "I just got nervous that's all. Was it the breaker?"

"Yeah, it's the weirdest thing," Jared explained, "Somehow the breaker hadn't been triggered by the wind or extra current, and it had been switched off. I have no clue how that happened," Jared responded scratching his head.

"I think I know," Nicole whispered under her breathe.

"Did you say something?"

"Uh, no honey. I'm just glad it wasn't anything serious. Come on, let's go to bed. I'm not in the mood for a bath anymore," she said as she turned to go open up the tub's drain.

"Okay, I guess I'm not either."

He turned to follow his wife's lead out of the bathroom, then stopped and looked back at the tub and window.

"Man, she' got to learn to close the blinds around here," he mumbled as he reached back over the tub and with the flip of his hand, closed the blinds and left the room.

Nicole made her way to their bedroom and slid under the sheets of their queen size bed. Taking her lead, Jared discarded his clothes and joined her. Within moments, Jared had forgotten about the blown circuit breaker and even Nicole wasn't thinking about the stranger that she had seen just minutes before. Both were caught up in the moment and everything else was trivial to them at that time. When they were finished, they collapsed into one another's arms and Jared was asleep almost instantly. It was only then that Nicole realized how much she still wanted to continue reading the entries in Rachel's journal. She silently slid out of bed, cautious not to wake her now snoring husband, and reached for her robe. Retrieving the book, she quickly descended the stairs and went into the library to curl up in her favorite chair. She popped open the diet coke that she had grabbed and took a few swallows before she sat down and started reading again.

May 30th

He was here again. I told him that I think I'm pregnant and he just laughed and wondered what I was going to tell Henry. He warned me that everyone would pay dearly if I ever divulged the truth to my dear Henry and from the look on his face, I know he meant it. I'm so ashamed and don't know what to do. Even Betty turned on me today when I tried to speak with her. She, of all people, shouldn't judge me. After all, she's the one who lives with a real life charlatan. I don't know how to read her sometimes but I do know that I need her friendship right now. Maybe I'll just tell Henry the truth about what's been going on ever since we moved here. Maybe he'll understand and take care of him once and for all. I'm truly worried about the impact this is having on my dear sweet Clarissa too. She doesn't admit it but truly thinks she understands, at least to some degree. She's never let on, but something inside her has changed. We used to be so close and now she hardly speaks to me. And now the eyes that were once filled with respect and admiration for me are full of hatred and bitterness. I truly think she thinks this is my fault. What will she think of me when she learns that we're having another baby? She already deeply resents her brother and the time he takes away from her needs. She'll never forgive me now. And poor Robert, how will take care of him and a baby too? Maybe I'm not strong enough to survive all this....

June 3rd

The bastard is lurking around the house every time Henry is gone. I wish we'd never bought this house and moved out here. I tried to tell Henry about the baby last night during our walk but we caught Clarissa eavesdropping by the ledge. After a firm scolding by her father, she reluctantly returned inside but by then I had lost my nerve. I've got several weeks before he'll suspect anything, so I'll just have to wait until the time is right again. That child, I don't know what's gotten into her. This is the third time we've caught her spying on us. She knows something is going on but she has no idea what. Luckily, she hasn't been exposed to him when he's here. If only I had extra money to give him, then maybe he'd leave us alone. If only Henry made more money selling his vacuum cleaners....

June 7th

Today is a good day. Henry surprised us by taking us on a picnic to Lake Ontario. My nausea has finally started to cease and though my breasts are becoming so extremely tender, I feel great. Being away from the house and the prospect of unwelcome guests makes me feel so much better. Robert and Clarissa enjoyed the change of pace and spent the day in and out of the water. I am truly grateful that they have learned to swim as well as they do. Clarissa is just such a natural in the water and little Robert is doing so well, all things considered. My dear Henry packed the lunch for us and when the children were down by the water's edge, he gave me a box that he had snuck into the basket without my knowledge. Inside was the most exquisite angel and dragonfly broach that I have ever seen. When I asked him why, he simply said that she was to be my guardian angel and protector and that she'd always be there when he couldn't be. He knows how much I love angels and dragonflies, and there aren't words enough to describe how much his token of love means to me. I will cherish the pin always.

Nicole gasped as she finished the entry and stared at the rough pencil sketch of the pin that Rachel had scrolled into the journal. It was identical to the cherubs handing on the wind chime that Jared had given her as a house warming present. Quickly dismissing it as mere coincidence, she reread the last two entries again. She tried to envision was it must have been like for Rachel, living day in and day out with that terrible secret looming over her and unable to tell her greatest love about it for fear of his reaction. Nicole's heart went out to the woman, though she'd been dead for thirty years. She couldn't even fathom what the young mother must have been going through. Nicole sat silently as she stared at the pages in front of her, and then looked out at the blackened sky. The rain had stopped but the sky remained darkened with luminous clouds hovering overhead. She thought about the passages and about the predicament Rachel had been in and who the mystery man in the journal was. Nicole had a few opinions about who her regular visitor was but decided not to formulate any conclusions until she had read the entire contents of the journal. Just as she was about to resume her reading, she glanced back outside to see the dim lights of a car approaching the house. Startled, she jumped out of her seat and quickly hid the book.

As the headlights grew larger, Nicole's heart raced. Who would be coming to see her at this hour? She called for her husband but realized it was useless as he continued to snore. Functioning on pure adrenaline, she grabbed the closest object she could find, a fireplace poker, and made her way to the front door. She quickly decided that she would use the element of surprise against this uninvited intruder. She waited until the car's lights went off and counted the seconds in her head that it should take for its driver to reach her front door. As the second's passed, Nicole could feel the beads of perspiration forming on her brow. She raised the poker overhead as she heard footsteps coming up the front stoop and an unseen hand turning the doorknob. Complete fear paralyzed her momentarily as the door started to open. Nicole took a deep breath and closed her eyes, trying to focus all of her energy into the blow she was about to deliver to the intruder.

"Nicole Rose, what are you doing?" the voice shrieked.

Catching her off guard, the piercing voice caused her to swing haphazardly in the air, hitting the wall. Nicole opened her eyes to find herself standing inches from her mother-in-law.

"Oh my God."

"Nicole, what has gotten into you? You almost killed me!"

"Oh my God."

"Hey Nicki, what's going on down there?" Rubbing his eyes, Jared looked down at the three of them standing in the foyer. "Hi mom and dad. Is everything all right? You look kind of pale. And Nicki," his eyes now focused. "Why are you holding that fireplace poker?"

"Your wife practically killed me just then," his mother chimed, glaring directly at Nicole.

"I am so sorry mom Brentwood. I heard a noise and was half awake and forgot that you and dad Brentwood were coming back and I panicked. I am so sorry that I frightened you."

"I don't care that you scared me half out of my wits, it's that you almost split my head open that bothers me," she sarcastically interjected.

Standing there, still with the fireplace poker in her hand, Nicole looked pleadingly into her husband's eyes for support. Not knowing quite what to say or do, he reached over and took the poker form her and motioned for his father, who was still standing in the doorway to come inside. Once he was in, Jared closed the door and turned back to his mother.

"Well," he said coyly, "Now that we've had a little excitement to wake us up, how about we call it a night and all get some rest?"

Taking the opportunity to remove herself from the whole situation, Nicole jumped at the chance to escape.

"Yes, I'm exhausted and you must be too, after the long day you've put in," she said as she looked at her in-laws, finally making direct eye contact with them. Jared's father was the first to speak, "Yes Nicole, it has been a long day and everyone is tired. I think you're right, so I'm heading up to bed. Do you still want us in the back bedroom?"

"Uh, yes; I put your things up in the bedroom overlooking the lake dad Brentwood."

"Okay, thanks. Good night. Come on dear, say good night and let's head up to bed."

"Night" she said coldly and followed her spouse up the stairs, turning once more to look back at Nicole.

"Don't think you scored any good daughter-in-law points tonight honey," Jared joked once they were out of earshot. "I know my mother gets on your nerves, but whacking her in the head with an iron poker is a little extreme, don't you think?"

"Oh Jared," she replied, still horrified at the thought of what she almost did. "I don't know what happened. I thought that she was a burglar or prowler or I don't know what. I just know I saw the headlights approaching and freaked. I'm so sorry."

Putting his arm around her, he smiled. "Come on, let's go to bed."

"Okay, but wait one second, I have to get the light in the library."

"Okay, go get it and I'll wait right here. Or do you want me to get it?"

No," she snapped, not meaning for it to come out so gruff, "I'll get it."

Within a split second, she was back at his side and heading up the stairs. She put her left arm around his side and held onto the journal, under her robe, with her right. Once inside the sanctity of their bedroom, she excused herself to use the bathroom and once behind closed doors, she removed the journal from under her robe and stuffed it in between two clean towels in the linen closet. She flushed the toilet, ran the sink water, and waited a moment before joining her husband who was already back in bed, half asleep. Once she joined him, he turned to her and smiled.

"Next time you try to kill off my mother, would you be a little more discreet?" he joked.

"You're a jerk Jared Brentwood," she responded under her voice. "An absolute jerk!"

"Yes, but I'm your jerk," he teased as he reached over and grabbed her by the side. They both broke out in subdued laughter as they started their usual horseplay that led into more serious lovemaking. Belong long, neither seemed to think about what had just transpired downstairs and Jared's parents were the farthest things from their mind.

Chapter 33

Henry woke bright and early; still disappointed that they had to cancel their trip out to Brynmar to visit Robert due to a last minute emergency call that Clarissa had to handle. Henry was anxious to get the morning started and even though Richard had offered to drive him out himself; Claire had insisted that she should be present when they saw Robert after all of these years. She promised that she would reschedule everything in her day so that she would have the afternoon free and that she would pick Henry up at 1pm sharp and drive him there herself. He graciously accepted her invitation and decided that he would reacquaint himself with the area. Richard had offered to drive him around but Henry simply wanted to take a long bike ride, something he hadn't had the pleasure of doing in quite some time. Richard had reluctantly agreed and also promised to work on getting Henry's driver's license reinstated. Once dressed, Henry reviewed a road map over breakfast and devoured his meal quickly so that he could start out. Not quite sure where he was going, he folded the map into his shirt pocket. The house was quiet except for the ticking of the clock on the wall and the occasional hum of their housekeeper. As he finished up his meal, Rosa entered the kitchen, arms full of brushes and dust rags. Taking note, Henry hopped up and went to her side.

"Let me take those from you mam. You're going to hurt yourself."

"Thank you senior Harteman. You're very kind."

Setting them on the counter, he looked at the stout, smiling woman in front of him and smiled back.

"I don't know about kind or not, but I do know that you were carrying too much and it's a wonder you didn't trip and hurt yourself."

"Ah, no senior, I'm fine. I do it all the time; it's my job."

"Well Rosa, you won't be able to do your job if you fall and break an arm or leg, so let me help you while I'm doing nothing but sitting around, okay?"

"Gracious senior, Thank You."

Henry stared at the heavyset woman for a brief moment and wondered how long she had been working for his daughter. She had a peaceful face and genuine smile which made her deeply set brown eyes sparkle when she showed her pristinely white teeth. Dressed in black, he estimated her to be in her mid to late fifties. He continued to stare at her for another moment, and then his eyes lit up as he came up with an idea.

"Say, the house looks immaculate. How would you like to help me out with something?"

Somewhat hesitantly, she responded, "Do you have laundry to be washed or isn't your room in satisfactory condition?"

"No, no, all that is fine. What I was wondering is, how would you like to go for a ride with me? That is, would you like to drive around town with me, since I don't have my license yet? I was going to ride Richard's bike but I'm sure I'd get lost, so much has changed. Come on, it'll be fun and we won't be gone long. It's such a beautiful morning out" he added enthusiastically.

"Ah, okay, if you think Senora Drake will approve?"

"Certainly; I'll tell Richard that you offered to drive me around since he wasn't too keen on me biking alone. You just saved the day Rosa! This is going to be fun and I'd love the company!"

Blushing, she added, "Okay."

"Good, then it's settled. Give me fifteen minutes and I'll be ready."

"Si. I'll put something else on and meet you back here in fifteen minutes."

"Great," he responded, now with a radiant smile. There was something genuine about Rosa and he looked forward to her company as he scurried off toward his bedroom to brush his hair and teeth, whistling as he went.

Rosa was standing nervously in the kitchen as he made his way to her within their designated time frame. He was sporting a lightweight jacket and looked quite dapper, all things considered. Richard had went clothes shopping prior to Henry's release from the hospital and although he had never known his father-in-law prior to the riot and Henry's hospitalization, he had done an excellent job in choosing attire that Henry himself would have purchased. Rosa had changed into a cream colored wool blouse and plaid slacks which she accented with a beautiful copper pendant hanging on a long braided chain. She had removed her hair from its usual confine of a bun and had pulled it back into a simple French twist. As Henry smiled approvingly at her, she blushed again and thought he noticed a hint of makeup on her bronzed face. She truly looked stunning as she stood in the kitchen, looking silently over at him. Not quite sure what to say, he started to zip his jacket and reached for the keys that were resting on the counter.

"Shall we?" he said as he motioned toward the door.

Once in Rosa's car, Henry looked over at the woman behind the wheel and smiled. She had never questioned his character, from the moment he entered his daughter's home and for that he was eternally grateful. He was also grateful because it appeared that slowly, his life was regaining some resemblance of normalcy. Now he and Rosa were going to spend the morning together with no schedule or anyone dictating what had to be done and that prospect delighted him to no end. Looking at Rosa, he realized that no woman could or would ever replace his first love; but Henry suddenly realized that he had in fact missed the relationship that is shared between two people who care about each other.

"If nothing more, she will become a good friend," he thought to himself and smiled. Not quite sure where they were off to, Rosa stopped at the end of the neighborhood and looked over at Henry.

"Sir, would you like to go for a drive in the city or a drive in the country?"

"Miss Gonzales, please call me Henry. And if it's okay with you, I'd love to go for a ride in the country."

"Please call me Rosa, and okay to the country. I've always loved it better than the city anyways."

With that, they pulled away from the Drake residence and within moments were on the freeway heading out of the city. Still, with no destination in mind, she just followed the flow of traffic and made small talk with her new friend. Before long, both were feeling comfortable and the conversation freely flowed. Henry found that Rosa was not only intelligent, but articulate and well educated. He berated himself for assuming that she was simply a housekeeper who was content cleaning houses for a living. He was shocked to learn that she had worked as a Registered Nurse back in her homeland of Brazil. The more he listened to her, the more he liked her and the more respect he had for her. As he listened intently, he said a silent prayer of thanks, thanking God that his daughter had turned out so well, in spite of the odds.

Claire too, was talking to God that morning. As she sat at her desk trying to sort through the paperwork in front of her, her mind wandered back to her childhood. Bits and pieces of information came rushing back against her will. Taking care of her brother, the humiliation she felt from kids at school about Robert, the good and bad times at the lake house and him. Her mind raced when she thought of her mother's friend. Why now, was his face coming back to her? But what was his name. She knew that she knew who he was but her brain wouldn't divulge the information. She closed her eyes and tried to retrieve the information that she had blocked for so long. Slowly, she started remembering fragments of images from so long ago. Gifts he used to bring her and her brother; he was always showering them with gifts. And crying; she clearly remembered now how her mother was always crying after he would visit. As a child she had always thought that it was because he didn't always bring her mother a gift, but now, Claire started to put the pieces together. Her mother's nervousness when he came around, even if their father was home. But he was their neighbor, their friend. And the crying---why was it that their mother was always crying? She remembered the one time that she got a ride home early from school and he had been there when she walked in. Her mother had looked so upset and her usually neatly pressed outfit was so wrinkled and disheveled.

"Why, why am I remembering this now?" Claire thought to herself as she placed her hands on her head as if it was about to explode. "And what does it mean?" she thought to herself as she once again tried to close her eyes and remember more. As she sat there, she started remembering the last few days of her mother's life. She had been so upset those last days. She seemed like she was so sick and always distraught; or so it appeared to the child she had been at the time. As she sat there, she recalled a conversation that she and her mother had had shortly before her death. Rachel tried to explain to Claire that things weren't always what they appeared to be and that things were about to permanently change around their home and that they might be moving to a different house soon. Caught up in adolescence and herself, Claire hadn't really listened to what her mother was trying to say, nor had she cared. Over the last few months, she had become increasingly distant from her mother. The little girl who had been her mother's best friend had grown into a resentful, bitter, self-centered teenager who became not only cynical of her mother's actions, but of her mother herself. Claire felt the tears well up in her eyes when she thought of that terrible fight that she and Rachel had had less than a week before her demise. Rachel hadn't slept much the night before and was exhausted. When she asked Clarissa to watch Robert for a bit after school so that she could rest, Claire flippantly remarked that "Maybe you should have him come over and do it cause for all we know maybe he's Robert's father." Rachel, without thinking, slapped Clarissa across the mouth and screamed for her to never make such a statement again. And as the tears freely flowed down her cheek back then as they were now, she screamed back at her mother that she wish she were dead.

"Oh mother, I never meant it. I never meant it, you have to know that…" she whispered as she held her head in her hands. Sobbing, she pushed herself away from her desk in order to stand up and retrieve a tissue. As she did so, she inadvertently knocked over the stack of papers on the corner of her desk. "Damn it," she said as she bent down to pick them up, wiping her moist nose on her linen blazer. As she started to shove the papers back into a stack, she saw it. There, right under her nose. Unable to believe the coincidence, she stared down at the name for what seemed like eternity.

"Nicholas Carelli. Holy shit, that's him. That's the bastard that was fucking my mother. I wonder," she said as she pulled the paper containing Carelli's name out from the rest of the stack, "what he's in jail for." She took a moment to read the article as the wheels continued to turn in her head. Racketeering, extortion, bribery, the list went on and on. Running an illegal gambling ring and ties to the Mafia rounded out his fact sheet.

"A real outstanding citizen," she thought to herself as she resumed picking up the last of the papers. Quickly dialing her cell, she barked as soon as her secretary answered; "Jane, do me a favor and pull everything you can on a Mr. Nicholas Carelli, and do it ASAP."

"Right away Miss Drake."

Claire sat back down at her desk and stared at the photo in front of her. It was as if thirty years had been erased and she was again the little girl who had looked up to her father's friend and one-time employer. Claire's mind raced wildly when she thought of the prospect that her father had been involved in organized crime, or at least had been employed by someone within the organization. What if her own father was directly involved. Maybe she had been right all along; maybe she didn't know her own father as well as she had thought. And if he was involved in something like that, maybe he could have been capable of murder. Her head was starting to spin with speculations and theories as her phone rang, breaking the trance.

"Hello."

"Hi Claire, it's me."

"Richard, "she blurted out as soon as she realized it was him, "I think my father might have been involved in organized crime. Or at least was employed by someone who was, or is involved."

"What?" Richard snapped, feeling a strange sensation come over his body and beads of perspiration forming on his forehead. "Where'd that come from?"

"I found an article on one of my father's employer's, a Nicholas Carelli."

"Jesus Claire, your father was employed by Nicholas Carelli?"

"You know him?"

"Of course I know of him. He's one of the players in the Dorella family. He's as crooked as they come, but he's not known for his violence but for his way with the women."

As her husband spoke, she suddenly felt sick as her stomach flipped upside down.

"I've heard through the grapevine that he's on at least wife number five or six and when he sets his sights on someone, he doesn't quit until he's got her. Of course, two of his wives' went missing while they were going through divorce proceedings, never to be heard from again.

"Richard, I think," her voice quivering, "that he was involved with my mother and that she was trying to break it off with him, just before her death."

Richard cleared his throat and addressed his wife's statement, "Do you realize what you're saying Claire?"

"Yes Richard, I do. I'm saying that we just discovered someone other than my father who might have wanted to kill her."

"Claire, he's known for his womanizing and his explosive temper. Its common knowledge that he's probably responsible for those missing ex-wives' disappearance and probable deaths so if your mother was breaking it off with him, who knows how it took it. Could it have been enough to set him off and kill her?"

"Might have been if she had told him that she was pregnant. Oh my God, what if it was his baby?" Claire shrieked as the thought once again turned her stomach.

"I suppose there's a possibility that the baby your mother was carrying could in fact, been his," Richard responded logically. "I'm sure her getting pregnant certainly wasn't part of Carelli's plan."

"Richard, what if she told him and he killed her? Maybe she wasn't trying to end it, but when she told him that she was pregnant, he lost it? Or maybe, "her head once again spinning with ideas," "Maybe she told him that she was pregnant and that it was over. Regardless of the circumstances behind what he knew, if Carelli was sleeping with my mother, that adds him to the list of suspects. My

God Richard, why didn't Carelli's association with my father come out during Henry's trial?"

"Well," Richard responded, trying to choose his words carefully, "I took the liberty of reading the manuscript of the trial, and sorry to say, your father didn't stand a chance. The public defender appointed to represent him was fresh out of school and inexperienced and incompetent. To him and everyone else, Henry was the most logical suspect and with that mentality, your father was convicted before he even got to court. The whole trial was a sham and Henry the scapegoat."

Changing the subject, Richard changed the tone in his voice; when you get home, let's wait together for Henry to come back from his ride and then we'll go take him to see Robert. That will give us a chance to ask your father directly about his relationship with Nicholas Carelli."

As soon as Claire said goodbye and hung up, Richard was on the phone to the warden at Jefferson Prison. What he had failed to tell his wife is that he knew that Carelli was already doing time there awaiting his next trial on the new charges. After a brief exchange, Judge Drake explained what it was that he was after and the warden assured him that he could get the information he requested. Feeling satisfied with the response, he tied up a few remaining loose ends and headed home.

When Claire walked in the front door and spotted his wife, he could tell that she'd been crying.

"What's wrong Claire?"

"Everything," she burst out, unable to contain her pent up emotion any longer. "I have hated my father for years for a crime he probably didn't commit. I disowned by only brother. My last childhood memories of my mother were of the horrible fight we had, and now I find out that a mobster probably fathered my sister or brother who died when my mother did. I'd say just about everything is wrong right about now," she sobbed. "But how do we prove it?" she asked as she looked over at her husband sitting silently beside her.

"Leave that part up to me honey. I may be able to get the answers to some of the questions that your father can't answer. Dry your eyes," he said warmly, offering her a tissue. "Your father will be home shortly and we'll talk to him then."

Henry and Rosa rode along several country roads laughing and making small talk. Both spoke of their childhood and other happy moments in their lives. Unbeknownst to Henry, Rosa told of her short-lived marriage to a man name Rafael. Henry listened somberly as Rosa told of her wedding to her childhood sweetheart at the young age of seventeen and becoming a widow before her nineteenth birthday. Her voice started to break when she told of giving up her dream of having children and loving again. For the first time in a long time, Henry realized that everyone, no matter how they look from outward appearances, might have pain and sorrow that they're living with. He also realized that even though he lost his one and only true love, her legacy still lives on in her children. Now, more than ever, he wanted to be reunited with his only son. As he listened to Rosa speak, he got wrapped up in how articulate she was and didn't pay attention to where she was turning. The next thing he knew, she had entered a dead end street that he had been down hundreds of times before. Realizing what she had done, his face paled as he stared off into space.

"Senior Harteman, is anything wrong?"

"No Rosa. And please call me Henry. It's just," he stammered, "Well it seems that I was so caught up listening to you and didn't pay attention to where we were."

"Oh. I wasn't paying attention either and appear to have gotten us lost on a dead end street."

"No Rosa, we're not lost. I used to live right down at the end of the street," he said as he stared ahead.

"You mean the house where," she gulped, "Where Mrs. Harteman died?" He turned toward Rosa and smiled meekly, "I'm sorry. I didn't mean to put you in an uncomfortable situation. It's just that,"

Before he could finish, she smiled in a warm, comforting smile and put her hand to his lips.

"It's alright. I am not uncomfortable. You loved Mrs. Harteman and it's natural that you would be shocked that I accidentally drove here. Would you like to go see the house?" she asked, not sure if she wanted to hear his reply. He looked deep into her golden brown eyes and smiled. He reached up and took the hand that was still close to his lips and without hesitating, kissed it gently.

"Thank you Rosa. I would like to show it to you, but are you sure you're okay with it?" he asked, suddenly thinking about his companion.

"Yes, Henry; I'm fine with it," she replied, feeling something come over her that she hadn't felt in many, many years.

As they pulled back onto to the road and slowly made their way to the end of the dead end street, both Rosa and Henry sensed that they had started something that was very good.

Chapter 34

Jared and his father had snuck out of the house immediately after breakfast, leaving Nicole and her still disgruntled mother-in-law alone in the kitchen. Nicole tried to make small talk but the elder Brentwood remained aloof. After several attempts at conversation, Nicole gave up and excused herself while her mother-in-law sat reading the paper. Just as she was about to go upstairs to tidy up, her mother-in-law finally broke the cold spell that she had cast.

"Do you think the woman who lived in your house was really murdered by her husband?"

Caught off guard by her question, Nicole studied her face and realized that she was asking not out of fear but genuine compassion for the deceased woman. Nicole seized the opportunity to talk about Rachel as she looked at her mother-in-law who was waiting with baited breath for her response.

"No mom Brentwood. I solemnly believe that Henry Harteman is innocent of murder. I think that someone else pushed his wife off that cliff and I think that someday the truth will come out; it eventually always does. But," she said, not wanting to dwell on the subject too long. "I have to go back to work in a few days and I've got a lot more to unpack. I can't be worried by events that occurred before I was born.

"You're right dear but if that man didn't do it that means there's a murderer walking around free today."

"I'm sure there are numerous murderers still stalking our streets all over the country. But with any luck, it's just a matter of time before they're caught."

Content in her response, Nicole left the room and proceeded up the back stairwell. Once upstairs, she sighed loudly, when she saw that either Jared or her in-laws had left the back bedroom light on. She entered the room, not only to shut the light off but also to open the window to change the air. As she proceeded over to the window she glanced out at the crystal clear water below her. The lake was brimming with fishing boats, all trying to take advantage of the previous night's rough seas. As she opened the window, a blast of fresh air engulfed her nostrils as she took a deep breath. Adjusting the screen into place, she strained her ears, trying to determine if the engine sound she could hear coming down the road was that of her husband. Unsure, she made her way to their bedroom to get a look. After last night's fiasco, she didn't want to jump to any conclusions about anything, so she walked briskly to her room without hesitation. Not recognizing the vehicle slowly making its way toward her house, she bolted out of the room, skipping steps on her way downstairs and mentally prepared herself for a confrontation. She was becoming frustrated with all of the traffic that she was seeing on her supposed dead end street and was becoming increasingly concerned that her neighbors would complain. As she opened the door, the car had already come to a complete stop right in front of her door. Not recognizing its occupants, she stepped outside, ready for a fight.

Seeing Nicole step out onto the landing, Henry's fear faded and he opened the car door. Unsure of what was transpiring, Rosa sat frozen in the front seat of the car.

"Good morning Miss Brentwood; I hope that I'm not disturbing you this lovely morning."

Realizing then who the uninvited intruder was, Nicole smiled radiantly back.

"Well good morning to you to Mr. Harteman. Of course you're not disturbing me. What brings you out of this neck of the woods so early?" she asked as she approached the car.

"Well I, I mean we," he said as he looked back at Rosa, who still remained motionless inside the car, "Decided that it was a beautiful morning to go for a ride and we inadvertently wound up here. I truly didn't mean to interrupt you this morning, I just wanted to show my friend where I had once lived and to show her how beautiful the countryside is." His coy smile and sparking eyes revealed more to Nicole than his words. Something about Henry was very different from the man she had met for the first time just a few days prior. There was life in his eyes and an eagerness about him. Maybe, Nicole thought to herself, it was his way of starting over and getting on with his life. She smiled back at Henry, whose eye contact never broke from hers except for a brief second he glanced to the right of her shoulder. Spontaneously, she looked to see what had caught his attention but when she didn't see anything, she looked back at the man in front of her.

"The countryside is beautiful this morning Mr. Harteman. Please, would you like to show your friend around," Nicole asked, curious to see who was hidden behind the tinted windows of the car.

"Oh thank you very much Mrs. Brentwood, but we've got to be heading home. Rosa and I will be listed as missing in action if we don't get home soon; but it sure was nice to see you again. Are you getting settled in okay?" he asked as he looked at the house that had once been his.

"Yes, thank you. Say, Mr. Harteman, now that we've met and you're going to need furniture for an apartment eventually, is there anything that we have in storage in the attic that you'd like to keep? After all, it is rightfully yours."

"No Nicole," he sighed, "Any furniture that came with the house is legally yours and besides, it all holds too many memories. It's time for me to buy new furniture and make new memories."

"You have no idea how many memories from the past that furniture holds," Nicole thought to herself as she just smiled as Henry got back into the car.

"But thank you anyways," he shouted as he waved from the window as his friend started down the driveway. As they left the property, the car slowed momentarily near the same spot in the woods that had caught his attention just a few moments earlier when he had been speaking with Nicole. But nothing seemed out of the ordinary now. Nicole gazed into the woods at the same time but also didn't see anything there. Then she thought of it.

"Wait!" she shouted as she sprung off the landing and toward the departing car. Seeing the commotion in her rear view window, Rosa stopped the car and within a moment, Nicole was standing beside the driver's side window, which she approached deliberately so that she could get a view of Henry's companion. She held her side as she caught her breath as Rosa fumbled with the automatic window.

"Nicole, what is it?" Henry asked, somewhat surprised by her outburst. "I nearly forgot to tell you. Someone came by the house the other day looking for you, a Gary Danbarry. Said he was a friend of yours," she responded watching Henry's face for his expression. Henry's eye lit up as he looked at Rosa and then Nicole.

"Yes, Gary is a good friend of mine. He's one of the few people who have stood by my side for a number of years. He's an honest, hardworking man and I care about him like a brother."

"Well," Nicole said, "I think the feeling is mutual. He boasted to me that if it weren't for you, he'd be dead right now. He said that you saved his life."

Rosa looked admiringly at Henry as he blushed and blew off the statement.

"Gary's a good person and I couldn't just let him die. He got hurt very badly in the riot and I did what any human being would do, I did what needed to be done to get help to a friend in need."

"Yeah, and he says you risked your neck doing so and that's how you ended up hurt as well."

Rosa listened intently to their conversation, formulating and even better opinion of the man sitting beside her as she listened to Nicole brag about his heroics and Henry down play the risks that he had taken to save a friend.

"Well, Gary and his wife stopped by the other day and wanted me to give you his number. He said that he really needs to speak with you and something urgent."

"Did he say what it was Nicole?"

"Not exactly, but he did indicate that it had something to do with your wrongful imprisonment."

"Wrongful imprisonment?" Henry asked, somewhat confused.

"Yes. He, I mean we, both know that you didn't do anything to harm Rachel and I think that he might have some new evidence proving just that. I don't want to get your hopes up, but I know that he said that it was urgent that he speak with you."

"Thank you for being so kind Nicole. But out of curiosity, why do you believe I'm innocent?"

"I know it sounds ridiculous, but your wife told me. Her spirit is still in this house Henry; and I firmly believe that she's been sending me messages. She wants everyone to know that you're innocent and that you never harmed her."

Henry said nothing but turned to find Rosa smiling as she sat silently in the driver's seat. She had listened intently to the young woman's proclamation of Henry's innocence and had been convinced completely that Henry was indeed a decent person that society had unjustly convicted. She stared into his weathered but still young looking face and studied his eyes. Even prison had failed to dull the sparkle in his eyes. She wondered momentarily to herself what he must have been like before this terrible injustice had been forced upon him. What he must have looked like, what kind of father he had been and what kind of husband. As she sat, transfixed within her own thoughts, Henry looked back at her and smiled. He knew without words that Rosa trusted his sincerity and that meant a great deal. As he looked at her, he not only saw his daughter housekeeper, but a beautiful woman. To break her spell, he reached over for her hand, which was resting in her lap and squeezed it gently. She never flinched as he took her hand, instead she covered his hand with her other one. They sat frozen in the moment until Nicole coughed, feeling uncomfortable sharing this intimate moment.

"I'll go grab that number for you Henry."

Gone only a minute or two, Nicole returned with Gary's name and number.

"It was nice seeing you again Henry; and remember, you and your friend are welcome here anytime."

"Thank you."

And with that, Henry and Rosa headed back down the dead end street and back toward Syracuse where he knew Claire would be waiting for them.

They rode in silence as both Henry's and Rosa's minds were filled with questions and thoughts. Could Gary Danbarry really know something that could clear his name once and for all? He tried to force the thoughts from his mind as he drove along the freeway, afraid to get his hopes up. Rosa on the other hand, was also trying to force certain thoughts from her mind. She was unsure why she was feeling so funny inside and wasn't certain that she wanted to feel that way. As she glanced over at the man beside her, those feelings came back again, against her will and finally she decided not to resist them, for maybe feeling something for a man after all these years was not all that bad. Besides, how harmful could it be for her, at her age? She accepted the fact that she was indeed attracted to him and decided to let fate take its' course. She just silently prayed that her fate wouldn't be the same as his late wives...

Claire and Richard waited impatiently at their home for Henry's arrival. Richard tried to read a journal that he had brought back with him from the office and Claire tried to focus on the stack of mail in front of her, but neither could get their mind off of Nicolas Carelli and his association with Henry. Just when Claire thought she couldn't take the waiting anymore, they both jumped up to the sound of the garage door opening. Rosa hadn't even shut off the engine when she looked up to see Claire and Richard standing in the doorway. Feeling very uncomfortable, Rosa looked over to Henry.

"Come on; let's tell them the good news," he smiled as he looked at her and then at them. "Hi guys. Am I past my curfew," he joked breaking the tenseness of the moment. Relieved that he was home safe and sound, Claire spoke first.

"No Henry. We're just glad you were able to get out for a little bit. And I see you must have had a great time by the smiles on both of your faces. Rosa, would you excuse us though because we need to speak with Henry privately. Besides, you must have some dusting or vacuuming to do around here."

Unsure why his daughter was being so rude, Henry turned back at Rosa and spoke softly, "Rosa, let me speak with them for a little bit and if it's okay with you; I would very much like it if you would accompany me for a stroll this evening."

"Si, I mean yes; yes, I would like that very much," she whispered as she turned to make her way inside.

"Seven o'clock sharp then," he shouted back so that everyone could hear as she hustled past Claire and Richard and hurried to her room to change.

Before he even had a chance to confront his daughter about her behavior toward Rosa, Richard was already chastising her.

"Claire, there was no reason for you to be so rude to Rosa. It didn't hurt anything for her to go out with your father for a few hours."

"We're paying her to be here and work, not run the roads using up our gas."

"Oh bull shit Claire! You said that just to remind her who's boss and it was uncalled for and rude. Now come on, we've got more important things to talk about, but I expect you to apologize to her when you see her in a few minutes and I expect you to keep your nose out of Henry's and Rosa's business," he said as he scowled at this wife and then turned around and winked at his father-in-law. Henry's face remained solemn but inside he was bursting at the seams at how red his daughter's face got but she didn't argue.

"You're right Richard," she finally said as she turned to look at her father.

"Come on inside Henry, we need to speak with you about something of utmost importance."

Henry glanced over at Richard as he made his way toward the house. Richard smiled reassuringly back at him and stepped aside to let him pass. Claire was already heading toward the study and once everyone was inside, she looked out into the foyer and closed the mahogany doors behind her. Henry studied their faces as he was motioned to sit down. Unsure where or how to start the conversation, Claire just blurted out the question: "Henry, what was your association with Nicolas Carelli?"

"Nicolas Carelli? What has he got to do with anything?"

"Father, please. What was your association with him?"

"Clarissa, you were old enough to remember. I used to make deliveries for him on weekends and sometimes in the evening; why?"

"Did you realize that he has mob connections Henry?" Richard asked gingerly.

"Why yes, I realize that now. But when I worked for him, there was no such connection. Or at least, I never knew of it. Look, I simply ran errands for the man; nothing more, and nothing less. He treated our family well. Always brought you kids and Rachel presents and he paid me very well for the amount of time it took to run his packages to their destinations.

"Yeah, he was giving mother something alright," Claire said under her breath.

"What did you say Clarissa?" Henry asked hesitantly.

"I said, he was giving mother something alright. Henry," she said as she looked into her father's eyes, "I think that mother was willingly or maybe unwillingly involved with Nicolas Carelli. And I think that she tried to end it with him and that infuriated him; maybe enough to kill her."

Not wanting to hear what she was saying; Henry bounded to his feet from the high back chair.

"No! Your mother was a good woman and I won't sit here and listen to your blasphemy!"

"Maybe she had no choice. Maybe he forced himself upon her or maybe he had some way of blackmailing her into doing it. Maybe you didn't realize what it was that you were transporting all over town for him and he told her that you'd be arrested if he wanted you to be. I don't know father, but I do know that when she died she was pregnant and it wasn't yours, so she was doing it with somebody. And" she said as tears filled up in both her and Henry's eyes, "I can remember numerous occasions when that asshole used to wait for you to leave and he'd come over to pay a visit. She'd beg him to leave but he wouldn't and then she'd shoo both Robert and myself away for a while and usually when we'd come back, she'd be sobbing. I'm sorry, but it's the truth. Mother was sleeping with Carelli and he probably was the father of the baby she was carrying when she died."

"No. I won't believe it. He's involved with illegal things now but back then he was kind and generous. Why; he even gave us the money for the down payment on this house. Back then, it was a large sum of money. I always intended to pay him back and then everything happened."

"He gave you a large sum of money without some form of loan agreement?" Richard asked.

"Yes and never once did he ask me for a penny; he was like that."

"Do you think," Richard spoke softly, "That it's possible that he was using the loan to hang over Rachel's head. Maybe he told her that if she didn't service his needs; that he'd never let her go and he'd make you pay off the loan, and take your house? You said yourself how tight money was then and how hard it was to make ends meet. Is it possible that he was indeed blackmailing her?"

Taking a moment to give his son-in-law's question some thought, Henry tried to recall some of those now so distant memories of conversations that he and Rachel had had regarding Carelli. She had begged him not to accept any money that he wasn't entitled to from him, but Henry knew how much she had wanted the house and had good intentions of paying the loan back in full. Whenever he had mentioned the money to Carelli, he had always said that he didn't want the money back and was happy with their arrangement.

Not until now, had Henry really understood what the bastard had meant by his choice of words.

"Yes," Henry replied, bowing his head in to his hands, "I believe that it's possible that he was using something against her. I will never believe that Rachel would have done it willingly. Not my Rachel. She was kind, and considerate and a good woman. She would never have done that to me, to us, if she wasn't forced to. I refuse to believe otherwise..."

"She was always friends with that crazy neighbor next door too father. You know, Mr. Langhorne," Claire piped in, and then realized that she shouldn't have.

"Oh Bart was harmless enough. He idolized Rachel, simply adored her, but he couldn't get within two feet of her without his bitch wife breathing down his neck. Betty had a jealous streak a mile long and she never allowed him anywhere near Rachel or any other woman for that matter."

"Is that why she was always so mean to Robert and me?"

"She didn't intend to be deliberately mean to you honey. That was just her way. I believe that old Bart had stepped out on her once or twice before we moved into the house on Sycamore Lane, so we when we moved in next door and she saw how beautiful your mother was, it was only natural that she'd be jealous. But she was that way with everyone. God, I wonder if the old coot is still alive."

"Which one?"

"Both of them."

"Doesn't matter. What matters is that we need to find out Carelli's true relationship with mother."

"But how are you going to do that? Your mother has been dead for nearly thirty years and the last I knew Carelli was in prison for something or other."

"Racketeering and extortion," Richard offered.

"How do you know that?"

"I had his file pulled. He's a dangerous man Henry, and you're lucky to be alive. Many of his past associates have wound up with bullet holes in their temples. Promise us Henry, you'll never attempt to contact him or anyone associated with him," Richard said half asking and half pleading.

"If I saw the man, I'd probably kill him with my bare hands for what you're implying."

"Stay away from him father, do you understand me?"

"Yes Clarissa, I hear you and understand, but listen to me. If that man is responsible for your mother's death and the death of her child, I will make sure he gets what he deserves."

"That is what the court system is for Henry."

"Yeah, it did right by me, now didn't it? All I'm saying is if that fucker killed my Rachel; I will kill him. My life didn't end when I went to prison; my life ended the day Rachel died. She was my world, that simple. I loved you kids with my heart and soul, but she was my world..."

"That was different Henry, and for that I'm truly sorry. But we can't change the terrible injustice that was done to you but we can avenge your wife's death in other ways."

"Richard, you don't want to hear it; but after 30 years in prison, trust me I know how to kill someone and if I find out he murdered Rachel, he will die."

Trying to change to subject that was getting too much for her to hear, Claire stepped toward her father and touched his arm, "I'm sorry that you had to learn all about his father, but it needed to come out. Let's try to forget about it for a few hours and let's go see Robert like we had planned. I know that he'll be thrilled to see you."

"He won't even recognize me or you for that matter Claire. That's just another part of my life that was taken away from me.

"Let's make up for that now. I'd like to meet my brother-in-law Henry. Are you up to it?"

"Yes. Yes, I am. Just give me a moment to freshen up a bit and I'll be all set to go. And," Henry said as he headed toward the door, "I'd like to have a word with Rosa before we leave, and it wouldn't hurt you to apologize to her either Clarissa."

"Fine; I'll apologize."

"Good, thank you." Henry turned and shut the door behind him, leaving Richard and Claire alone in the study.

"Don't say it Richard. Just don't say it."

"I wasn't going to say anything except that I wouldn't be so quick to discourage a friendship between your father and Rosa. He needs someone and she's as safe as they come."

"But she's our housekeeper!"

"Who cares? Whether she's a socialite, cashier or housekeeper, if she makes your father happy, who cares? He deserves all the happiness he can get. I have a feeling that this is going to get uglier before it gets better, and I want both you and Henry to be ready for that."

"I can handle it, and I think he will too. Remember, he's a fighter."

"Good; he's going to have to be. Come on; let's go see your brother."

Within a few minutes, the three had set off towards Brynmar Facility where Robert resided. Henry entered the kitchen prior to their departure to find Claire stumbling thru a forced apology. After she excused herself, Henry also apologized for his daughter's rude behavior and promised Rosa that he'd be back in time for their evening plans. Back in her housekeeper's attire, she looked older but still refined, and Henry couldn't help but notice how attractive she truly was. Once she heard where he was going, she rushed him out the door and wished him luck. Then she sat silently in the massive kitchen and pondered on why she was feeling the way that she was. The last week had brought about such changes in her life, along with all the residents of the Drake household. Feeling the urge to discuss her feelings with someone, she quickly phoned her sister as the threesome pulled out of the drive.

The drive took less than an hour, despite the heavy afternoon traffic. They drove the entire distance in silence, everyone keeping their own thought and emotions to themselves. An extremely nervous person by nature, Claire could feel her chest tightening, and her heart rate quickening as they approached the entrance to The Brynmar Campus. After receiving directions from the attendant at the gated front entrance, they slowly made their way around the campus toward their intended destination. Then they saw it, the Brigham house was directly in front of them. Richard slowed the Escalade momentarily as they stared at the quaint white Cape Cod. The house looked homey enough, with its hunter green shingles and shutters that matched the wide front porch, lined with white wicker furniture. The windows had shadow boxes which were overflowing with greenery and tulips, and the lawn was manicured, almost to the state of perfection. The curtains in the windows were all uniform and gave the appearance of something out of Better Homes and Gardens. The three momentarily studied the faces of the two gentlemen sitting on the front porch off to the right. As they scrutinized their appearances, the men never looked up, for they were oblivious to the company, and were completely focused on their game of checkers. Richard looked over at Claire, trying to determine if she recognized their faces, but within a moment, she turned toward him and silently nodded her head no. Richard took her cue and accelerated slowly forward, trying not to disturb the residents. Once the SUV was stopped and they were outside the vehicle, all three simultaneously took deep breaths and started toward the front door. It was only when the older of the two gentlemen involved in the game heard their footsteps that he even acknowledged their present.

"Howdy strangers; can I help you?" he asked as he diverted his eyes momentarily away from the game, but never stood.

Henry spoke first. "Yes, good afternoon," he said with his voice quivering to the point of trembling. "We're here to visit Robert," he paused. "Robert Harteman."

"Well then, you'd better go inside," the old man said as he glanced at his watch. "You might have already missed him thou, because he usually heads over to the pool this time of day to go swim laps. The boy can't seem to stay out of the damn water."

Astonished at the thought that Robert was not only alive, but in good enough physical health that he still is able to swim made Henry's heart beat a little faster. He quickly thanked the gentleman and increased his gait toward the front door.

The anticipation was killing Claire. She had never been more fearful in her life, scared of his rejection of her and petrified of what childhood memories he might have retained. She was almost frozen in time as her husband nudged her to catch up to her father. "What will he remember about that night and about me?" she kept repeating in her head as she obliged her husband and slowly moved toward the front door.

"Don't knock, just go right in," the younger gentleman on the porch finally spoke up as he saw Henry pausing by the door. "Sarah is inside and will log you all in the visitor log."

Henry smiled in appreciation, and as he was reaching for the handle, the door started to open from inside. Henry backed up as the person on the other side stepped out onto the porch.

"Well, there you go," the older man quipped. "You don't have to go looking for Robert, because there he is."

Everyone froze and for a brief moment, the three forgot to breathe. Robert stared back at the two men and the woman standing just feet away from them. As they stared at the man in front of them, Claire instantly felt her eyes filling with tears. Taller than he had expected for some reason, Henry surveyed the young man from head to toe, still unable to formulate any words. Sensing the awkwardness of the situation, Richard stepped forward and extended his hand.

"Robert Harteman?" he inquired.

"Yes, I'm Robert Harteman," the curious man answered back, not quite sure what to make of the commotion around him.

Richard shook Robert's now extended hand and smiled. "You don't know me, but my name is Richard, Richard Drake and I've, I mean we've, come to visit you."

Taking a brief moment to recall where he had heard that name before, the light quickly went on and he gasped as his eyes darted at the other members of the group. Seeing his almost instantaneous recognition of the name, Richard spoke softly.

"Robert, I've brought your sister Clarissa and your father," Before the words left his lips, Robert was already at Henry's side, bypassing Claire altogether. Robert positioned himself directly in front of Henry and with his slightly crooked smile gave him the biggest grin possible as his bottom lip started to quiver.

"Father is it really you? He spoke softly, glancing over at Richard for confirmation.

Unable to speak, Henry felt lightheaded as he slowly nodded his head yes. Both had waited or this day for so long and now that it was actually here, neither dared to move for fear of it being a dream. Finally Robert reached his hand up and delicately touched his father's face as the tears streamed down his face. The two elderly residents on the porch, who didn't know what to think of the situation, folded up their game and quickly excused themselves, although the four were oblivious to their departure. As Robert and Henry embraced, Claire remained frozen, terrified of how her brother was going to respond to her. After what seemed like eternity, the two Hartemans finally stepped back from one another and both evaluated the other with glowing smiles. Then Robert remembered Clarissa, and turned his attention to her. She trembled as she made eye contact with her long lost brother, not quite sure whether or not she should approach him, but with a little nudge from her spouse, she finally took a step in his direction. Hesitantly, Robert stepped toward his only sister. His head spun at seeing her again, as his mind raced to retrieve control over his emotions. As he stood face to face with the last link to his past, he didn't know whether to hug her or hit her. She was after all the person who abandoned her. Sensing the awkwardness of the situation, Henry stepped in and addressed Robert.

"Doesn't your sister look great Robert? She's a very important person and extremely busy but didn't hesitate to take the time off to come down here with me to see you."

"Excuse me father, but wasn't that mighty gracious of her? He replied snidely. "Hope this little reunion isn't ruining your professional image or taking up too much of your precious time. But hey, look at it this way sis, you've done your duty and that should suffice for another twenty years or so.

"Robert," Clarissa said softly, "our aunt and I put you in here because we thought that we were doing what was best for you. For Christ sake, she shipped me off too. Granted, it was a boarding school, but none-the-less, she didn't want me either!"

"Is that it? Not being wanted?" Robert said as this tone of voice rose. "And here, for all these years as I read about you in the paper, in legal journals and on the news, I thought it was because you'd forgotten about me, or that I would have tarnished your golden reputation. I'm not sure why you're here now Clarissa; but I am glad you're here and I know it's been hard on you too so I'm sorry about sounding so cold." Feeling a momentary rush of relief, she approached her brother and embraced his waiting arms. As she hugged him, he softly whispered into her ear so that neither Henry nor her husband could hear him.

"I know about you and mother and you will pay dearly sister. I've waited thirty years and it's about time the truth came out about what really happened to our mother don't you think?"

Petrified after hearing the words that she'd been dreading, Claire backed away from Robert. Her ashen white face revealed more to her husband that she imagined and she quickly turned and stepped out into the front yard.

"This is a little too much for me honey," she reassured her concerned husband, "I just need a little air."

Content with her statement, Richard turned back toward his father-in-law and brother-in-law. The three men smiled without saying a word, and Claire retreated to the sanctity of the truck.

"It sure is wonderful meeting you Robert. I only wish that it had been sooner. I'm not making excuses with Claire, but this whole thing has been extremely hard on your sister. I am embarrassed to say it, but you were right about her. When we were married, I came from a very wealthy and powerful family and she decided on her own, whether her decision was rash or not, to come into the marriage as an only child and an orphan. Somehow in her head, that was the easiest way. 'I'm genuinely sorry, but I didn't know of your existence until she told me about Henry, after the riot."

"So, in other words," Robert asked stunned, "She and our father haven't been in touch throughout these years either?"

"I'm afraid not."

"Now that's the self-centered, manipulative sister I remember."

The three men, uncomfortable with their conversation, changed the subject and made small talk. Henry asked Robert once again to join them for lunch, and even with Richard's coaxing, he remained solemn. Explaining that the entire situation was happening too fast for him to handle, he took a rain check but said that he'd definitely consider Henry's and Richard's gracious offer in the near future. Content with Robert's response, they ended their conversation with him and headed back toward the truck where Claire remained. Robert followed just to taunt his still visibly distraught sister a little more.

"Feeling better sis?"

"I'm fine, thank you."

"I'm so glad. We'll have to get together soon and play catch up on the old times, okay?" he asked dryly with a somewhat sinister smile appearing on his face.

"Sure Robert, anytime. I'll look forward to it," she replied; up to the challenge.

"So do I Claire, so do I. We have so much to catch up on."

"Yes we do little brother."

And with the last of the snide remarks sent, he turned to Richard. "It's been very nice meeting you Richard Drake. I'm very grateful to you for bringing my father to me. Thank you from the bottom of my heart."

"Robert, the pleasure is all mine; and you are welcome at our home anytime so please don't hesitate to call."

"I will do just that, Thank You. And father," he said as he stepped closer to Henry. "God has answered my prayers. Thank you for coming back to me. I've missed you so."

As the tears welled up once again in Henry's eyes, he smiled back at his only son. "I have missed you so Robert and I'm so very sorry that I haven't been able to be here for you. Please forgive me."

"You've done nothing wrong father, so there's nothing to forgive. And father, the people who wrongly imprisoned you will pay soon, I'm sure of it."

Not understanding why his son had make that kind of statement, Henry only smiled and said good-bye. Once everyone was inside the truck, Robert waved and turned back toward his home. Within a moment, Henry, Robert and Richard were exiting the facility and heading back toward the city. Everyone was once again silent, trying to absorb the magnitude of the visit.

Chapter 35

Nicole had spent the remainder of the afternoon tucked away in her bedroom, rummaging through boxes and closets. She made rattling and banging sounds for the first hour or so just so that her mother-in-law would think that she was still hard at work, but in reality, she was doing nothing of the sort. Nicole felt bad about the deception, but she desperately wanted to resume reading Rachel's journal. Her husband made it easier for her once he returned with his father from the store. Upon their arrival, her mother-in-law joined them outside to see what they were up to. Nicole opened her bedroom window and acknowledged their presence, stating that she'd be down in a few minutes. Explaining that they'd be tied up for a half hour or so, Nicole felt comfortable in retrieving the journal and opening it once more.

July 2nd

We spent the entire day down by the lake. The sky was a beautiful shade of baby blue and there wasn't a cloud in the sky. Even Clarissa appeared to enjoy herself since I let her girlfriend spend the night. Little Robert is getting so strong these days and the water is a natural therapy for him. His muscle tone and coordination is becoming stronger and more refined and I'm so proud of him. Clarissa is growing into a young woman right before my eyes and the changes in her body frighten me so. She's more developed that I'd hoped she be and I only pray that others don't notice the changes. Richard promised to be home early for supper this evening but then at the last minute he phoned to say that he had to run an errand. I knew what that meant and I went up to the house to mentally prepare myself. I prayed I was wrong but before I had even made my way up the stairs from the lake, there he was lurking in the shadows. Half startled, half furious, I tried to make him leave but as usual, he wouldn't. I decided that it wasn't going to happen today and when I started struggling, he not only hit me but threatened my Clarissa. My worst fear has come true; he has set his sights on her. When I begged him to leave her alone, he just laughed. I swear, I will kill this man. Maybe first, I should tell his wife the truth about her husband. I don't know if she'd believe me or not.

July 4th

Henry spent the day with us today and we had a party for the neighbors. It was a wonderful event until they showed up. I can't believe Henry extended an invitation to them, even after I asked him not to. He tried to rationalize his motives by stating that we couldn't invite some of the neighbors and not others. If only he knew the truth about his dear neighbor. Somehow I think that his wife already suspects something; but she doesn't seem to care. She laughs it off and says he's a natural flirt with all the ladies~~ if she only knew...

I just don't know what to do. I feel like my life is spinning out of control and it's getting to the point where I'm going to have to tell Henry about the baby. I'm beginning to show and he'll figure it out soon enough. Even Clarissa commented that I'm looking heavier and she never pays attention to me anymore. So I must be showing. Henry promised me today that he'd be home early every night this week so I will tell him soon. I love him so and though I'm going through hell right now; I pray that he doesn't blame me for what has been happening.

July 6th

Henry and I went for a moonlight stroll this evening and it was very peaceful. I started to tell him, and again we caught Clarissa eavesdropping. I'm under so much stress these days that I couldn't help it; I started screaming at her to mind her own business. Her one word response summed everything up for me. As she glared at me and screamed "slut" before retreating back to the house, I could tell from her eyes that she knew everything. Or so she thought she did. Henry stood silent, very confused and after I tried to explain his daughter's reaction, I was too mentally drained to tell him the truth. Clarissa and I are going to have to talk this out tomorrow and I pray that she'll listen and then understand.

July 7th

After confronting our daughter this afternoon, I have lost all hope of Henry understanding. Though I thought my love for Clarissa was strong enough to overcome this obstacle between us, obviously it isn't. I tried to make her understand the situation that she's been exposed to, isn't what it seems but she flew into a rage and called me all sorts of horrible names. She threatened me that if I told her father and hurt him; she'd get even with me. She wants me to leave Henry and go away. I've never seen her so angry and when I tried being rational with her, she shoved me out of her way and nearly pushed me down the stairs. Luckily I only fell down the first step before hitting the banister. I have no idea what's gotten into her but I know that it scares me. She never even acknowledged the potential harm that she could have caused me or the baby. Something has got to give...

July 8th

I've been up all night and have decided that this horrible secret needs to come out in the open once and for all. Clarissa hasn't spoken to me since yesterday and hasn't even asked about the bruises that she inflicted. Her temper has become so volatile lately; I'm not sure what we're going to do with her.

As Nicole continued to read the last entry in Rachel's journal, it dawned on her that Rachel had written it just hours before she died. Nicole continued to read the words, flipped back a few pages and then reread those last few entries again. Suddenly it all made sense to her. As she read the passages, she came to the only logical conclusion as to who had really pushed Rachel off that cliff so many years ago. Irritated with herself for not figuring it out sooner, and more irate that the police had not investigated anyone other than Henry, Nicole stretched as she held the journal in the air as a sign of triumph.

"Now how do I get all the players in one room," she thought to herself as she stood to join her family. As she tucked the diary away, she thought of telling Jared what she concluded. And then she thought of Gary Danbarry and his lawyer nephew. Deciding hastily that the fewer people who knew what she was going to do, the better. She skipped down the front stairs, pausing momentarily to look at the banister where Claire had pushed her mother. "That bitch" she thought to herself as she continued down the stairs and out the front door to meet her husband. As she approached the garage, she found her husband and father-in-law working on something resembling a riding mower.

"What is that? And what are you doing?"

"It's our new tractor honey. Dad and I saw an ad in the paper and that's where we went this morning to look at it. Isn't it a beauty?"

"I guess so. That is if tractors can be beautiful. Why is it all apart?"

"Oh we're just greasing it up so it runs smoothly for you Nicole."

"I don't think so Dad Brentwood. I don't do tractors and I don't do lawns."

"You do now. You wanted this big house and big lawn, remember?"

"Yeah right Jared. Say honey, while we're on the subject of being outdoors, why don't we have a barbecue this weekend? We could invite some of the neighbors since it would be a great way to introduce ourselves and to meet everyone. I want people to be comfortable around this house and a party would be a great ice-breaker."

"I don't know Nicki. We've still got so much to do around here. The place isn't quite ready for a party yet, don't you think?"

"No one expects the place to be perfect Jared. Besides, I want to invite Henry Harteman over and allow him to spend some time around his old friends and neighbors."

"Wait a minute Nicole," Jared responded as he quickly made his way to his feet and stared directly at Nicole. "I know that you're doing what you think is right, but Nicole, we don't even know the man for Christ sake, and he just got out of prison remember?"

"Even more reason that we should include him honey. A great injustice was done to him and his family and if inviting Henry into our home, his former home, could somehow heal a few of his wounds, I think it would be worth it. "Please," she smiled coyly, "It would mean a lot to me."

"Oh why not Jared," his father intervened. "He's paid his debt to society, and even if he did kill her; he's no threat to you."

"What? Are you out of your mind?" Jared retorted, without even thinking of whom he was addressing.

"No son, I'm not" he huffed. "I think that sometimes we need to give people second chances and if your wife believes that strongly in his character and his innocence, I think we should give her the benefit of the doubt and let her trust her instincts. She was right about you, wasn't she?" Knowing that he was defeated, Jared reluctantly shook his head and grated his teeth together as he answered his father's question.

-273-

"Fine. We'll have a party here this weekend and Henry Harteman can come."

"Thanks Jared. You won't regret it, I promise."

Nicole skipped out of the garage and back toward the house before her husband could say another word, and he stood silently, still gazing at the path that she had taken. He hoped and prayed that his wife's intuition didn't fail them on this one, because if she was wrong about the man, then he had just given his wife permission to invite a murderer into their home. The thought made him shutter as he crouched back down to work on the dismantled tractor.

Nicole quickly made her way back into the kitchen and retrieved her cell phone. Checking to make sure she was alone, she opened up the phone book. She fumbled momentarily with the pages until she found the number that she was looking for and without hesitation, dialed the number as it appeared on the page. Within two rings, the call was answered by a familiar voice on the other end of the line.

"Hello."

"Hello. This is Nicole Brentwood. Is your husband in?"

"Sure Miss; hold a second and I'll get him for you."

"Certainly, take your time."

The silence on the other end was killing Nicole as she waited for him to come to the phone. She second guessed herself briefly, then assured herself that yes she was doing what was right for everyone. She started to hear footsteps approaching on the other end of the line and her heart rate increased as she waited to hear his voice.

"Hello Mrs. Brentwood; Gary Danbarry here."

"Hello Mr. Danbarry. Sorry to bother you but I just had to tell someone and you're the only one I can trust with the information."

Excited by the tone of her voice, Gary could feel his palms beginning to sweat.

"What is it Nicole? I mean Mrs. Brentwood. What is this all about?"

"I can't explain everything over the phone, but I think I know who really killed Rachel Harteman and I need your help to prove it! Can we meet this evening so I can show you what I've found?"

"Sure. Just say when and where and we'll be there."

"Great! But I also need you and your wife to be present at a housewarming party I've throwing this Saturday afternoon. I believe that the truth will come out then."

"Absolutely, we wouldn't miss it for the world! Miss, are you sure about this?"

"Surer than I've ever been in my life."

After Nicole and Gary decided on a place to meet, she went about making the other necessary phone calls and then sat down to phone her next door neighbor Betty. Being there the longest, she knew that Mrs. Langhorne would have everyone's names and numbers on the street; and Nicole had determined early on that Betty was the local gossip so she'd have the scoop on who to invite and who to avoid.

"Mrs. Langhorne, this is your neighbor Nicole Brentwood. I was wondering if you could help me."

Before either knew what was happening, Nicole had smooth talked her way into obtaining all the necessary phone numbers from her unsuspecting neighbor. Betty did seem a little skeptical of her new neighbor inviting people that they hadn't even met to a party for no reason, but when Nicole assured her that she needn't bring anything, her reluctant neighbor quickly warmed up. Nicole's plan was falling into place perfectly. She thanked Betty and after hanging up with her, phoned each neighbor, explaining who she was and what she was doing. Young and old, all of Brentwood's neighbors graciously accepted her invitation; many of whom she believed accepted the invite more out of curiosity than desire to meet the new owners. Unbeknownst to them, they were not only going to see the Harteman's house again, but the remaining Harteman family, in a way they never imagined.

Now that the neighbors were all accounted for, Nicole made the most crucial call of all. As she waited for someone to answer the phone at the Drake household, her heart began to pound. The anticipation was so intense that she felt more and more nauseous with each ring of the phone. Just as she was about to hang up in despair, she heard a voice pick up on the other end. Fearing that the female voice was Claire herself, she strained to identify the speaker.

"Hello, Drake residence."

"Ah yes, is Mr. Drake in?"

"Yes, may I ask who's calling?"

"Yes, my name is Nicole Brentwood and I am a friend of his father-in-law." Hearing Henry's name mentioned, Rosa immediately warmed up to the voice on the other end.

"Just one moment Senora Brentwood; this is Rosa; we sort of met the other day."

"Yes, Rosa, we did. You were the driver when Henry stopped by. It was very nice of you to do that for him and I hope that I will be seeing you again real soon. The invite that I'm extending to Mr. Drake includes you as Henry's guest; just so you know. And I believe that you'll be very happy if you accept it and come with him."

"Thank you Mrs. Brentwood. Please wait one moment and I'll get Mr. Drake for you."

"It will be nicer than you think Rosa, especially when I reveal who the real murderer is. Your life is about to get even better than you thought possible Rosa," Nicole said to herself as she waited for Richard Drake to come to the phone.

"Hello, this is Richard Drake."

"Mr. Drake, this is Nicole Brentwood, and I'm calling you to ask your presence along with your wife and father-in-law at my house this Saturday. Please let me explain why."

After giving the Honorable Richard Drake the best snow job that she could think of, but doing it with such sincerity, Nicole waited with baited breath to see if he'd bite. The tension mounted as the seconds passed. After thinking it over in his head, Richard hesitantly said but one word.

"Yes."

"Yes? Are you serious?" Nicole rejoiced. "You'll really help me prove Henry's innocence? Oh, how can I ever thank you?"

"You already have Miss Brentwood if what you're saying is true. You already have."

After giving him the additional details, she added one last request and upon hearing it, Richard smiled to himself as he complied.

"Yes Miss Bentwood, I'll see to it that Henry invites Rosa too. You're right, she is a special person."

After the brief exchange was over, Nicole felt like she had won the battle but now knew she must prepare herself for the war of her life. She didn't envy Richard Drake's position either for she knew that his wife would be very reluctant to set foot in her childhood home again. She wasn't even sure if Henry himself would be up to the event but she believed in her heart that what she was about to do was for the best. Realizing that the truth was going to destroy a family but reunite another, Nicole felt almost remorseful about what she was undertaking, but the wheel had already been set in motion and there was no way of stopping it now. She couldn't allow her mind to second guess herself. And she suddenly realized how much was needed in order to get the house and grounds ready for the number of people she had invited. As she hung up the phone, she glanced out at the wind chime, hanging motionless above the veranda.

"I'm doing this for you Rachel. I hope that you can rest in peace after Saturday," she thought to herself as she stared at the dainty angels.

While lost in thought, Nicole jumped at the ring of her cell phone.

"Yes, hey Miss Brentwood, this is Betty Langhorne again."

"Hello Mrs. Langhorne, what can I do for you?"

"Two things; first of all call me Betty and don't say no when I tell you I'm going to bring some of my famous chocolate chip cookies to the party and second, there's one more number that I have for you that I didn't give you before. You see, I thought that she was still in Florida visiting her son Tony but Bart says she got back just this week."

"Oh, okay, sure. Who's that Betty?"

"Angela Carelli. She's the last house on our street before you intersect Maple. She's a little crazy but is usually the life of any party; you'll like her, she's spunky like you!"

Nicole gasped as she heard the last name. Trying to contain her surprise and shock, she asked nonchalantly, "I've heard that name before, is she related to anyone famous?" she asked, trying to play ignorant.

"More like infamous if you ask me. Her ex-husband is Nicolas Carelli, the mobster. But rest assured miss, that was his business, not hers. She wasn't involved in any of that illegal stuff. She's just a good, down to earth kind of gal."

"I see. Well, thank you Betty. Why don't you give me her number and I'll certainly invite her. Thank You."

Upon getting her neighbor's phone number, Nicole thanked her busy body neighbor and hung up before her excitement became too evident. She couldn't believe that all along, Nicolas Carelli's ex-wife was living just a few doors down from her. Nicole wondered if they had lived there when Rachel and Henry occupied the house, although she was certain that she already knew the answer to her question. Rapidly the pieces of the puzzle were falling into place and Nicole was becoming more excited by the minute.

"So that's how come it was so easy for Carelli to sneak over to see Rachel when Henry was gone. Henry had to literally drive by their home on his way to anywhere. Carelli probably met Rachel and saw something he wanted, so he convinced Henry that he needed to live out here, when in reality is was for Carelli's convenience all along. "What a fucking asshole," Nicole thought to herself as she stared out at the lake below. "What a prick. Now how do I tell Henry that if he had never moved his wife out here, she'd probably still be alive today," Nicole asked silently of herself. "I don't. Henry's going to be shocked enough when this whole scenario unfolds and he realizes who really killed his wife. He doesn't need to know the details about Carelli too. Those secrets went to the grave with Rachel and that's where they'll stay."

The rest of the week went by quickly for both Jared and Nicole. Having returned to work, Nicole ran errands every night after leaving the hospital. The house was shaping up nicely and the yard looked presentable for the upcoming gathering. Nicole spent her evenings once home, baking and organizing her supplies for the party. Wednesday afternoon after work, she swung by the one neighbor that she hadn't spoken with on the phone, to invite her in person. With a loaf of homemade bread in hand, Nicole approached the Carelli home with apprehension and a bit of fear. She was anxious to see how the woman would not only receive her, but her invitation. Her stomach started to turn as she reached for the doorbell. Before she could get herself worked up into a frenzy, the door swing open and she was greeted by a smiling, very young appearing woman in spandex.

"If you're not selling anything, I bet you must be Nicole," the petite woman announced.

A little started that she knew who she was, Nicole stood silent for a moment, trying to gather her senses.

"Ah, yes, I'm Nicole, Nicole Brentwood, your new neighbor down the street."

"I know who you are and all about you; won't you come in?" she said as she swung the door open and motioned for Nicole to step inside. Still surprised and somewhat intimidated, she did as the middle aged woman asked but not before making a visual note of her surroundings. As she stepped out of the foyer and into the living area, she could see that even though this woman was divorced, she'd certainly done well for herself. The room revealed numerous oil paintings on the walls, some of which Nicole recognized as originals by a famous Italian artist, though she couldn't recall his name, and the furniture was not only exquisite, but very ornate in character. The white plush carpet set off the dark walls, creating a feeling of not only warmth, but serenity. Two German Shepherds sat at attention near the hearth of the marble fireplace but remained motionless as she approached the room. Realizing that she was still holding the loaf of bread, she turned to her neighbor and smiled.

"This is for you. It's Amish Friendship Bread, and I hope you like it."

"Thank you Nicole. I can call you Nicole, can't I?"

"But of course. Mrs. Brentwood is too formal, besides that's my mother-in-law," she said with a grin. "If you knew my name, and I assume you weren't surprised by me stopping here, then I assume you know the nature of my visit?"

"Yes. Betty informed me that you were having a little get together for the neighbors in your new home. And the answer is yes, if" she responded.

"If? If what?"

"IF, and only if, I can bring something," the dark haired woman responded as her deep set brown eyes sparkled. "I know that you're a working woman, and all I do it sit around here and go with the gals to Bunko night and weekly golf lessons, which I might add, haven't helped me improve in my game for the last ten years," she added with a wink. "I have so much free time on my hands and I do so love a good party; I insist on bringing a dish or two to pass around."

Thrilled by not only the acceptance of the invitation; but also the offer, Nicole answer showed in her smile. "If you'd like to bring something that would be great and would be much appreciated, thank you. I'm not a very good cook so I won't pass up free home cooked food!"

"Well then it's settled. I'll bring two trays of Lasagna, one traditional and one vegetable, and a big ass tray of homemade cannolis, if that's okay with you."

"Are you serious? That would be great, but I don't want to put you to too much trouble Mrs. Carelli."

"Please call me Angelina or Angie for short. I hate the name Carelli and though it was once my name, I don't admit to it anymore. I've since remarried and divorced a couple of times, so technically, my last name is Smith. Don't ya just love it? About as Italian as it gets for a last name, and now as American as apple pie! I got rid of that last name as soon as we divorced; got tired of the association."

"I'm very sorry Angelina," Nicole responded, somewhat embarrassed. "I was told that your name was Carelli, and I apologize for the misunderstanding."

"It's okay, I know that Betty told you about me, as she's notorious for spreading anything she considers juicy information. She used to have a field day when I was married to Nicholas. Funny thing is, she should have paid more attention to what was happening under her own roof and not worried so much about her neighbor's business."

Curious, Nicole asked meekly, "What do you mean Angelina?"

"Nothing honey. I sometimes ramble far too much. It's ancient history and really not important anymore. The past is the past and that's where it should stay." Shifting her petite frame on the sofa and petting the half asleep dog resting his head in her lap, Angelina smiled as she continued. "A lot of terrible and crazy things occurred around here years ago, some of which I'm sure you already know about. You'd have to since you bought Rachel's old house, and that's one thing I want to commend you on. You and your husband have done a wonderful job in restoring her house and I know she's very proud of what you've done."

Confused by her statement being in present tense but not wanting to end the conversation, Nicole let her comments go and tried desperately to keep her host talking. Nicole smiled at the dog now completely asleep and snoring in Angelina's lap.

"What was Rachel like Angelina? I sense from the house that she was a very strong woman, yet very refined."

"That woman had more sophistication in her little pinky than most people could ever hope for. She was beautiful and articulate and could charm the skin off an alligator if she wanted to. But most of all, she was a dear friend and a wonderful mother. She had a baby who was born ill you know. Everyone said that she should award him to the state, but she wouldn't hear of it. She treated him just like she'd treat anyone and never admitted to him or herself that he had limitations. Before she died, he was making such strides and I've always wondered what became of him. Shame, isn't it? I mean, shortly after her tragic accident, Henry's gone, Robert's gone and all's that left is Henry's insane sister and his snotty spoiled daughter to inherit everything."

"He's institutionalized at Brymar Institute," Nicole said off the cuff, quickly realizing that she probably should have kept her mouth shut.

Curious, Angelina looked at her guest in amazement, "How do you know about Robert" And what else do you know about the Harteman family?"

Stumbling, trying to find the appropriate words, Nicole simply answered with the truth.

"I went to the library and researched the murder prior to us buying the house. A few of the articles mentioned the children and how old they were at the time of the accident."

Taking the opportunity to press her luck, Nicole asked the next question.

"Speaking of children, what was Clarissa like?"

"She was a spoiled rotten little brat. I couldn't stand her, especially in the way she treated her mother. That girl needed a good beating with a belt and she would have straightened out but Rachel never saw the devil in her. She loved her children with all her heart and soul and to her, that little bitch could do no wrong." Angelina stared down at her dog and started petting the sleeping animal as she tried to calm herself down. She had never liked Henry and Rachel's first born and made no qualms about it back then, and certainly not now.

"And I'll tell you another thing. The only good thing that kid did was become a lawyer because it was her that kept my son of a bitch ex-husband right where he should be, that is, in jail. Of course, I know of a few other people that the law needs to catch up with besides him, but that's another story."

Knowing when to not push the issue any further, Nicole just smiled and kept her thoughts to herself. She liked Angelina Carelli-Smith and was glad that the woman was going to attend her party but she couldn't help but wonder if she knew that her ex-husband had been sleeping with her so-called good friend. Though friendly on the outside, she realized that this woman was more than what met the eye.

"What about Bart and Betty Langhorne? Have they lived here long?" Nicole asked innocently, knowing full well what the answer was. "They seem like really nice people."

"Oh Bart's a wonderful man," Angelina quickly responded with a twinkle appearing in her eye, "But Betty's one tough old bird. She's always after him for one thing or another. She's always treated him badly but after she became ill with cancer a few years back, she became worse. She hardly lets him out of her sight without giving him the Spanish Inquisition when he returns. He used to come over and do odd jobs for me now that I'm alone here, but she won't even let him do that anymore. She must be pitching a fit now that she' got you living right next door; you being Rachel's double and all."

"What do you mean?"

"Well," Angelina said as if she was finding great pleasure in the conversation, "Betty used to be insanely jealous of Rachel, even though they were good friends. She was always accusing Bart of sleeping around but little did she know it wasn't Rachel that he was messing with. He had several female friends over the years, but he never once touched Rachel. She loved her husband and he worshipped her you know. Bet you didn't find that in any newspaper articles?"

"No I didn't. But I did read that Rachel was pregnant with another man's baby at the time of her death," Nicole said softly.

"Yeah, I know. My scum of a husband was poking her whenever he had a chance. But that relationship was all one sided. He was obsessed with her. When I found out and threatened to tell Henry and leave him, all hell broke loose and before I knew it, Rachel was dead."

"Why didn't you tell the police about your husband's affair and motive for killing her?" Nicole blurted out.

"And wind up dead like Rachel? Why would I? She was dead and she wasn't coming back, and besides, they would never have believed me. I had a pretty shady past before I married Nicholas, one that we won't get into here, and my wonderful husband, according to the general public was an upstanding citizen, a pillar of the community. They would have never believed me and back then they didn't have DNA analysis like they do now. I would have lost everything so be it morally wrong or not; I kept my mouth shut and got a quick but profitable divorce as soon as possible."

"And Henry got life," Nicole flippantly responded back with unintended sarcasm in her tone.

"Yes, he did. And for that, I'm truly sorry. I've corresponded with Henry over the years you know. I even set up a trust fund in his name for the day he gets out of prison," Angelina said solemnly, looking genuinely remorseful. "I'm sure the day will come when he's finally freed and when he is, he'll be a very rich man."

Realizing that Angelina had been in Florida during the time of the riot and Henry's subsequent pardon, Nicole quickly surmised that Angelina had no idea that he was already a free man.

"That was a very kind thing to do Angelina, especially in light of the fact that some of your husband's actions are what caused Henry to be in prison in the first place. But let's not get into that," Nicole interjected quickly. "Let's just hope and pray that Henry's able to use that money in the near future."

"Nicholas didn't kill Rachel if that's what you're insinuating Miss Brentwod. He was a womanizer and a loser, but he idolized Rachel. Sure it pissed me off that he was sleeping with someone else, but the way he looked at her wasn't sexual, it was almost mystical. There was something about Rachel that drew men in, just the way it did my husband, Henry and even Bart. She possessed such charm that it was ever consuming and men couldn't help but be attracted to her."

"I'm sorry Angelina," Nicole said, softening the tone of her voice. "I never meant to throw your husband up in your face, but it seems only logical that if he was in fact messing around with Rachel and she was pregnant, that he would be a natural suspect."

"Yes, but as I said before, he idolized her and would never have harmed her. Deep down I think he was in love with her but didn't even know it. But I do know that if Henry didn't do it, I don't know who did. And I know that as much as I hate the bastard, I'd stake my life on the fact that Nicholas didn't do it either."

Standing to leave, Nicole stared deeply into the mascara riddled dark brown eyes that suddenly showed a lot of pain.

"Thank you for sharing that with me. I know that bringing up the past must be hard on you and I promise I'll never mention it again, nor will I ever mention what we discussed in this room. I must get going before my husband wonders where I've been, but before I leave, you've got to promise me that you'll make it to our party this Saturday, with or without your Lasagna and Canoli's," Nicole asked shining her pearly white teeth.

"The answer is yes and with the food," the older woman smiled back as she made her way toward the door. "If your husband is as full of life and energy as you are, I can't wait to meet him! Thank you again for the invitation and I'll see you in a few days."

"Great, I'll see you then."

With that, Nicole was out the door and heading to her car. Her head was spinning wildly reviewing their conversation again and again. Something Angelina had said now made sense out of one of Rachel's passages. But what was it? Nicole tried to retrieve the bit of information from her subconscious unsuccessfully as she got into her car and headed in the direction of her house. "Oh well, it'll come back to me when I least expect it."

The rest of the week flew by and before Jared and Nicole knew it, it was Saturday morning. They woke to the sound of birds chirping outside their window. As Nicole got up and pulled back the shade to catch a glimpse at the source of the noise, she glanced out over the water, which was dead calm. There were only a few fishing boats still out on the water. Nicole realized that it was probably later than she thought. The sky had a deep blue hue to it and had a few scattered clouds surrounding the sun. Overall, the day looked like it was going to be a perfect day for a picnic. As she sprung out of bed, her husband stirred and started to wake up. By the time he was fully conscious, she was already in the shower. As he stretched, he stated thinking about all the last minute things that needed to be accomplished before the afternoon and starting to panic; he jumped out of bed and joined her in the bathroom.

"Whose dumb idea was this to have a party anyway?" he said as he lathered up his face.

"Mine and it's going to be a party that no one's ever going to forget, trust me on that one," the voice said from the steamy shower stall.

"Why do you say that Nicole? What are you up to now?" he asked, showing concern in his voice.

"I'm not up to anything honey. Relax. It's just going to be a great party that's all," she replied, feeling somewhat guilty about lying to her husband. But she also knew that if she confided in him with her suspicions, he'd never allow the event to take place. "Now why don't you stop worrying and join me in here. I'll wash your back..." she said in her best seductive voice. "We don't have time for that right now Nicole. We've got to get the tables set up, and pick up the half keg, and arrange the vegetable platters, and" he stopped mid-sentence as Nicole opened up the shower door and used her sudsy hands to caress her breasts and abdomen. Jared stared as she made additional gestures that he could not refuse. Within a minute, he was immersed under the flow of the water and had warmth of her flesh against his. He had never been able to refuse her charm, nor did he really try to. Soon the honey-do list was far from his mind as he reached ecstasy with his best friend and lover.

The rest of the morning was not nearly as much fun for the two of them but regardless, still passed surprisingly fast. Jared left with Nicole's brother to pick up the ice and beer, while Nicole and Gwen set up the tables once they were delivered. They worked together silently for quite some time when Gwen blurted out something that surprised Nicole and even herself.

"I'm really falling for Jimmy you know."

"I know, and I think it's great" Nicole replied nonchalantly. "I just don't want to see either of you hurt that's all. After all, he's my brother, and you're my best friend."

"I'm a big girl now Nicki and I'm not going to get hurt. With a little luck," she said with a grin, "Maybe I'll become a little girl someday. All of a sudden, I have a desire to shed a few pounds, and the way your brother is in bed, it might be a lot more fun losing weight. It certainly beats aerobics," she said as they both laughed.

"Just be careful Gwen."

"Always Nicki, always. Say, why the sudden desire to have a party right after moving in anyway?" Gwen asked, changing the subject away from her weight.

"Can you keep a secret Gwen? I mean, you've got to swear to keep your mouth shut no matter what I tell you," Nicole asked with a devilish look in her eyes.

Now , intrigued, Gwen stopped what she was doing and gave Nicole a serious look. "Of course I can Nicki. What's going on?"

"You can't even tell Jimmy Gwen, promise?"

"Nicole, I promise. What?"

Nicole squared herself in front of her friend and reached over and touched her hand. She took a deep breath and slowly revealed her well-kept secret.

"Gwen, you know how I've said all along that Henry Harteman didn't murder his wife. Well, I'm positive now and today I'm going to prove it. The real murderer will be at the party along with Henry Harteman and today is the day that Henry will be vindicated."

"What the hell are you talking about Nicole?" Gwen shrieked in disbelief. "'Just what I said Gwen; I've invited all the neighbors, along with Henry and his family, and today Henry's going to find out who really killed his wife."

"Holy shit Nicole; and just how are you going to do that? It's not like the murderer is going to confess to a crime that he committed thirty years ago."

"No, but she will if I play my cards right."

"She; you said she! Nicole, who do you think killed Rachel?"

"I'm not ready to say yet because I haven't quite worked out all the details yet. The murderer has been carrying around the guilt for such a long time and I think that's why she's the way she is. She's been a bitch ever since I met her and I couldn't understand why she was so miserable and cold, now I know why."

"You think it's Claire Drake don't you?" Gwen exclaimed triumphantly. "I knew it. I thought that woman was hiding something. Why else would a smart individual like herself sell this house for such a miniscule amount of money? She was hiding something and wanted to get rid of it and the memories."

Gwen sat confidently as Nicole just shook her head. "I've never said that Claire Drake murdered her mother, but I will admit, that woman's one cold bitch. And I'll give you the fact that this place does indeed hold terrible memories for her. But I never said that I think she did it. I don't like her and that's why I have a few surprises in for her. We'll see how calm and cool our little D.A. is when I get through with her."

"I knew it," Gwen continued to squeal. "I just knew it."

"Gwen, maybe she is the one and maybe she isn't. But for now, you've got to promise me to keep your mouth shut and your ears open once the guests start arriving. Deal?"

"My lips are sealed," Gwen said as she made the gesture to button her lips.

"Good."

"But can't you give me just a little hint?" Gwen teased.

Nicole's glare told her the answer and Gwen responded back by again buttoning her lips and smiling. The women went back to work without discussing the subject any further. As they worked in silence, they were interrupted when Nicole heard the phone ringing. As she raced in through the veranda, she glanced up at her beautiful wind chime that was hanging motionless by the atrium doors. Racing to get her cell, she didn't bother to admire their state of perfection as they hung suspended in air. Within a few moments, she exited the house to resume the preparation to find Gwen nowhere in sight. As she neared the bluff, she found her lounging in one of the hunter green Adirondack chairs that came with the house. Practically asleep, Gwen didn't stir until Nicole was planting herself by her side. Without even turning her head, Gwen asked her one last question.

"Just a little hint?"

"You're a pain in the ass."

"No, that would be your brother Nicki."

"Ah gross Gwen I don't want to hear that; he's my brother for god sake so spare me the details! Yuck!"

"I wasn't going to give you the details. Hey, look it's been three years since I've been laid so I'll take it any way I can get it."

Changing the subject, Nicole got up and started back towards the house.

"Come on, we've got celery to chop and carrots to peel. You can tell me about your sexual romps with my brother later."

"Yeah, yeah, yeah," Gwen said as she made her way to her feet. "You got any fat free dressing for those veggies?"

"Bottom shelf, on the right," Nicole responded suddenly thinking that maybe her brother hooking up with Gwen wasn't such a bad idea. If it gave Gwen incentive to take better care of herself, and Jimmy incentive to remain sober, then the matchup would be worth it.

Before they knew it, Jared and Jimmy were back from their beer run. Everything was coming together nicely for the party. As they finished the final preparations, Nicole gasped when she realized that it was already 3:30pm and her guests would be arriving within an hour or so. She rushed outside to find Gwen, Jimmy and Jared all talking around the keg. As she approached them, she got a sinking feeling in her stomach when she saw her brother with a beer glass in his hand. Almost ready her mind, he smiled and tipped it in her direction His 6'2" body hovered over her as she got closer.

"Relax sis, it's only soda. I'm being good. I've got a reason to be good now," he said as he glanced over at Gwen.

"Sorry Jimmy; guess I was playing mom again huh?"

"Yeah, but it's okay. Say, shouldn't we get ready soon. What time does this shin dig start?"

"In about an hour."

"What?" Jared exclaimed, looking at his watch and simultaneously jumping up.

Everyone took their cues and headed inside. Nicole and Jared entered their bedroom after directing their guests to the spare bedrooms. Jimmy thanked his sister, grabbed his towel and rushed to Gwen's bath once his sister shut her bedroom door. As the remaining minutes flew by, everyone hustled to get ready. As Nicole dressed, she could hear noises coming from outside. As she looked out the window, she was slightly irritated at the thought of guest arriving nearly a half an hour early but quickly diffused once she realized that it was only a few of her brothers and their families. Fastening the remaining buttons on her blouse as she bounded down the stairs to answer the door, she was greeted by Jimmy in the foyer.

"Hey Nick," he asked with a serious tone in his voice. "Are you okay with Gwen and me?"

She smiled softly, "Yes Jimmy. I only want you to be happy."

"Oh Nicki," he gleamed, I've never been happier."

"Then I'm happy for you, for both of you." She awkwardly put her arm around her brother and smiled again. "Let's get outside and start this party!"

"Let's do this little sis," he agreed as he reached for the door as the doorbell chime resonated in the foyer.

Nicole opened the door and welcomed in her first guest and family members. She saw that Bart and Betty increased their pace to be part of the first group inside, which didn't surprise her in the least. She greeted each individual guest and with Jared now at her side, welcomed them into their new home.

As Bart and Betty entered the house for the first time in years, Betty's mouth dropped open when she realized that the house had been restored almost exactly as Rachel had once had it. She stood awestruck at the colors Nicole had chosen and the furnishings. As she tapped Bart on the shoulder to get his attention, her eyes left the Brentwood's dining room and scanned their formal living room. Now that she finally had her husband's attention diverted away from Nicole, she leaned over whispering into his ear.

"Look at this place. It's as if she never left. How'd she do it?"

"I don't know how she did it, but isn't it wonderful? It's as if Rachel's back," he replied as a grin formed on his narrow face. "She's back in her home where she belongs."

"Oh damn Rachel! She must have seen pictures of how they had it and copied them, that's all," Betty reassured herself.

"No, I don't think so," the voice from behind them whispered. Stunned, they turned around to be face to face with Angelina Carelli. She was dressed in a silver and white sequined T-shirt and white tight fitting slacks that held her aging body together nicely. Her mascara covered eyelashes and dark brown eyes opened wide as she addressed her neighbors.

"It's eerie isn't it? She's been gone for so long and now she's back to haunt us through Nicole and this damn house. I told you long ago Betty; we hadn't seen the last of her. Even death couldn't keep her from this house."

"What are you talking about Angie? You're crazy. She's dead, God rest her soul, and she's not coming back."

"What about what happened to you out on the bluff," Angelina asked quietly moving them away from the foyer and out of earshot. Betty turned to glare at Bart who remained silent.

"Don't get mad at your husband. Yes, he told me about your fall; he was just so relieved to have you back relatively unharmed."

"I wasn't exactly unharmed Angie."

"Well you made out better than poor Rachel did on that cliff, wouldn't you say?"

"Stop it, both of you," Bart shouted over the other commotion in the foyer. "Would you two just stop it, he repeated as he fretted nervously. "We're here for a party, not to relive that horrible event. Let's forget about both accidents, and that's what they both were, just terrible accidents."

"What makes you so sure Bart darling?" Angelina asked with a cynical tone in her voice, trying to catch the feeble minded man off guard."

"Because I was there! Now drop it! What's done is done and we can't change the past."

"You witnessed Rachel's murder," Angelina pried, trying to contain her excitement.

"Of course not," Betty snapped. "He witnessed my accident from the upstairs window and if he hadn't I would have been a goner. Isn't that what you meant Bart?" she asked as she glared at her husband.

Taking her direct cue, Bart's eyes darted toward the floor as he felt more beads of perspiration forming on his brow.

"Of course that's what I meant Angie," he said with a forced half grin.

"Besides, everyone knows that your husband was the second most logical suspect, that is after Henry, of course," Betty interjected.

"Look, just because my husband was fucking her doesn't mean he killed her off. That doesn't even make sense Betty."

Nicole stood frozen beside Gary Danberry listening to the entire conversation between the three older neighbors, oblivious to the fact that their voices easily carried across the room.

"Actually it does Betty. It makes a lot of sense for Nick to have killed her once she started showing with that baby she was carrying," snickering with an antagonistic grin.

"People who live in glass houses shouldn't throw stones toots," Angie replied back as she looked over Betty's shoulder to see Nicole and a slightly heavy set dark haired gentleman standing but a few feet away. In their heated discussion, they had become completely oblivious to the influx of guests who had entered the house. Anxious to end their conversation anyway, Angelina straightened the bottom of her blouse, puffed her voluptuous bosom out, put on her best smile and strutted toward Nicole.

"Well good evening Nicole. You didn't tell me you were going to have Chippendale models here. What's this one's name?" she asked extending her hand to the now beet red faced man.

"My name is Gary mam, Gary Danbarry and it's a pleasure to meet you."

Taking his hand into hers and placing her left hand on top, she smiled and batted her eyelashes, revealing her heavily shadow covered lids.

"Angelina, Angelina Smith and the pleasure's all mine."

Moving in closer, she flashed her perfect teeth again and continued her flirting.

"Say, you're not the one who moved into the Shelby house are you?"

"No mam, I don't live in this neck of the woods."

"Oh," she replied, somewhat puzzled. "I thought the Brentwoods were just having neighbors over."

Stepping back into the conversation, Nicole interceded on Gary's behalf. "Gary's my second cousin, once removed. You're going to see a lot of my family roaming around here Angelina. I wanted to show everyone the new place."

"I think that's great; just wished he was a new neighbor," she said as she winked quickly at Gary and then excused herself.

"Wow! What was that all about?" he said as he shook his hand out. She had such a death grip on me; I didn't think she'd ever let go."

"By the sounds of it, she wanted to get hold of a few other things too. Good thing Mrs. Danbarry's outside; could have turned into a cat fight!"

Turning red again, he quickly asked "Did you hear the conversation those three were having? Who are the other two anyway?"

"They are my next door neighbors, Bart and Betty Langhorne."

"What's up with their discussion? He asked still puzzled.

"Well, for starters, Angelina's former married name was Carelli, as in Nicholas Carelli's ex."

"No shit! I mean, really?"

"Yeah and I sort of have the feeling that there's a little more going on between Bart and Angelina than meets the eye."

"You mean that old man and her? No way," he said as he shook his head in disbelief. "There's no way she'd go for someone as frumpy as him."

"Oh, that's right, you're more her style Mr. Chippendale," she winked. "I didn't mean that I think that they're currently involved. I just think that they're been something between them in the past.

After all, her husband was off screwing women all over the place, why shouldn't she get a little on the side too?"

"Now you're confusing me. Carelli was screwing Henry's wife and his wife was getting it on with her husband and the neighbor and whoever else?"

"Right."

"So this place is better than Payton Place?"

"Right."

"Wow; maybe I need to move into this neighborhood."

"Mr. Danbarry," Nicole exclaimed somewhat exasperated.

"Just kidding; so do you think that this Carelli dame knocked off Rachel for sleeping with her husband or what? Or do you think Carelli did the dirty work himself or had her killed?"

"I don't think Angelina cared what her former husband was doing, nor with whom as long as she continued to reap the benefits of his empire. And as I said before, I think she had companionship on the side too, so she was content."

"Well then, who do you think killed Rachel Harteman?"

Before she was forced to respond, her husband entered the room. With majority of their guests now out on the veranda and scattered throughout the yard, Nicole quickly made her way toward him after excusing herself. As she passed the atrium door, she glanced outside to see that many of her guests and family members had indeed arrived without her knowledge. Feeling that they must have come when her attention was diverted on Gary and Angelina's conversation, she hastened her pace toward her spouse.

-300-

"What is it Jared?"

"There's someone here to see you," he said with a somber face.

"As Nicole listened to his words and rounded the corner, she came face to face with Henry and Richard Drake. Claire and Rosa remained back behind them as if frozen in the parlor. Unaware of Nicole's presence, Claire stood motionless, staring up the stairwell as if expecting to see her mother at any moment. Breaking the silence, Nicole greeted her guest and it was only then that Claire snapped out of her spell.

"I am so glad you could make it Mr. Harteman, I mean Henry. Welcome home."

As the words left her lips, Nicole could see the emotional impact it was having on Henry. She directed her attention toward Claire who remained unmoved by the events unfolding.

"Beautiful day for your party Miss Brentwood; Thank you for including us," Richard offered.

"Yes, thank you Nicole for making the house look alive again," Henry smiled. "Rachel will be very happy."

"Father," Claire snapped. "Mother's dead so she can't be happy. I told you coming here was a bad idea. I think we should leave," she dictated to her father as she gave her husband an evil glare. "Don't you agree Richard?"

Clearing this throat, he ignored his wife and spoke directly to his father-in-law.

"Henry, I'm more than willing to stay if you're okay with being here."

Before Henry had a chance to answer, he looked past his son-in-law and a look of shock came over his face. Unable to say a word, Henry remained speechless as Claire, Rosa and Richard turned to see what was holding Henry's attention. Claire felt the color drain from her face as she watched in horror as her brother entered the room. Still in a state of disbelief, Henry slowly replaced his shock with joy as his long lost son approached him.

"Surprise father."

"Robert, Oh my God! How did you?"

Turning toward Nicole, he finished his question as he took his son in his arms.

"How did you know about Robert and where to find him Nicole?" he whispered. "Are you some sort of angel or something?" Henry uttered as he pulled his son in closer.

Nicole, with tears in her eyes simply smiled at the two men.

"No Henry, I'm not an angel but I think I've had one on my side for some time now; and her name is Rachel. But in regards to locating your son, Rosa was the one who led me to him."

Claire glared at her hostess as a look of hatred came over her face.

"How dare you! How dare you bring up my mother! You didn't even know her or know what she was like."

"Clarissa!"

"No, Mr. Harteman, it's all right," Nicole reassured him as Jared stood helpless as his wife directed her response straight at Claire who was ready to spit her venom at anyone within striking distance.

"Contrary to your belief Mrs. Drake, I know a lot more about your mother than you might think. And I know a lot more about her murder, not accident," she offered as she glanced over at Angelina and the Langhorne's who were within ear shot. "And Mrs. Drake, I know a lot more about you and what really happened that night."

Sensing that she was definitely getting under her skin, Nicole continued on her attack on Claire's composure.

"Did you know that your mother kept a journal right up until the day that she was murdered?"

Nicole watched what was left of the color in her face slowly drain out, in self-satisfaction while Henry spoke up.

"I remember that journal. I bought it for my dear Rachel after we moved into this house."

"I know Henry. I hope you don't mind, but I've read her entries."

"You had no right," Claire screamed like a caged animal; not meaning to let her anger and lack of control come through.

"She had every right," Richard finally spoke up after listening to the debate in silence up to that point.

"Yeah sis, afraid there's something in there that the world shouldn't know," Robert snickered, thoroughly enjoying his sister's melt down.

"Fuck you Robert!"

"Oh my Claire, my darling sister; what's the matter? Can't the DA take a little heat?"

"Why don't you just shut up Robert? And you Richard, what makes you think she had a right meddling in our personal affairs?"

"Anything that she read in your mother's journal, she had a legal right to Claire. After all, you were the one who sold all the furniture with the house; and if your mother's journal was inside this house or a piece of furniture, that fact in and of itself makes it legally Nicole's. Now come on, we came here for a party, let's go mingle and enjoy ourselves."

"You're right Richard. I'll be right there. Why don't you take my father, Rosa and my brother outside, I'll catch up with you in a moment."

Richard decided that fresh air was probably what everyone needed, so he obliged his still fuming wife. Taking his cue, everyone quickly evacuated the room following Jared's lead. The Langhorne's and Angelina, still in shock at seeing not only Henry but his son, quickly followed the foursome outside, leaving Nicole alone with Claire. Once everyone was out of earshot, Claire turned back toward Nicole who never flinched.

"You little bitch. You had this planned all along didn't you?"

"I don't know what you're talking about Mrs. Drake."

"Cut your little innocent act with me. And don't play games, especially games you can't win."

Nicole smiled smugly and waited a few long seconds before replying. The room grew suddenly colder as the two women sized up the opposition.

"You know Claire; I never play a game I can't win, so that's where you're wrong. I've already won. I know all about your relationship with your mother. How you hated her so much that you shoved her down the stairs. Yes, don't look so surprised. She was a very expressive and emotional woman and she put all of her thoughts and fears on paper. And you know what else. You knew nothing about what she was going through. You were too busy being a spoiled, selfish little brat to see what was really happening right underneath your nose."

"What do you know? You weren't even born yet. My mother was nothing but a two bit whore who had been warned to never have any more kids but what did she do?" Claire said as she moved to within inches of Nicole's face. "She started screwing the neighbor when my father wasn't looking and wound up pregnant again. It was hard enough taking care of my brother all the time, and I was going to have to take care of another one!"

"So you killed her?"

"What?"

"You heard me Claire. Your mother spilled everything out in her journal and that's the one thing you didn't realize, no, actually there were several things that you didn't realize. You think you knew your mother so well. Well let me tell you something you self-righteous rich bitch, you knew nothing!"

Nicole heard a noise and glanced over Claire's should as the woman breathed down her neck. Oblivious to everything around her, Claire stood with her arms folded tightly in front of her chest and her knees locked. Assuming that she was simply hearing the wooden floor just settling, Nicole looked back into the woman's cold eyes.

"You thought your mother was cheating on your father, well you were wrong. She loved your father and you two children with all her heart. She was being raped Claire, not having an affair. Nicholas Carelli was blackmailing her and forcing her to have sex; it was never consensual. "

Letting the words sink in, Nicole quickly saw a slight change in the once lifeless but hateful eyes. Claire looked at the young woman standing in front of her and gave Nicole a blank stare.

"Could it be what's she's saying is true?" Claire asked herself as she searched Nicole's eyes for the answer. "Could it be that through all these years of hating both her father and her mother for what happened, could it be that neither of them had control of the situations around them? Was it possible that her mother really hadn't abandoned her and her father?"

"Yes Mrs. Drake," Nicole said softly as if reading her mind. "Your mother loved you and the rest of her family very much. She wouldn't have intentionally betrayed you. Your neighbor was an evil man and had something over her. She wrote about his blackmail in her journal but never came out with the exact details; but it all revolves around this house."

"But he was married, and he was our neighbor and friend. He used to constantly give us presents; for Christ sake, we used to play with his kids."

"I know."

"Do you think he killed her?"

"No. You and I know who the real killer is and that person is here today and before the party is over, I promise you Claire, your mother's killer will be revealed."

"How can you be so sure?"

"It was quite easy, thanks in part to Rachel. She was well aware of what could happen to her and she implicated her murderer before she died."

"Who else knows about the journal Mrs. Brentwood? Claire asked as the tone in her voice changed.

"Just your family and me; but after tonight, everyone will know the truth."

"Hey, is everything alright in here?" Jared asked as he looked at the two women, still frozen where he had left them a few minutes earlier.

"Everything's fine honey, "Nicole smiled. "I was just telling Mrs. Drake about some of the surprises that I have in store for the evening."

"What surprises?" Jared asked, somewhat puzzled.

"Oh nothing Jared; you'll find out soon enough." Turning back to Claire, Nicole smiled. "Now if you'll excuse me Mrs. Drake, it was nice talking with you and we'll talk again later, okay? But for right now, I have other guests to attend to."

Without waiting for a response, Nicole took Jared's arm and walked out of the room, leaving Claire with her demons. As she stood in the room that had once held so many childhood memories, Claire thought about the young woman's words and accusations.

"Could it be possible that she knows everything that happened here?" Claire thought silently as she tried to analyze Nicole's remarks. "If she knows the truth and lets it out, it'll destroy everything. I can't let that happen," Claire said under her breath as she looked out the bay window facing the lake.

Nicole and Jared mingled with both their family and their new neighbors, while Angelina continued her pursuit of Gary Danberry. Everyone appeared to be enjoying themselves and Nicole had even noticed Henry smiling frequently, mostly when Rosa was by his side. She had been so leery of bring Robert back here again, but when her brother Daniel had mentioned the event to him, Robert was all for it. "Thank goodness for brothers," Nicole thought to herself. Of course it didn't hurt that her cousin was the regional director of the entire Brynmar facility either. There seemed to be so many strange coincidences pulling her to this house. Nicole had dismissed many of them in the beginning but when she discovered Robert Harteman's place of residence a conversation with her brother, she knew it was more than coincidence.

It was fate and simply her destiny to occupy Rachel's home. And now it was Nicole's turn to do something for Rachel. As the afternoon quickly passed, Jared went around to the various groups of guest, obtaining their meat preferences for the grill. Nicole continued to mingle and socialize, absorbing the various interactions of individuals. Angelina continued to stay close to Officer Danbarry, even when his wife was present; Jimmy and Gwen remained inseparable, and the Langhorne's stayed within listening range of Henry and Rosa the entire afternoon. Every time Bart tried to strike up a conversation with another neighbor, Betty would rudely cut the conversation short. Henry didn't seem to mind the barrage of questions Betty was always throwing at him. After all, it was bittersweet but enjoyable to see everyone all in one area. And for a few brief moments, it was like old times for the original neighbors.

Claire wasn't enjoying the festivities quite as much as the rest of her family. Seeing the house restored into its original state, coupled with seeing so many faces from the past was too overwhelming. She wandered away from the crowd shortly after everyone finished eating. Unfamiliar with the surroundings, her husband had no idea where to find her as she disappeared toward the bluff. Seeing her making an exit, Nicole quickly got Gary's attention, and then slipped away from the commotion of the guests who were still enjoying their dessert. As the sun started to set, Nicole noticed her shadow as she made her way to where Claire had last been seen. Assuming that the additional shadow she thought she'd seen was Gary, she never looked back but quickened her pace, preparing herself for the confrontation that lay ahead. As she approached the cliff's edge, expecting to find Claire in the chairs overlooking the lake, she not only found them empty, but also noticed that the wind was definitely picking up. As she squinted, trying to locate Claire, she looked back at the house in the distance, now lit up for her guests. Jared had not only turned on the floodlights but had turned every inside light on. As she glanced at the trail adjoining her house with the Langhornes; her eyes honed in on a slight movement off in the woods. Her first impulse was to wait for Gary to catch up but afraid of losing the opportunity to confront Rachel's killer once and for all, she took a deep breath and started down the trail after her. When she got within shouting range, Nicole addressed her in a tone she had never used before.

"They say the killer always returns to the scene of the crime!"

"What are you talking about," the voice responded back in a droll, monotone response.

"You heard me. I just wonder how many times you've come to this very spot and looked out at the water, just thinking that you might see her again."

As Nicole moved closer, she continued her verbal attack on the shadow standing in the darkness.

"You know exactly what happened that night so why don't you tell me the truth; tell me your version of what happened."

"No! I don't know what you think you know. I wasn't there so I didn't see anything."

"Yes, yes you did Claire. You saw Rachel go off that cliff and for thirty years you've let your father rot in prison for something he didn't do. Now you and I both know who the murderer is and it's time the truth comes out. I've already called the police and they'll be here in a minute and when they arrive, you and I are going to have a talk with them. You owe that much to your father and your mother's memory."

Before she had a chance to respond, both Claire and Nicole jumped as they heard a blood curdling scream come from the darkness of the woods beside them. Both froze, trying to determine the source of the terrible noise.

"No! You will not ruin my life like she did!"

Claire gasped as she realized who the voice belonged to, and her heart started beating wildly as her eyes focused on the raised butcher's knife locked around her ashen white knuckles.

"She made my life hell and she got what she deserved!"

Remaining outwardly calm, Nicole remained motionless as the knife toting intruder came out into the clearing.

"Rachel did not destroy your life. Your own husband did and your jealousy."

"But she was sleeping with my husband!"

"No Betty, she wasn't. She was pregnant by the man who was blackmailing her and continuously raping her and even though your husband was having an affair, it wasn't with Rachel, it was with Angelina," Nicole said as she backed away from the crazed woman. Claire herself had silently backed up toward the bluff's edge as she watched Betty circling in on Nicole. Unsure what was transpiring before her eyes, the one thing Claire knew was that she was not going to suffer the same fate as her mother.

Betty stopped momentarily approaching the two women as the words left Nicole's lips. Nicole took the opportunity to try and both diffuse the situation and buy them time until Gary and the police could find them.

"Betty's, Rachel's death could be viewed as an accident. Give yourself up and I'm sure in light of your age and medical conditions, Claire will see to it that they go easy on you. Please, think of what you're doing."

"Please Mrs. Langhorne," Claire stumbled, trying to find the right words; I'll see to it that you get exactly what you deserve."

"To hell with both of you" she screamed as she lunged at the two women hovering on the cliff's edge. As she swung the knife, she was suddenly blinded by a ship's spotlight coming from the water below. Seizing the moment, Nicole screamed for her husband as she dove out of the way, pushing Claire to the ground on her way down. Still temporarily blinded, Betty swung the knife frantically in the dark. Nicole panicked as she heard Jared's voice.

"Nicki where are you?"

"Stay back! She's got a knife!"

"Shut up," Betty yelled. "It's too late for you," she snickered as she regained her vision and again raised the knife and proceeded toward them.

"Betty, stop!"

Hearing her name, she spun around quickly. Standing just yards away in the woods was Bart who had followed her.

"How could you?" he asked as he approached the three women.

Seeing her attention clearly focused on her husband, Nicole didn't think, just reacted by diving at the irrational woman, knocking her backwards. The knife flung from Betty's good hand and disappeared over the edge of the cliff. With Nicole still in a death grip around her legs, Betty kicked frantically to get free. Neither Bart nor Claire knew what to do so they remained motionless watching the drama play out in slow motion. Betty continued to struggle, finally getting her one foot free. Before Nicole knew what hit her, she felt the sharp burning sensation of Betty's boot on her face. Hearing her cheekbone snap, she cried out in pain, loosening her grip on the immobile leg. Using every bit of strength she had remaining, Betty kicked up dirt into Nicole's eyes, bent her legs and with all her might, gave the temporarily blinded woman a mule kick directly in the chest. Bart shouted frantically as the blow knocked Nicole backwards, and partially off the bluff. As Bart raced toward Nicole who was struggling to get her footing, Claire go to her feet and looked at Betty with hatred she didn't know possible.

"You fucking bitch; you killed my mother!" she screamed as she dove toward the woman still on the ground. Trying to avoid the woman's attack, Betty quickly rolled to her right; unaware of how close she was to the edge. She gasped as she rolled onto the loose soil below her and within a second was gone. Realizing what was happening; Bart screamed for his wife and raced to the cliff's edge, leaving Nicole to fend for herself.

By now, the commotion had caught the attention of several guests. As Jared and Jimmy raced past the area where Betty had fallen, desperately trying to reach Nicole, Clare and Bart forced themselves to look over the edge. As Gary led the troopers who had arrived moments before, to Nicole, who by now was on solid ground, Bart stared down at his wife below and silently wept. Claire too wept as she looked at the semiconscious woman lying only ten feet below her on a protrusion of the cliff. As the waves crashed against the rocks below her, Betty opened her eyes.

"Bart, do you hear her?"

Bart wiped his eyes on his shirtsleeve and looked down in disbelief at this wife of forty years. Having thought her dead, he called out to her in a trembling voice.

"Stay still honey. Help's on the way."

Still fixed on her husband, Betty closed her eyes and smiled.

"It's okay Bart. Rachel's here now. She's come for me, and she's not even angry with me," she said as she tried to get up.

"Why'd you hurt Rachel Betty? It was an accident right Betty? Please tell us about what happened to Rachel," Nicole asked in a soothing tone, playing into the injured woman's delusion.

Betty once again opened her eyes and pulling herself to a sitting position, looked out at the water, addressing it like an old friend.

"Rachel, I'm so sorry. I never meant to hurt you. I just wanted you to leave my Bart alone."

"What?" Bart cried out. "I never laid a finger on Rachel, ever! I loved her like a sister. But I was never involved with her in any way."

Nicole once again addressed Betty. By now, Henry had joined his daughter and held Claire tightly as he looked down at his former neighbor and listened in disbelief. Noticing his wife going into shock, Richard quickly motioned for her to move away from the cliff and sit down, but she was too transfixed on Betty.

"Betty," Nicole said in a softer tone, "Everyone knows it was an accident. Tell us what happened that night."

"It was so long ago, I can't."

"Please Betty; I need to know what happened to Rachel that night. Please," Henry pleaded, dropping to his knees.

"Please forgive me," Betty sighed. I never meant to. You and Rachel were arguing. She had just told you about the baby and since I knew it couldn't be yours and I knew that Bart was stepping out on me, I assumed it was his. When you went inside for her sweater, I confronted her."

Betty, still sitting precariously on the ledge, looked up at Henry and then Bart before turning her back to them. Looking out at the water, she continued.

"She denied it and said that it was Angelina's husband who was having his way with her against her will and that she and Bart were only good friends."

"Is that true?" Henry whispered to the man now kneeling beside him.

"Yes, I was seeing someone, actually two women; but I never touched your Rachel, I swear."

"Thank You," Henry forced the words from his mouth as Betty took a deep breath and finished her tale.

"We exchanged words and she got mad and tried to go inside but I was blocking the path. She pushed me and I pushed her back, in self-defense I guess, and I pushed her harder than I thought. She fell backwards and screamed out your name as she went over the bluff. I rushed down the path to the lake but never saw her again. I swear I never meant to hurt her, much less kill her. Ask your daughter, she was there and saw the whole thing!"

All eyes turned to focus on Clarissa as she stared off blankly into space. As if unable to react, she remained motionless as she acknowledged by a nod what the woman was saying. Robert, listening to what was being said, slowly walked over to his only sister, put his arms around her and wept silently with her.

By now the paramedics were in position and implementing a rescue. Seeing them getting ready to approach her, Betty shouted for them to heave her along and stepped back as if to get away. The gravel gave way under her feet as the spotlight from the lone boat on the water once again lit up the ledge and part of the evening sky. Everyone present had a solemn look at the distraught woman as she toppled off the tiny ledge and into the rough waters below. As if on cue, the boat's light went black as her body hit the cold water's surface. By the time the troopers, EMT's, Jared and Gary reached the boat dock at the water's edge, Betty, like Rachel was already out of sight and resting in her watery grave.

Gwen remained at the house with a few of the other guest as the drama played out. The whole ordeal was too eerie for her to deal with so she paced nervously on the veranda, with a tight grip on her glass of wine. The only sound she was able to hear over the wind was Betty's last desperate scream, which was then replaced by the hum of Nicole's angelic wind chime dancing in the wind. After Betty was gone and everyone had dispersed, Jared and Nicole slowly walked back toward their home. They both looked up as the upstairs bedroom light dimmed and then went out. Joining hands, they entered their now darkened home......

....

I hope you enjoyed Bittersweet Justice, and will follow Nicole through the next chapter of her life. ~~~~ Erin Maine ~~~~

Excerpt from Masquerading Justice:

Prelude

"Nicki, Ellen needs to see you at the desk."

"Why does she need to see me?"

"I don't know Nick," Sarah answered solemnly.

Nicole couldn't think of anything she'd done wrong, nor had she volunteered to work a double; so she knew whatever the nursing supervisor had to talk to her about couldn't be good news. She quickly approached her and figured it was better to just get it over with.

"Hey Ellen; what can I do for you?" Nicole asked tentatively.

Not sugarcoating anything, the supervisor got right to the point. "Nicole, I need for you to come to the E.R. with me right away. There was a multi-car pile-up on 481 and your husband was involved in the crash."

Seeing the color drain from her face, she grabbed Nicole's arms to keep her focused and upright. "Nicole, he's alive but he's seriously injured. Come on, we need to get down there RIGHT NOW."

And with that, Nicole's world shattered...

Chapter 1

"Jared. Jared, can you hear me? Damn it! Open your eyes. Don't you dare leave me!" she whispered, trying to hold back tears as her trembling hands clasped his.

Nicole looked down at the broken shell of the man that was her husband, her rock, her only love for the last eight years; as the emergency room nurse scurried around in the cramped trauma room. Many of his injuries were obvious as he fought to, and she begged him to regain consciousness. As she closed her eyes momentarily to pray, she felt a slight squeeze on her hand.

"Hey gorgeous," he whispered in a voice that was barely audible.

"Ah baby; you scared me half to death," she responded with the floodgate of tears finally opening.

"Shhh, listen to me Nicki; listen to me my love." He said softly, wincing in pain as he fought to form the words.

"Rest Jared; we'll talk later,"

"No time Nicki. Rachel's here Nic. You were right; she's so beautiful Nicole, just like you said."

Thinking the drugs were taking effect, Nicole smiled down and reassured her husband. "Jared, Rachel's dead honey; and she's in heaven at peace," she said as she quickly scanned the tiny room, not sure what she thought she might see.

Having always believed in some type of afterlife and suddenly realizing what Jared's vision could mean, Nicole squared her shoulders, did a second look around the room and when the E.D. nurse stepped out, she said in her most authoritative voice:

"Rachel, if you are here, go away! He's mine Rachel, just as Henry was yours. Leave us alone and go back to where you came from!"

"No Nicole. She's here for me; and to thank you for saving her Henry. She said that she will always be with you Nicole to protect you. It's okay Nicole; it's my time and I'm okay. Don't worry about me; I love you Nicki and I always will. Rachel and I will watch over you always."

Jared Brentwood took his last breathe while holding onto the love of his life. Rachel Harteman, who'd been dead for thirty years wept silently beside him.

Chapter 2

The two gunmen made their way up the back stairwell leading to their destination. One driven by hated and drugs, the other focused solely on revenge; they whispered silently, reviewing their plan for the hundredth time. Russ had always been simple, for lack of a better term, and a follower; so when his brother ranted about the "bitch nurse" who wouldn't let them in to see their mother when she was there dying, he listened. And then, when the same nurse called security and had him thrown off the unit; he made up his mind that she must pay, and pay dearly. Now standing here, in a back stairwell waiting for his brother's signal to go in, Russ began to have second thoughts about the whole thing. Alvin, his older brother by seven years envisioned "lighting the place up in a hail of bullets and going out a martyr for his cause," while Russ was beginning to realize that it was simply a suicide mission. They had no way of knowing if that damn nurse, Nicole he believed her name was, was even on duty that day. Before Russ could voice his hesitancy and uncertainty of their quest, Alvin spoke up and with that, all hell broke loose on Nicole's unit.

"Code W 4 South. Code W 4 South. Code W 4 South!" the switchboard operator announced, practically screaming into the intercom system.

Never in the eighty-six year history of the hospital had they ever had active shooters within the facility. Sure, they'd had a few attempted baby kidnappings by estranged fathers and several domestic disputes mainly in the E.D. and occasionally on the units; but never had anyone actually brought in a gun and opened fire. Although all the staff had had to review the hospital's mandatory net learning module regarding it, no one had been prepared for the day that Russ and Alvin Lewis would invade and destroy so many peoples' lives.

Hearing the code, Nicole, still sobbing and holding her husband's hand as it grew colder in hers; tried to focus on what was happening around her. "Code W; Oh My God, someone has a gun on my unit," she realized. Before she could even react, she felt a firm push on her shoulders, forcing back into a sitting position.

"What the hell?" she thought; again searching the room as she felt the presence beside her.

Hearing her before seeing her, Nicole whipped around at the sound of the voice. There, not three feet in front of her was Rachel, the apparition of the woman murdered in the home that Nicole and Jared had shared for the past year.

"You must stay Nicole. There is nothing you can do for them now. I promised Jared that I would protect you; so please, stay here. It's too late for your friends," the woman softly said.

"NO! I have to get up there to help them," Nicole screamed as she pushed at the form of the woman standing in front of her, feeling her hands pushing through nothing but air.

Nicole, looking back one last time at her deceased husband, burst out of the trauma room and took off at a near sprint towards the stairwell leading to her unit....

21550033R00184

Made in the USA
Middletown, DE
03 July 2015